Serendipitous

Craig L. Andrews

Solstice Publishing - www.solsticepublishing.com

Serendipitous

by

Craig L. Andrews

Dedication

To Pat

Chapter One

His gaze reached toward the people who watched him. He grinned back at them. Bryan Northfield stuck out his elbow and pushed the camping trailer's screen door closed. The orange glow of the fire was only a few steps away. He clutched three bottles of beer and a bottle of soda with the deftness of a circus juggler. The fire flashed off his eyes as he moved to deliver refreshments to Olivia and Lee Carson, and his wife, Louise, all sitting in metal camp chairs. The chairs encircled a small fire pit. Terpsichorean shadows flickered off the surroundings even as the fire receded from the initial torrent to more tranquil flames and glowing embers.

***

The fire's glow warmed his face as he approached. The aromatic smell of burning mesquite wood drifting on the evening air captured him like a comforting cloud. This was his first encounter with the outdoors under the evening sky, relishing the pine scent from the nearby ten-foot trees that the campground owner had placed throughout the trailer rental zones. Even as a youth, he had never had the opportunity to experience this type of spatial openness, a sky without a city's halo, and the adventure of exploring. At last, he and his wife had an evening under night's canopy, reaching out and grabbing time, and holding it motionless, instead of dashing down halls of research buildings. And they were sharing it with new friends.

He sent a satisfied smile to Louise as he held a bottle out to her and then he surrendered his curiosity to the sky again, taking in the star-speckled heavens. The only planet, which he could locate without help, appeared so much brighter here outside Sedona, Arizona, compared to back on the east coast. The difference amazed him. Of course, he doubted he was more amazed than Louise. Back east, sitting out on their patio, admiring the sky, she complained constantly about the glow from city lights ruining good observations with her telescope. He took one more upward glance and turned to their new acquaintances, presenting a bottle of cherry soda to Olivia and a beer to Lee.

"Thank you, sir," said Olivia, sitting with her feet curled under her small frame that couldn't have been taller the five feet and maybe three inches. Her body matched her small voice, electric eyes, and shoulder-length, wavy, ash-blonde hair. She had a youngish easy smile, and a small mouth with pink lip coloring of some sort that glistened in the firelight.

"You're most welcome," Bryan said. Louise removed a bottle from his hand.

"Yeah, thanks for the beer," Lee said. "I think we might have some chips. I could go get them."

"Don't bother," Bryan said. "I'm good with the beer… unless you folks want them." He looked up. "I can't believe how clear the sky is."

"Lee, those chips are gone," Olivia said. Her eyes brightened comically. "I finished that bag yesterday."

"You devil," Lee said.

In their brief time together, Bryan had made a connection with Lee. Bryan thought of Lee as the type who would help a neighbor remove a blown-over tree without being asked. Bryan flashed back to a small farm where he grew up in Pennsylvania, a time when his dad worked in a factory during the day, and during free time farmed twenty acres. By farm standards, Bryan wasn't a big farmhand, only medium build, standing five-feet ten inches, but if his brain had gone another direction he could have been happy on a farm.

Lee shifted himself in his chair. "Olivia, these chairs you bought are a little small for me."

"Lee, could it be that you're too big?" Olivia said, grinning.

Looking at Lee, sitting sprawled with all of his six-foot stature overpowering the small camp chair, Bryan laughed to himself. However, as a twist of nature, despite Lee's height and football player's massive shoulders, his voice was soft. Bryan felt a little sorry for Lee's thinning brown hair. They fell close in years but he was blessed with a full head of hair.

Bryan looked at Louise and found her gazing up at the sky.

Louise held a hand to her forehead, shading the camper and fire pit's light from her eyes. "The sky is wondrous," she said. "The stars are really visible, honey. I'm glad you talked me into this trip. This is the next best thing to a telescope. I would go and get the binoculars, but I'm too comfortable."

"I'm glad you surrendered." Bryan grinned at her, wondering if she would eventually acknowledge he'd been right in their conversations over several dinners that a trip out west would be fun. She had protested because of her expectation of boredom and the unknown problems associated with using a camping trailer. In coaxing her, he had done his best to compose visions of adventure, beauty, and romance. It took a lot of convincing to eliminate her fear of critters such as snakes and scorpions.

"So, Bryan, what do you do for a day job?" Lee asked, and tipped up his beer, taking a drink.

Bryan thought for a moment, stopping himself from blurting out a technical specialty and decided on using a broad label. "I'm a professor at Princeton in the artificial intelligence area." He wondered if Lee knew what he meant. Bryan found it easier to talk about stars than to discuss rules for making decisions in the computer logic engine or neural networks. Even with Louise, he didn't have a lot of luck. Their discussions heated up on the future danger of artificial intelligence to humans, a system reaching the singularity of self-awareness. She never stopped giving examples of disasters that could come to fruition at the hands of a silly computer scientist.

"Isn't that the stuff with computers some of the futurists are fussing about, computers taking over?" Lee's eyes widened.

"Yep." Bryan sat down in his chair next to Louise. He touched his bottle against hers. "Cheers, babe. By the way, you look fantastic in the firelight."

"Lean over here and give me a kiss," Louise said as Olivia and Lee watched with warm smiles.

The chair's aluminum tubing scratched through the gravel as Bryan slid his over next to Louise's. He stared at her sparkling blue eyes and her glistening reddish-blonde hair for a moment. She smiled. He loved the way her eyes appeared exceptionally large and inviting in the firelight. He leaned over and kissed her lips, lips she refused to cover with what she considered obtrusive lipstick.

"Now, I understand Louise wearing the shirt with Princeton written on it," Lee said.

Louise looked down at the embroidered name on her shirt. "One of my favorite shirts."

Olivia glanced at Lee and back at Louise. "Are you two newlyweds?"

"Nah, just having a good time," Louise said, beaming at Bryan.

Bryan patted Louise's hand. "This is a nice campground, huh, babe. Especially with these fire pits and the firewood already cut and piled."

Louise smiled contentedly. "I'm really surprised how nice it is."

Bryan nodded and noticed again how the fire reflected off the highlights in her hair.

"This excursion has been great," Louise said. "The bright stars with new friends on a warm night make it special. This is wonderfully peaceful. We've not gone on a vacation, a real one, since taking our posts at Princeton. Of course, I talked Bryan into going to an area of Texas that has virtually no lights fouling the night sky, so stellar observations should be amazing. I had misgivings about renting a camping trailer but it's been fun and luckily we haven't hit any other cars on the highway. After seeing the nice trailer you folks have, I think we could have done much better."

"This is our second time at this campground," Olivia said. "We like it here and we like walking around in town. There are so many nice shops with crafts."

"Louise, what do you do?" Lee asked.

"I'm also a professor at Princeton."

"That's interesting... both of you," Olivia said. Her voice rose in pitch.

Bryan leaned forward a little, glanced at Louise, and then at Lee and Olivia. "I must confess that I play second fiddle in our family," Bryan said. "Louise is the heavy hitter. She's a professor in astrophysics. She's happiest talking about stars, black holes, dark matter, and such. On top of that, she makes the best meatballs you could ever eat." He grinned. "However, I do have her beat when it comes to fried chicken in the old cast iron skillet."

"Yeah, true," Louise said, offering a self-deprecating smile.

"Wow, astrophysics, that does sound heavy," Lee said.

"Bryan, you make me sound like... uh, I don't know..." Louise frowned and shook her head. "What do you folks do? Did I hear you tell Bryan that you live in Indiana?"

Olivia flashed her brow at him and said, "Bloomington is home. I'm a second grade teacher and

Lee's an assistant principal at another school." She clutched her soda bottle between her hands.

"So we all dabble in education to one extent or another," Bryan said, watching Olivia and Lee. He turned to Olivia, who he could visualize as a second grade teacher. "Are second grade children hard to handle? They must be a lot of work."

"No, no. They're fun and eager to learn. You have to have a little variety for them and keep things fresh, but they are eager."

Louise glanced at Bryan, smiled, and then met Olivia's eyes. "We both love children."

Bryan nodded, "Someday we'll have a couple. Right, babe? Soon would be good."

"Well… maybe in a couple years. I have to finish a research grant first."

Bryan raised his beer to his lips and sipped as he craned his neck backward, thinking to search for a star constellation that he could identify. "Babe, is that Orion?" he asked, pointing the neck of his bottle toward the sky, feeling good that he could remember the name of a constellation for Louise.

They all looked in the direction he had indicated.

"Yes, honey. That's where it's supposed to be for July."

Lee, remaining in his chair, craned his neck, searching the western sky. "Is that bright one up there anything special?"

Bryan turned with Louise, locating and studying Lee's object.

"Huh," Louise said. "That's strange. It's almost too bright."

"What babe?" Bryan said.

"I don't know anything that bright in that location this time of the year. On top of that… I think… I think it's moving."

Bryan found comfort in her dismissing the object as something she could identify. He wasn't going to plunge into one of her astrophysics scientific investigations, defiling their vacation. "It's probably just a plane," he said.

Louise stood motionless, watching the object with her usual determination to find an explanation. "It's not a plane. Not with that light."

With Bryan and Louise entranced, Lee lumbered from his chair. He placed a hand on Olivia's shoulder as he tipped his head back in serious observation. "What on earth?" Lee said. "Is that a chopper?"

"Come on, Lee, sit down and forget about it," Olivia said, refusing to participate, sitting comfortably and gazing into the fire. "I was just thinking. If they had benches with backs, couples could cuddle in front of the fire and not need to bring chairs."

Louise turned to Olivia. "That would be nice."

"Why don't all you airplane gawkers come back to the fire conversation," Olivia said.

Bryan stepped alongside Louise and wrapped his arms around her, staring at the light with her, watching it approach closer. *It couldn't be a chopper*, he thought, *there isn't any rotor noise and a plane can't move that slow and that quietly.* Of course there was the possibility of a special government stealth chopper, but even that must make a little sound from moving air.

"Bryan, I don't understand," Louise said. Her words came out edgy, uneven with excitement and confusion. "It's not up where the commercial planes fly. I'm wondering if it's a stealth something or other."

"I thought that same thing," Bryan said. "But I don't here air movement."

"It's not like any plane, meteor, or star. I should get my camera." Suddenly, Louise clasped her mouth with an anxious hand.

"What is it, babe?" Bryan said. "Is it…" He paused. "Maybe we should go inside, babe."

"What do you think it is?" Lee asked. His tone showed his apprehension. He stabbed the sky with his finger. "It stopped. It's just hovering… over there."

"This is fantastic," Louise whispered, staring at the light. "The staff at school won't believe me. Bryan, do you have your cell phone on you?"

Bryan figured they were observing the brilliant object at an angle of perhaps thirty or forty degrees from the ground. The blue-white light crashed on them so strongly that he couldn't hold his eyes on it. It was like looking at the sun. "How far is it from us? It looks like somewhere around a thousand or fifteen hundred yards to me." He paused. "Hey, this thing is giving me a strange feeling."

Louise grabbed Bryan's arm. "It's as if the object is observing us."

Bryan felt a tingle on the back of his neck. "What do you think? Maybe we should go to the camper. Come on, babe, let's go to the camper."

Louise flailed her hand. "Honey, do you have your cell phone so I can take a few pictures?"

He studied the object, his fear rising from their standing around while some intelligence examined them. "You already asked that. I don't want to leave you here. I don't have my phone with me. Maybe we should be careful."

"I left my phone inside our camper too," Lee snapped, his voice nearly breathless with excitement. "So I can't help you."

Olivia stood, reaching out, grabbing Lee's hand. "I don't like the way this feels. I'm scared. I want to go inside, now!" She pulled on Lee's arm. "Let's go. Please let's go in. I don't like it. Please."

As Olivia pulled Lee toward their camper, he looked over his shoulder, checking on the airborne object. At their silver Airstream camper, Olivia yanked open the door and disappeared inside. Lee paused in the door, watching the thing in the sky.

She returned, grabbed his shirt, and pulled. "Lee, close the door."

Lee shouted from the door, "You two might want to take shelter… just in case." He waved at Bryan, closed the camper door, and killed their lights.

"Come on, babe, we should go inside too," Bryan said. "They may not be a welcoming committee." He knew he was being paranoid and failing her with his distinctly unscientific behavior, permitting his fear to destroy curiosity. He didn't care. He had no answers. She worried him with the way she was so disconnected from an analysis of the situation. She seemed out of control like a child in a candy shop, all caution buried under the adrenaline of discovery.

"Come on, Bryan, why would highly intelligent beings want to harm us? Besides, how many people get to see a UFO?"

Bryan was breathless. His mind raced for an answer to what he saw. He feared horribly for Louise. She watched the object like a child, oblivious to her own safety. "Think about it! What concern do you have about stepping on a bug on the sidewalk? They could scoop up a bunch of us and push us into an ant farm and watch us go berserk."

She dismissed him with a wave of her hand. "What? Are you seeing this?"

Just as Bryan thought of slamming down his husbandly authoritarian-boot, ordering Louise to safety, going for the trailer, the object's single white light became three yellow lights that blinked on and off in a repeating sequential pattern.

"Look, Bryan," Louise said excitedly in a gasping voice.

"Please come, babe. You've seen it. It's time to be sensible."

The object moved toward them in ghostly silence, filling Bryan's field of view of the sky directly overhead. Up above him was something that drove fear through his bones. Two dishes on top of each other, one upside down and one right side up formed a craft. He stared at the object, fighting his growing mental paralysis. The bottom appeared flattened a little. There was a circular area in the underside of the saucer with lights along its edge. He heard a faint hum and felt a change in the air as if it had taken on static electricity. "Louise please, for God sakes, let's go. Now!"

A circular area on the underside of the craft opened, sliding away like a cloud moving past the sun, leaving a circle of light. A column of brilliant white descended, not instantaneously in a blot, but spilling like a liquid to the ground, the light having a finite demarcation as it moved. It encapsulated Louise and him. Bryan felt tingles over his body and then inside his head. He watched Louise become a mannequin, her head directed upward gripped in an insane stare, as if those above had paralyzed her. Bryan felt weightless and his hearing faded. The sounds reaching him sounded muffled. His vision narrowed as if he looked down a tunnel. He thought of Louise and saving her. The tunnel turned into a dot of light and then nothing.

In his mind Bryan said, "Louise."

He blacked out.

Chapter Two

Bryan became aware. He realized he was conscious and hearing something. The muscles to lift his eyelids failed him. They felt glued shut. Cold air flowed over him. The sound he heard was a faint hum, like a machine. Had he blacked-out or fallen asleep for hours?

Get yourself up.

He tried to organize his thinking, return his body and mind to a normal state. He was lying on his back and the surface was hard. The inside of his mouth felt dry and rough against his tongue. A strange unpleasant odor found his nose. He swallowed to rid his dry and irritated throat. Again, he tried to lift his eyelids. They started to open and stopped. He had to get up. Wait. What did he hear? Again he heard a hum. The machine was close to him.

I must open my eyes!

"Take your time," a voice said. It was a soft female voice, whispery with a melodic tone.

The voice was near him.

"Louise?" Bryan asked.

He turned his head toward the voice and thought of the night at the campground.

"Oh, God."

His memory connected to his fear for Louise. She had been standing near him. He reached up to his eyes with his hands and began rubbing.

"Louise?"

"No. You must try hard to open your eyes."

"Who… who are you?"

"I call myself Liana."

Bryan pushed his muscles, raising his brow, using it to lift his eyelids. He rubbed his eyes with the palm of his hand again. At last he looked through slits, squinting against the light that splashed everything before him. The brightness forced him to close his eyes for a moment.

"That is it. Keep trying."

Reopening his eyes, he saw a female figure standing before him. A gossamer gray haze clouded his vision, giving him an unfocused image. After a moment, he saw a tall and trim young woman with blue eyes. Although indistinct, her hair appeared a light color, a reddish-blonde.

"Louise?"

He moved his arms, pushing himself up on his elbows. His arms hurt. He bent at his waist, lifting his head. Nausea started in his stomach, forcing him to drop back down.

With a scratchy voice he said, "I don't feel good. What's wrong with me? Where am I?" He closed his eyes. "Where's Louise?"

"Focus. It will get better. I have something for you to drink. It should help you."

He felt a gentle hand lifting his head and an object pressed against his lips.

"Drink this."

Bryan parted his lips and took in a small quantity of liquid, finding it slightly sweet and minty. He swallowed. Warmth followed the liquid as it descended into his stomach. The heat radiated out slowly, warming his arms and legs, and then it warmed his face as if caressed by a hot wet cloth. For several moments, he felt warmth spreading throughout his body. He drew a long breath as his head cleared. Again he opened his eyes, this time unhampered by weak muscles. The light sensitivity had passed. He sat up and looked up at the woman helping him.

"Sensing yourself better?" asked the young woman. Her tone was plain as if given by a medical professional.

The situation brought him to think he was in a hospital—but how?

"Yes, I'm better."

"I am not Louise. I call myself Liana."

The way she phrased her identification was strange, although it wasn't the first time Bryan had heard people express their names like that.

"I am here to help you. I am here for you."

"What day is it? What's the date?" His throat was raspy.

"It is a short time increment before the new solar day. In your measurement, it is approaching the morning time of nine o'clock."

"Date?"

"In earth human calculation based on the solar cycle is called August. It is the tenth day in the August period."

He grabbed his head with both hands, rubbing and squeezing. He studied her, the way her reddish-blonde hair dropped in straight strands, which she had cut horizontally at her shoulders. Her eyes seemed different from any girl he'd seen. They looked larger than most, dark blue, like magnetic pools. Her pupils seemed normal, but the colored parts of her eyes stood out so blue. As they settled on him they seemed to swallow him. He had heard of beautiful girls with large eyes. She had full lips, not a pressed line, and no lines or age wrinkles appearing on her oval symmetric face, as if she had never matured from youth. She had a delicate chin just like his Louise. If he had to guess, her features seemed northern European, Swedish or Danish, in origin and her height had to be at least five-foot eight or ten. Although it was covered by her hair and beautifully proportioned, he got the impression her head might have been slightly large but nevertheless she was utterly beautiful, easily as attractive as his Louise. He thought of the legend of the Amazon women. She was exceptional and captivating. Her eyes, electric and dancing, said she was intelligent.

She looked at him strangely with a sudden focus that could have been mistaken for surprise.

"Louise," Bryan said. "Where is she?"

"Do you feel better?" Liana asked, her eyes dropping down as if with reluctance or held by sadness.

"Yes, I feel better. Thank you." He closed his eyes and took a breath. "Where am I?"

His mind climbed a hill, laboring, pushing thoughts up the hill, struggling to make connections.

"Take your time. There is no time constraint."

He looked up at the woman, fighting to make sense of what had happened. She wore what looked like a form-fitting exercise leotard. It was light blue with a high neck. The fit sculpted her smallish breasts. The lower part, the gray pants with pockets, wrapped around her hips with the same form-fitting design. He swallowed hard.

"Tell me your name again, please?"

"Liana."

"Liana, where am I? I'm confused. Am I in a hospital in Arizona?"

"You are now in a government facility," she said, clasping her hands at her waist with the comportment of a subordinate.

Bryan looked off in the distance, past her, off into the room. He gasped. His head started to spin.

"Oh, God." He closed his eyes. "My wife! Please, where's Louise? I want to see Louise."

"See if you can move your legs over the edge of the table."

He moved his legs. They felt achy and stiff. Sitting on the edge of the table and bending his legs made his leg muscles feel better.

"Why are my legs so stiff? My head is still a little dizzy."

Liana spoke softly, "What is your name? Think about who you are. Breathe deeply. Your anxiety will dissipate and your head will clear."

Beyond the beautiful creature in front of him a cavernous room stretched out for at least seventy-five feet. With his awareness improving by the minute he couldn't avoid recognizing its strangeness and its clammy feeling. He took a few deep breaths.

"Feeling better?" Liana asked.

"I want to see Louise." He scoured her face for understanding. He saw no sign of encouragement.

The answer he wanted to hear from her seemed hidden behind her curious eyes, an answer he feared she was trying to avoid.

"I have to see my wife. Where is she? Take me to my wife." He watched her. Nothing. "Where is Louise?"

Looking around for Louise, he again gazed across the room. Rows of tables filled the space. They extended down the room, uniformly spaced, counting twenty or perhaps thirty in a line. The large space held six such rows. A translucent cover, like a plastic film, enclosed each table, dropping from a conduit that extended from the ceiling above each table. Across the ceiling was a surprise. Curiously, the occupants used antiquated incandescent bulbs, which struggled to provide even meager light. A spider web of pipes and wire blanketed the ceiling. He had lain under the same oppressive plastic covering, a closure which had connected in some manner at the surface of the table.

The female who was helping him had apparently pushed open his closure, moving it to the side of the table to wake him. The table smelled like a mix of deteriorating organic material and a chemical cleanser. He looked down past his thigh at the table top and discovered its surface was concave, slanted to one end, and had an evenly distributed array of holes apparently for drainage of a liquid.

In his still lethargic mind, he realized he was one of a multitude of occupants. On the table next to his, he saw a man. That person's plastic cover appeared clearer, about like his, as if the occupant was recently added. Others down the room looked clouded. The man's clothes looked like something worn on a farm. Bryan thought the variation between him and the other occupant curious but too tiring to analyze at this moment.

"What is this place?" he asked, his voice becoming thin and strained with his fear. His breathing labored. "Where am I? Where's my wife? Where is Louise?"

"Control your breathing. Try to relax." The woman held up her hand to him. "Think about who you are. What is your name?"

"Uh... Bryan Northfield." When he said his name he thought it odd and distant.

"Do I address you as Bryan?"

"Yes, please. Please tell me what this place is?"

"Perhaps at a later time. You are secure. You are safe." She frowned. "Does your name have a meaning?"

"Uh, what... I guess it comes from Celtic origin... brave or virtuous or something like that."

"Interesting."

"Why am I here?" He wanted answers now. His irritation felt good, energizing. It woke more of his head. "Where is my wife, Louise? I want to see her now!"

"Bryan, you sound agitated. It is not a productive state of mind." Liana rubbed her hands together for an instant and abruptly stopped as if realizing it was improper. "I can tell you that you are part of a research program. I am trying to help you. I am here for you."

"Dammit, where's Louise?" Bryan's eyes began to tear. "The last thing I remember is standing with my wife in a light." He gasped. "Oh God, we were looking at an object in the sky, at a UFO, an alien craft."

"The woman with you, who you call, Louise, is not with us."

Bryan didn't like the change in Liana's face as her brow wrinkled.

"Liana, please explain," he said in a conciliatory tone.

He stared at the young woman who was attending him. Her eyes and mouth drew tight, making him think something was wrong.

Liana stared somberly at him. She blinked as if uncomfortable. "The Louise person did not survive."

Bryan fell back onto the table, clutching his face in horror, sobbing.

"Not my Louise," he cried. "Oh God, no, no, no." He pulled his legs to his chest and sobbed.

In his mind, he saw Louise standing beside him at the campground, happy and carefree, before the damn light flew overhead. That had to be what happened. The damn aliens had abducted them. Olivia had feared something would happen. Why could he remember? Didn't aliens wipe away people's memory? But, their friends had the common sense. Olivia made Lee race to the trailer. If he had gone to the camper with Louise, he wouldn't be where he was, and this woman would not have any reason to tell him a horror story about his Louise. His chest heaved as he pushed his anguished hand into his teeth. Why didn't he force Louise into the camper? They could have fought any aliens from inside the metal trailer.

For several minutes Liana watched him, studying him, her manner attentive and slightly distant except for a momentary hint of concern. She said nothing.

Life had just drained from Bryan all his energy to keep living. After a few minutes he sat up again with his legs over the table. He wiped the tears from his eyes and looked severely at Liana.

"Was she hurt? Were you part of the abduction? Was it aliens from another planet? A UFO took us, didn't it?"

"I don't know what UFO means."

"An alien craft from another planet," he said, his words racing with anger.

"Yes. It was a craft."

"Was she hurt?"

"She had no conscious pain." Liana wet her lips. She watched Bryan's chest shudder.

"Thank God for that."

"You loved her greatly?"

"Yes. She was my life."

"She was your life partner."

Bryan nodded.

Liana's forehead wrinkled. "She loved you with equal devotion?"

"Yes. We loved each other for more than three years. These creatures have stolen my wife and left my soul bleeding, draining my blood." He gathered a breath. "What happened to her?" His breathing shuddered again. He clenched his teeth, fighting his grief.

Liana looked off across the room as if evaluating what Bryan had said.

"Liana."

Liana turned to Bryan, seemingly pulled from a deep thought. "Yes."

"How long have I been here?

"You—and I—have been here the same length of time, two years."

"Two years!"

She looked at him as if afraid of his reaction. "Beings from another star system collected you."

Bryan's eyes grew wildly large. "Oh God! It happened. We were abducted."

"You are safe now."

Bryan hung his head. "How can I be safe if I have lost my wife?"

The pain of losing his Louise and the news of losing two years of life held in a government research facility tore a hole in his gut. Did he want to continue living? The question of struggling to stay alive took him to Louise's memory and ignited burning hatred for those responsible. As he thought of giving up, he remembered Louise's mental toughness. She was a fighter, never giving up on theories, never giving up on completing her doctorate after pneumonia sidelined her, and never giving up on research funding. He could do no less. His heart ached for her. Making those holding him pay for her loss was a good reason to push forward. Retribution seemed a good reason to survive. He had to make them pay, if he could. Louise would have screamed at him to fight on.

Bryan looked at the woman. She gazed back at him. The way she answered him previously, about her two years of residency, struck him as bizarre. If she had worked for that short of time at the facility, what had she done before coming there? Why was she working for such soulless animals?

"How did my wife die?" Bryan met Liana's eyes with a demanding gaze.

"I am not permitted to say," Liana said, her voice diminishing. She turned away for a moment and then returned to him.

Bryan found her gaze had softened as if saddened. Had her manner changed to that of expressing sympathy?

"Did my wife die here?"

Liana's mouth moved with a slight quiver. "She did die here. Two years ago."

Bryan swallowed hard. "Am I going to die here?"

"I am sorry. The probability is high that you will."

"Why will I die?"

"Your DNA contribution will end at some point." Liana hesitated, breaking her composure. "Your usefulness for brain study will end. When that happens they dispose of the subject."

"How long do I have?"

"I should not tell you but... you are an intelligent being." She spoke in a low voice. "The aliens here follow the same pattern with nearly all subjects. Subjects usually experience some type of surgery for tissue study or organ removal. Following the tissue study, the subjects participate in mental tests, if they are found worthy. Moving to the next phase depends on the results of those tests. The length of time varies." She looked sadly at him.

"What is the next phase? Death?"

"Very well," she said coldly. "In the next phase, subjects are exposed to any of an assortment of hormones, drugs, chemicals, including cellular DNA alterations. After that, the subjects may be taken to a tank room or they may be brought back to this room of tables for rendering into their constituent protein."

"Not that it makes a damn bit of difference, but what do they do with the protein?"

"They eat—"

Bryan leaned forward incredulous, nearly shouting. "What? The aliens eat the protein soup. My God, what insanity."

He sighed, fighting to hold himself together. Evil creatures exercising such ghoulish behavior deserved to face the wrath of God. Perhaps he could help God with that service. He sighed again. At the present moment, he needed to learn more—all he could. To carry out an escape he needed to understand the environment; he had to scratch for information, possibly a clue to a weakness that he could utilize to his advantage.

"What happens if I try to escape?"

"The statistics for escaping are not good. The aliens could punish you in some severe manner. There are observation drones, hybrids, and many aliens throughout these floors. The stairs have sealed access doors beyond the eleventh floor. The freight elevator is the only route all the way to the surface from the bottom four floors."

"The last thing I saw with my Louise was a UFO and you said I was in a government facility. Would I be wrong in concluding this place is operated in some sort of mutual agreement with aliens?"

"Yes is operated in that manner."

"So, I'm a subject for various experiments carried out by these aliens from another planet. I have been abducted to serve as a specimen in an alien genetics or body parts program. They are going to cut me into pieces. And my government is giving its blessing, not unlike another government that marched humans into gas chambers."

"Yes. As I said, they may study your brain, genetics, or anatomy." Liana stepped back, watching him with wide eyes as if surprised by his logic. "Your government is allowing alien Greys to work here."

"Greys?"

"Yes, from the Zeta 2 Reticuli. It is part of a binary star system."

"I thought that was science fiction."

"On the contrary, it is real."

He frowned at her. "Why tell me all this?"

"So you know the conditions of your imprisonment, the risks and probabilities. You must also know that I am not your enemy. I merely work for them."

"You say, 'them' as if you weren't pleased."

"How could I, I have feelings?"

"How did you get here? Were you abducted?"

"No."

"Then how?"

"The Greys made me."

Bryan pressed a fist to his mouth as he looked at her. "Oh my God," he said under is hand.

Silence enclosed them for several moments.

"Liana, how did they make you?"

"The Greys created me to serve them as, what your culture calls, a slave. The Greys made me from their DNA and human DNA. Their DNA isn't like human DNA but its molecular structure contains similar units in a different order. They used a human egg and inserted Grey DNA to fertilize it." She stopped and gazed into his eyes. Her eyes glistened. "They used DNA from your wife to create me."

"Her egg!"

"Yes. I am sorry." Her face was still and somber.

"Oh, Louise... my dear wife." He held his head in his hands and cried. Several moments passed before he found courage to look at her. "If they used Grey DNA to make you, why are so you human?"

"That is what they did."

"You don't look like anything other than a human female," he said, his voice thick and uneven. As he looked at Liana he felt sympathy for her. In his brain he thought of a hybrid and then a clone. "That doesn't sound like you were cloned."

"No. I am not a clone. I am essentially a different human. They made me to be like you by using an egg from your wife, her DNA, and Reticulan alien DNA. They manipulated the genetic code so I would look more human and still have the brain capacity of a Grey. They placed the fertilized egg in a surrogate human female. After several weeks, they took me from the surrogate and placed me in a machine, where I developed rapidly with their unique nourishment fluids until they extracted me. Their unique fluids made me mature at a high rate. I do not know the female who carried me as a fetus for several weeks, but I wish I did. I was not cloned."

"If you are a slave… ah, how long… never mind."

"Thank you for your sensitivity."

"Your name is human sounding. How did you come to learn to speak English?"

"Liana is the name I chose. To those for whom I work, I am known in your language as, Mettui Ouicil. All the creations like me, hybrids and clones, must learn English on the teaching machine."

"Your Grey name is, Mettui Ouicil?"

"Yes. It is Mettui Ouicil. Perhaps it is time for your education to begin. "The word, 'met' means I am part Reticulan Grey and part human, and I was birthed. Their definition of birthed does not mean traveling down a birth canal. It means the fetus grows naturally in a female for a period of time and not completely by artificial means as with their clones. Also the clones are made from DNA and no eggs or sperm are used, just cellular components."

"But…"

"Please allow me to finish. The next word of my name, 'tui,' means I am advanced, as in intelligence, 'oui,' means I have broad range of responsibilities, including technical ones, and 'cil,' is the Grey genetic strain used with the female egg from which I came." She hesitated, merely looking at him. "In the Grey's data system, I am also listed as Genome-Sp-7311, which relates to the experiment they used to create me, the specific Grey DNA used in their experiment. But forget that.

Bryan's eyes met Liana's. The single word haunting him spilled from his mouth. "Louise."

He cried. Liana's eyes sank sadly and her mouth hung low. He wiped a tear from his cheek with the back of his hand.

"Liana, I do not have hatred for you."

"Thank you." She nodded and then glanced around the room as if on alert, seemingly checking whether her controllers had eyeballs on her.

Suddenly, Bryan's eyes grew wide with a troubling thought. A connection had skirted over his confused mind.

"You said you were created only two years ago?"

Liana drew back. "Yes, I was. The Grey's nourishment fluids facilitated my maturation." Her eyes grew intense. "Why did you love your wife? What made you love her?"

He found her question odd. She was asking him a question, penetrating into the nature of human relations, the base emotions. Was it that she wanted to know more about who she was?

"Of course there was physical attraction, her beauty and her body... but I loved to talk with her. She was loving." His voice rose with energy. "She had a wonderful personality, a sense of humor, and an expansive awareness of the world and universe... at least within the limits of our science. I loved her brilliance... not that I benefited, but it was like watching blooming flowers. I used to surprise her with a single rose on her dresser when she would get home from the university. I had a ritual of giving her new charms for a remembrance bracelet on the special days of the year."

"You mentioned physical attraction. What type of physical attraction did you have?"

"You mean like appearance or sexual in nature?"

Liana's brow pulled down as if she were wrestling with the subtleties of the human sociology. "Like urges to touch, visual stimulation, response to smells... or mating desires."

"I loved her face, her body, and the perfumes she wore."

"Oh... I understand," she said. Her tone was plain and clinical. "I hear your love for her in your words and the way you moved your eyes as you talked about her."

The woman helping him was lovely and he couldn't help wondering how she had matured so fast, even with special nutrients. She smiled at him as if she had heard what was running through his head. Despite feeling self-conscious and getting an eerie sense that she was eavesdropping on his thoughts, he confronted her with a long gaze, finding it was impossible to regard her as anything other than a beautiful human.

A thought of Louise sparked a rampaging morality question.

"Liana, as a rational being, do you believe it is proper and justified to take the life of an innocent beautiful spirit or imprison a being simply because another being may have superior technology or science? Doesn't the spirit of every being created in the universe have a right to its own peaceful freedom?"

Her brow raised a little. "You seem an intelligent human man. I observed that." Liana turned her head, surveying the room, looking off to her right and to the far end of the room. She brought her attention back in a smooth unrushed motion, appearing to check for something in the other direction. "I have reached a point in my maturity where I appreciate all spiritual beings, living beings," she said, her voice emerging soft and measured. "I have also studied records from a vast repository of information, analyzing the question on a universal scale... including the premise of societal punishment for heinous acts against the living."

"What?"

"I may have been created only two years ago, but I have been educated by a teaching machine of the Greys. My emotions are still maturing. It has been my task to undergo instruction so I can better serve them. They use me to communicate verbally with humans. I am a communication slave... and I carry out broad ranging technical assignments. The Greys only communicate mind-to-mind. They can make sounds but do not communicate that way."

Her words stunned Bryan. The picture of his new closed-in world had startling facets and Liana seemed more cooperative by the minute, and faintly supportive.

"Should you tell me such facts?"

"I have no fear of those who control me. Of course, they could end my existence at any moment."

"Even though aliens from another planet are your master, you must not surrender your existence to them. Besides, you are now part of my Louise."

"Yes, I suppose so."

"How many Greys are there in this facility?"

"Seven at the present time."

"Are there more like you?"

"Hybrids like me? Not quite. In addition to me, there are four males and three females. None of them are exactly like me. None have my... I have the most varied tasks and I have freedom to act on my own. The Greys understand that my intelligence requires more diversity and stimulation than the other hybrids. They are studying me. I'm another of their experiments."

"What about freedom? Don't you want to be free?"

"I do not know what freedom is other than the absence of Grey's control."

"Freedom is more than not being constantly observed."

"Were you free before the Greys brought you here?"

"Yes."

For a moment he imagined an open pasture of clover and grazing horses under a sunlit sky. He had never been to such a place. Perhaps the open space was somewhere in his subconscious and he wished he could share it with Liana to help her appreciate what it represented.

"Yes. In my country people live free. But, there are other regions on this planet where people are controlled as slaves just as under the Greys."

"What are the characteristics of being free?"

The question struck Bryan as something from a scientist, completely unexpected. He thought for a moment.

"No one watching, no one telling you what you can and cannot say, no one telling you how to think, no one stopping you from looking up at the open blue sky, not seeing any barriers or prison bars, traveling at will to a location of one's choosing, breathing the air, and looking over a vast expansive landscape." He paused. "Of course, some things are limited by social rules preventing infringing upon other people's freedoms. There is a balance… an attempt at a balance."

Liana's eyes grew heavy. Her face said she was evaluating and digesting what he'd said and that she had found it disturbing.

"Very interesting." Her voice dropped. "I have never seen the sky."

"You have never left this place?"

"I never experienced that need."

"I'm sorry to hear that. I'm so sorry for your existence." He gazed at her, searching for his own strength. He wiped a hand across his cheek, catching a remaining tear, leaving a wet smear. "I had those freedoms."

This biological entity apparently lived an enslaved way of life no different than some people on earth had endured under a despotic regime. The facility and thoughts about the aliens made a connection for him. If the aliens existed in a working relationship with his government in this facility, located in his country, then who had the authority and who had agreed to such a criminal arrangement? Someone in the government had approved the unlawful genocidal human abduction and butchery. He thought of the Nazis in Germany, trying to wipe out Jews. It looked as if horror had crawled out of hell once again.

If she was intelligent, could he trust her?

"Is this facility is located in America?" Bryan asked.

"Yes. And I can see another question in your eyes."

"I'm sorry to ask, but how long will they keep you?"

"I observe your sensitivity. They will keep me until they no longer need me. At that time, they will probably place a sample of my DNA in their archives and dispose of my remains."

"I'm sorry." He clasped his forehead and rubbed as if squeezing the lunacy away to leave behind a new reality.

The past minutes, all of them since Liana had brought him back from the catatonic state, had placed a radical scope on his existence and the earth's place in the universe. Walking the earth now meant living with a shrunken sense of pride and perhaps anxiousness that higher intelligent species might not subscribe to hands-off or cohabitation.

"I know."

He looked at her. "If you're allowed to say, what are the Reticulans doing here on this planet?"

"Repairing and perfecting their species..." Her voice became a whisper. "...and populating this world for future control. Perhaps ten thousand years ago, when they changed their DNA to double and triple, their lifespan they created a problem with their reproduction. By the time they discovered it, their species was in disastrous and near irreparable decline for DNA mutations."

A strange sound emerged from behind Bryan, at the far end of the room, thirty yards in the distance. He turned and looked across the dimly illuminated chasm of dangling, glistening covers, hanging like plastic flowers in a grotesque greenhouse where the tables with bodies served as seedpods. His eyes hit upon the source of the noise, a disturbance from one of the many suspended coverings. Liquid rained down from the top of the plastic compartment that covered a dark figure lying on the table. He could hear a whooshing sound as the fluid bubbled, foamed, and enveloped the unmoving horizontal figure.

"Oh no… that can't be happening," Bryan said.

He sent a fist to his mouth as he watched the horror. In a few moments, the bubbles became smaller, dissipating as the body completely dissolved. A humming noise and the sound of moving air marked the onset of a vacuum stage, which pulled the fluid down through the table. In a moment the table lay bare beneath the plastic canopy, leaving an unforgettable gruesome image in Bryan's brain. His mouth gapped.

"My God, they dissolved a body!"

It was the most ghoulish scene he had ever seen. He had seen black and white pictures of piles of corpses from the last world war, but the dissolving of a body before his eyes was heart-ripping.

Bryan stared at Liana with dumb astonishment.

Liana's brow moved down almost imperceptibly. She gave him the impression she had experienced the human emotion of sadness and perhaps revulsion.

"I am not happy you saw that," she said.

The reduction of a person to fluid foreshadowed an option Bryan could face in his final moments. The victim appeared unconscious but that didn't exculpate the murderers in any way. However, if they made him a victim, he would probably have no awareness, but if given the chance, he'd go to his death with a fierce battle.

"You should not have seen that," Liana whispered. She looked at a door a short distance away.

"So that's the way they do away with bodies?"

"Not all," she said, her voice more clinical. "Some do not even make it to this room. The Greys surgically operate on some subjects in their ship and simply dump them out when they are finished. Those subjects fall back to the surface."

"How can you tell me this? It's horrible."

"I agree it is distasteful." She paused as if hitting a reset button. "I have taken too much time with you. I must take you for inspection. Three Greys have asked for you. When you were acquired, they read your brain and know that you were working on, what you call computer artificial intelligence. They must think you have intelligence worthy of study. That is good. I am going to try to make your first visit with the Greys as stress free as possible to minimize your trauma. Try to act intelligent and they may find you have value."

"If they will dispose of you one day, I assume I will also die." Bryan looked crossly at Liana, meeting her eyes, feeling helpless again.

At that instant, he heard Liana whispering in his ear, but her mouth wasn't moving and her head was three or four feet away. He rubbed his ear. In his head, a voice told him to relax. The voice told him that he would not face pain or harm. The voice seemed to flow wavelike, undulating in volume and then it repeated. He closed his eyes and shook his head. After a moment, he opened his eyes, thinking that she had somehow talked directly into his brain. He felt like he had fallen asleep with his eyes open.

Liana took his hand.

Inside Bryan's head, he again heard a voice: "You are hearing me. This is Liana talking into your mind. Come with me. Be calm. The Greys talk like this. You will learn."

He walked beside her and a half-pace behind, pacing with her steps compliantly, telling himself to observe and memorize everything as if in a silent movie that he could replay before his eyes. He moved his gaze from the surroundings to Liana, noticing how her body moved as she walked. She marched down the hall, head up with purpose, her legs smoothly striding, her arms carried at her sides, and despite the formality she had a feminine grace; she moved like liquid steel.

Chapter Three

Bryan and Liana continued down the passageway of untouched bleak concrete, his thoughts fleeting over his fears and the approaching encounter with his abductors. How he should act? Would he have the courage to face them?

A curious connection struck him as he gazed ahead. This place put him in mind of an obsolete missile silo or something else he couldn't bring clearly to mind. The corridor was wide and poorly illuminated for such a facility. That miniscule fact surprised him. Liana walked with him in what appeared part of a large circular section of the building with the echo of their footsteps following their travel. The ceiling, perhaps fourteen-feet high, capped off the concrete walls like the closure of a mausoleum vault. Periodic rectangular concrete trusses marked the distance along the hall. The place also reminded him of a cheap parking garage he'd mistakenly encountered on a cold winter day in New Jersey. And like that garage, this facility smelled of dampness and something else Bryan couldn't place. Bizarrely, it seemed he was walking to his death.

The sheer scale of the architecture spawned the thought that his escape was problematic. If this was only one hallway, the whole facility must have had monstrous dimensions. How could he escape such a fortress?

Liana stopped outside two elevators. One door appeared for passenger use. Liana opened the wider second door. As they stepped in, Bryan realized it was used for freight, to accommodate large equipment or contractors during construction. He had seen similar elevators at his university. Liana touched the button for level fourteen on the control panel.

Fourteen levels that I can access. That's how many levels I'll have to negotiate to find my way to freedom.

The elevator dropped and as it did, his pulse quickened. A moment later, it made a loud rattling sound just prior to stopping. Upon exiting Bryan stepped into another sweeping circular hallway, duplicating the same floor pattern they had left. On the inner circumference, they walked past door after door several yards apart. The immensity of his imprisoning structure and its compartments shook his optimism, darkening any thoughts of reaching freedom because of a seemingly insurmountable challenge.

Liana had warned him about the meeting but had offered no details. He feared something extreme, but what? He started to whisper to her and was stopped by a stream of words overpowering his thought. In his mind he heard: "You must remain silent."

At last they approached an open door. Liana paused at the threshold.

Ahead of Bryan, the room had a snow-white ceiling and walls. The controlling aliens used brightened walls like humans in a hospital, probably for improved observation. It had to be some sort of laboratory. He moved his gaze across the floor.

There they stood, three aliens. They stared at him coldly.

Bryan felt his heart race as a tingle ran over him. Despite knowing that seeing them was really happening, it was hard to believe what filled his vision. Aliens. Grey aliens with short slender stature, grey-colored bulbous heads, and large almond-shaped eyes stood a few feet from him. Lifeless and empty, their eyes had no pupils or iris, just blackness. Their bony brows jutted outward over the eyes. Their tiny ears, an afterthought, appeared little more than openings in their skulls.

He looked away from them. He had to. Instead of looking at them, he examined the room, which appeared to be designed for medical procedures. Two three-foot-high, gray equipment cabinets sat next to each other a few feet from the center of the room. The patient platform, operating table, that occupied the center of the laboratory told Bryan it was for examining biological subjects and performing surgery. A few feet from the platform, two smaller tables held glowing vertical displays with white characters. The rectangular illumination, like a TV screen, had a bluish tinge and he could see through it. He guessed they were holograms, forming a type of three-dimensional control mechanism made from light. One table held a device with binocular viewing extensions similar to a microscope. A three or four-foot long, rod-shaped instrument hung from the ceiling at the center of the room above the table. Three probes extended from its end. A foot-square metal case, three or four inches thick, sat open on a table, filled with rows of small capped vials. A silvery sphere the size of a soccer ball floated past him up near the ceiling, seemingly traveling on a purposeful path.

They are going to do something to my body.

A whispering voice in his head told him to come forward and lie down on the table. The voice didn't seem to be from Liana. Its frequency and amplitude was harsher than her mental communication. He didn't have a choice. His life wasn't his own. Never could he have conceived of the feeling of utter helplessness, but he felt it now.

Liana remained at the door like guard, or perhaps a slave, on call to help with an uncontrollable subject.

Bryan moved toward the table and stopped two feet away. The voice repeated in his mind, compelling him to step toward the table. As he complied, another voice deep down in his head screamed at him to flee, to strike out with fury. He moved with a jerky motion, his body and mind conflicted. Another command, its source seemingly that of a Grey, entered his thinking, rolling over his own contemplation. The Grey's words told him to relax, that there wasn't anything he could do, and that they wouldn't hurt him. Bryan placed his hand on the table, noticing it was cold, and pushed himself up. He lay down on his back, quivering from his fright.

He looked up, squinting to see through the bright light, looking at the objects hanging from the ceiling. Three Grey aliens moved close to the table, one at his head, and one on each side. They leaned over him, glaring at him, their eyes pressing down on him like a demonic spell. They seemed to enjoy feasting on his terror and powerless body. The vertical lines at the corners of their small childlike mouths failed to camouflage their hideous intent and grim disregard for human life. He thought he saw the hint of a smile.

One of the Greys, the one near his head, reached toward Bryan with a slender grey hand extending three spindly fingers and thumb. Bryan looked toward it. The Grey blinked its glassy eyes. He had to look away, away from the eyes, and away from their repulsive heads. His head jittered left and right as if operated by a broken gear in his neck trying to turn it.

A voice slid snakelike into his head again, intertwining with the Grey's underlying controlling mantra, telling him to remain passive, telling him to relax to minimize harm. With intermittent vision he looked past his feet. Liana still stood at the edge of the room, ready, poised at attention to serve her masters. Her eyes connected with Bryan's for a moment, which seemed like she was urging courage and support rather than aimlessly linking with him.

A searing light blasted down at Bryan, washing out his vision. In a moment, he felt a stinging on his stomach, possibly from a needle. His skin moved. Within moments, they had enwrapped him deeper in their control, his senses seemingly functioning through the smoke of dulled nerves.

The sounds that reached him came muffled as if the Greys had covered his head with a blanket. The room, the bright white light, the dead-eyed Greys, and the creepy hands disappeared into an intermittent smeared image, like a movie moving in and out of focus.

Something moved within the light, changing its brightness. He stared eyeball-to-eyeball with a Grey alien. He thought it grinned its tiny mouth at him in sadistic amusement, creating a dreadful caricature face. He screamed but nothing came from his vocal cords; it was only inside his mind. His vision went blank. He fell unconscious.

***

Light, tinted yellow by dirt coating the glowing panel, fell on the gray concrete walls of a small room. Meager as it was it coaxed Bryan to open his eyes. He found himself lying on a cot. He looked around and concluded they had placed him in a small prison cell. His ordeal with the Greys probing his body had ended and he was still alive. He moved a little and felt soreness in his stomach. He ran a hand down to the spot; it was where the Greys moved his flesh. A small lump stood proud from his skin. On the same side, on his back, he felt a tight muscle and a little pain. He raised his side and explored his back with his hand. Another lump came under his fingers, a longer deviation. The Greys cut his body and with their technology they had rapidly healed it, although despite their phenomenal methods, his body revealed a chink in their invulnerability. By not preventing formation of scar tissue, his skin had betrayed their actions, and told him another potentially more important thing. Their behavior disproved the perfection in their intelligence, at least regarding humans.

Thinking back to the previous day, the first day of his resurrection, at least he wasn't back on the table where they would dissolve him and flush him down the drain.

He looked at his cell, wondering if they had placed him there in preparation for another trip to the operating theater. The room was about fifteen-feet square and was nothing more than uncovered concrete walls and floor. A single glowing, and dirty, light panel was in the center of the ceiling. The room smelled disgusting. The odors had a biological origin, at least that was his guess. Maybe they came from the previous occupants. A small metal toilet and tiny sink, similar to what he'd seen in recreational vehicles, occupied a back corner, opposite the door-side of the room. A downward flow of heat came from a duct near the ceiling. He was surprised the room was as warm as it was, since the barren concrete was a good heat sink, sucking away heat forever. Why did the Greys keep the room warm? Was it related to the aliens and their bodies, or was it merely a psychological tool to help prisoners relax and not cause trouble? They could have thrown him into a room and forced him to lie on bare cold concrete. Perhaps he would live another day.

Was anyone watching him? He looked over the walls and ceiling. He didn't see any cameras or such devices? Nothing obvious, but would they use cameras? They would probably use something considerably more advanced.

What time was it? He hated not having a way to measure time. And he was lost geographically. If, as Liana had said, he was in a government facility it was no doubt a secret from his country and the world. If it wasn't secret, the curious people of the journalistic media, the ones still in possession of consciences and ethics, would bulldog-dig and scratch until they had exposed it to the residing ethical law enforcers of the people's government. He laughed at himself for his optimistic thought.

In the momentary solitude, he began exploring scenarios of his impending relegation to the alien scrapheap. If only he had the power, he would use it to destroy the facility holding him and obliterate the soulless aliens—not just for him but for Louise. His hatred for the invaders wasn't merely because of his personal situation, it was their shattering of human freedom, and it was because of their ghoulish acts, their acting like gods. If he ever got the chance to talk with one of the big-headed Greys, he hoped he would have the courage to remind them that a highly intelligent form of life should have more reverence for the lesser species.

He ran a finger over the lump on his stomach, fueling his anger. He stood next to the cot, lifted his shirt, and found the one inch scar had healed as if made several months ago. He suspected he had something similar on his back.

The door latch clicked, drawing Bryan's eyes. He wondered if another excursion to the operating room was minutes away. Would he ask himself that same question every time the door opened, until the last time the latch turned?

The door opened. Liana stood there, looking at him for a moment, a wary expression in her eyes. She stepped slowly into the room, leaving the door slightly open. The cold air that wafted into the room smelled fresh to Bryan, although it too had a slightly dank character. Beyond the room in the hall, he caught sight of a silvery sphere hovering at the height of the door.

As Bryan gazed back at Liana, he again found her questioning eyes. Her expression showed a definite lack of trust and that of someone observing a curiosity, an oddity. Wrinkles formed on her forehead in a momentary display of analysis and then she appeared sad or sympathetic. It seemed she was distracted and conflicted by her emotions on how to deal with him. He found that aspect of her personality surprising and a little reassuring.

"Do you... perhaps have a question for me?" Bryan said. "You seem concerned."

The wrinkles on her forehead dissolved. "How do you feel?" Liana asked, standing motionless with her arms at her sides.

"I think I'm okay, except I have a new scar on my stomach and I believe on my back."

"You do have scars. They occurred yesterday when I took you to their operation procedure room."

"Yesterday? This is my second day after the table?" He sat back on his cot, looking at her, trying to get a sense of her, whether she was a friend or just a tool of the Greys. The loss of a day reinforced how vulnerable he was while under the Grey's control.

"Yes. You rested here until now. They gave you a drug to reduce your trauma. It has been nearly twenty-four of your hours. It is mid-morning."

"What did they do to me?" he said. His voice was just short of exploding.

"Calm yourself. If you are irrational, they will consider you to be poor DNA material and discard you quickly. Remember the room with the tables. They could also use you in a different manner. You must offer value to them if you are to stay alive."

His eyes focused in the distance as he glimpsed the silver sphere again. He sighed and cleared his throat. "Okay. Please tell me why I have a scar and a sore area on my body?"

"They removed one of your organs, the one you call a kidney. They wanted to test its reaction to radiation. Radiation on their planet along with genetic manipulation and cloning has produced DNA replication deviations, and problems with continuing the positive development of their species. It's one of the problems they are studying. They are trying to use DNA from the strongest, best humans to improve their species, in addition to colonization. They consider themselves mentally very advanced but bodily inferior."

Bryan heard her words flooding to him without the guarded coldness of her original manner and caution, which seemed to consider him little more than a low level species good only for experimentation.

"What do they consider you?"

"The probability is high that they consider me nothing more than a slightly educated tool. I'm no more significant to them than an artificial intelligence creation you had in your brain while you were in your dormant sleep state. They trust no one, so I am merely a tool." She turned toward the door. "See that silver sphere floating in the hall. It is one of their monitoring devices. They have several floating around, watching their own kind, other Greys, watching everything. Their society operates with a central focus and a controlling structure. They work toward specific goals of the collective."

"Does that sphere follow you all the time?"

"No. It varies with their concern. They probably wanted to study my interaction with you."

Her acknowledgement of being a slave and a tool again troubled him. A question about the unthinkable came to him.

"Were you able to get my thoughts while I was unconscious?"

"Yes. It is one of my advanced abilities—compared to your species. The Greys can do it too. It is similar to the mind-to-mind communication I told you about. That's probably why you are still alive. They examined your thoughts and saw that you are, what you call, a scientific human. You work with your advanced technology. It isn't advanced to them, though."

"But that wasn't enough to prevent them from stealing one of my organs," Bryan replied hastily. He snatched an angry breath.

"Yes."

"Why are you talking to me like this?"

"As I said, they want observations, mine and theirs."

"Is that why the sphere is still outside?"

"It will probably leave after the Grey making observations has completed its task. They find the individuality of humans interesting. They don't function that autonomously. They refer back to a central social controlling structure, which includes a collection of intelligence in their data system."

"Don't they worry about you describing their operation?"

"They are not concerned about anything or any threat. They believe they are superior to everything on this planet. They are confident they have total control."

Bryan, sensing her softening tone, decided to explore further. "Can you tell me where I'm being held? I still want to know." He stopped, thinking for a moment, and looked at her. "Can I have a clock to keep track of the time and date?"

"Why?"

"There is no natural light. This place is like living in a tomb. Time has meaning for people... humans."

"I might be able to make one."

He stared at her, confused and amazed by her comment. A moment passed. "So those in control aren't concerned about any threats?"

"As I said before, we are in your government's facility. We are deep below the ground. The complex is quite large, fourteen levels. It is constructed with two concrete cylinders penetrating down into the earth. There are two wings, a west wing cylinder and an east wing cylinder. We are in the west wing. The Greys are only in the west wing and have work areas on the bottom four levels. The east wing is a mechanical section... for power generation. Air is circulated through ducts running down the elevators, one pushing it down and one pulling it up. At this time, we are on the Grey's second level, level twelve of the west wing. I took you to the bottom level yesterday."

He never expected to hear such information. It stunned him and did nothing to remove his fears that he couldn't escape.

"What is down on the fourteenth level?"

Liana's attention reached out into the distance for a moment. "The sphere has gone." She turned to him. "I doubt what I tell you will remove any of your apprehension."

"Please."

"The Greys have operating rooms for analysis, for harvesting body parts from animals and other biological entities, a room for genetics restructuring, a room for biological component storage with cryogenics, a chemical storage, and a biological incinerator." She paused. "They have their food processing system in one room, which might be considered advanced by your standards. It is there they create various molecules, combining them into palatable proteins and carbohydrates. They don't eat like humans or hybrids."

He held his eyes on her, noting how she had just become uncomfortable. "What do you mean?"

"The Greys take food in through their skin and they also lose their waste through their pores."

"If they have existed for so long, why haven't they advanced beyond such a method?"

"I don't know. Perhaps they find it efficient. They consume a fluid that they formulate, which contains liquefied components from other, once living beings." Liana's head dropped a little.

"I think you are saying they eat animals in liquid form."

Liana nodded.

There was something in her face, telling him that she held something back. "They don't eat humans... do they?" he asked.

Liana looked away and continued. "The Grey's get electrical power from the military. In this underground military facility, the two wings share a common wall and heavy emergency access doors on each floor. On the other side of the concrete wall from the Grey's level twelve, the military operates a three hundred megawatt water cooled nuclear reactor that provides all the needed power. The power generation section extends from sublevel twelve down to fourteen. However, regarding the electrical power, since the Grey's equipment operates on a different frequency, potential, and what you call, amperage, they must run the electrical power through their conversion device."

"I find that interesting... that the Greys get their electrical power from the military?" Bryan wondered why Liana described the nuclear power, not keeping it secret, and then he dismissed it as part of her discipline for completeness, perhaps part of her Grey DNA.

"They also get their heat from the military, which is forced hot air from their multiple gas furnaces located on their level eleven. There is a flying craft storage area accessed from floor eleven. A long tunnel goes to it. The Greys fly in and out from there, through a hole in the mountainside. At least that is what is recorded in their data. I have never seen it."

"Is this whole facility completely underground?"

"Nearly all of it. From what I have learned from the teaching machine. They store fuel for vehicles below ground on level two of the east wing and natural gas lines enter the structure there. According to the records, it is all completely hidden from the rest of the world except for a truck access at ground level. Apparently, the facility is well disguised."

"You've never ever seen the outside?"

"No."

Bryan tried to fathom the unbelievable dark life limited to roaming these concrete tunnels, a mole's life. But a life not knowing what was missed, was still a life.

"Is the level below this one where I was held in a dormant state?" he asked.

"Yes. This is twelve. There are eleven floors above this one. One through ten are occupied by an estimated two hundred military personnel, according to Grey calculations."

He shook his head a little. *My chances of escaping are looking minuscule.* He had no idea how he'd start. And besides, he was powerless to destroy the complex, which was his dying hope.

"You are correct thinking that an escape by you would have a low probability as well as any attempt at the destruction of the whole installation."

"You picked up my thoughts."

"Yes."

"Are you going to report those thoughts to the Greys?"

"No."

He felt her gaze. She appeared to be evaluating him, appraising his thoughtfulness or intelligence. He didn't know for certain; it was only a feeling, but something was rolling around in her head. And despite the momentary tension, her face appeared porcelain-smooth.

"Every prisoner thinks of escape," he said.

"That is logical."

He found her reaction tantalizing. "What about you?"

She nodded imperceptibly and faintly smiled. "Interesting."

He laughed under his breath at their little dance. She could track his thoughts. He concluded she would know everything he ran through his mind. He no longer had private thoughts. He no longer had any freedom whatsoever, not even in his own mind.

"I do not listen to everything in your mind."

"What?"

"They gave me a directive to place you on their teaching machine. The Greys want to evaluate your brain. It will be a good thing for you. They have allocated me liberal contact time with you. In addition, I think they want to evaluate my relationship with you, examine if emotions emerge and have any influence. They are interested in emotions and relationships since they don't experience any social connections. Everything they do is related to the collective society evolution and reproduction is structured by their objectives. They are allowing me to train your mind for our type of communication, so you will be able to talk mind-to-mind like I do and like they do. They want to know if you can be taught to communicate as they do. However, it may be difficult for you. You may have to work hard to do it."

"You mean I won't have to listen with my ears or speak audibly?"

"Yes. The machine should activate your dormant brain functions. It worked with one other subject."

"How does mind-to-mind communication work? Does it have a scientific basis?"

"From my time on the teaching machine, I learned of scientific relationships. Our thoughts travel on the subatomic level, the most fundamental level in the universe."

"You mean quantum level?"

"That is what this planet calls it from what I saw in my research. One mind can exchange quantum with another mind." She smiled. "That will have to suffice for now."

Bryan felt a relationship forming between them, due principally to their positive communication, the simple act of talking. Was that part of the Greys study?

For a moment, he lowered his gaze, surrendering to a human curiosity. He looked over her breasts, her waist, her narrow hips, and her trim legs. He tried not to think, given her a mind-reading revelation, but before he could stop he had formed a thought. She was an exceptionally attractive female.

Liana looked down at herself as if following the path of his eyes. "You think I am attractive? Obviously, the term 'attractive' is not related to magnetism in, what you call, physics."

Bryan smiled, slightly embarrassed. "It's a form of human compliment. I'm sorry. It's an emotional aspect of being human and a male of my species. I suppose it evolved early so our species would reproduce. Men look at women. It means you look nice."

"I did feel faint warmth as a reaction to your observation." She paused, permitting her eyes to drift off for a moment. "Yes, after going to the teaching machine, you will learn how to develop a private mind, although it will be hard."

He thought to her: *Does that mean they won't remove another body part tomorrow?*

Liana stared at him.

A voice slipped into Bryan's mind: "You will receive training and probably will not have another surgery during the next phase of the Grey's evaluation, which is research into the function of your human brain."

He spoke aloud, "You sent me a thought."

"Does that activity interest to you?" Liana said.

"It sounds interesting. Thank you." He flashed on the thought that he needed anything that would help him escape. "Will it make me more valuable to the Greys?"

"It should." Liana paused and then moved her mouth, seemingly about to speak. Her eyes grew larger as if she had discovered something. She smiled faintly. "I think I like verbalizing. I like the physicality. I have not had a need until they assigned me to monitor you."

He wondered if she had heard his last thought. Bryan cocked his head, frowned, and pulled on his chin.

Liana looked at him amused.

"If the Greys are placing me on their teaching machine, does that mean they want to see how much my subspecies brain will retain? Is that part of the brain study?"

Liana acknowledged him with a faint movement of her head. "That has a high probability as a constituent of their study but there are more elements. For now, I will place you on the teaching machine."

"I suppose it makes sense from their perspective," Bryan said, his tone mocking. "I'll cooperate as long as they don't cut off more of my body."

The longer he worked with them the more chance he would have at escaping. He had to prolong his contributions to their studies. At that point he noticed a change in her eyes. She looked sharply at him and then glanced away. He sensed she had read his brief thought about longevity and escape.

Liana turned toward Bryan's cell door, took a step, and held up her hand, gesturing an invitation. "Please come for a meal and your first session on the teaching machine."

Bryan bristled to readiness, standing, flexing his hands eager to take hold of his life. "I am hungry. Thank you. What time of the day is it? I've lost all sense of time."

"It is morning and the day is the eleventh of your planet's month," she said plainly. "I will get you a time monitoring device. The Greys have this planet's astronomical data and this country's physical and social protocols... your calendar for example... provided by the military a long time ago. They use that monitoring function in their long range plans for future actions."

    "What actions?"

Chapter Four

Bryan walked with new energy alongside Liana as they traveled from his cell, along a hall shooting radially out toward the sweeping outermost circumferential corridor of the underground building. They stayed on the same floor. As he walked along at her side, he was taken by her graceful athletic motion. Her feet landed as if she practiced her movement for stealth.

She took him down the dreary unembellished passage. Along the corridor, always in the same minimal light, they passed several doors and every one of them was windowless. He couldn't gather a sense of any activity, although he heard a deep low-frequency hum. After fifty yards, they turned down a hall that ran at a right-angle to the outer curved hall and walked ten more yards to an open door.

Inside the room, the overhead panel lights dropped minimal brightness onto a twenty-foot square space with walls of untouched concrete. Five two-foot square metal compartments rested on a long counter that ran along one side of the room. Four wire mesh chairs were placed around a small table.

"This is where you will eat," Liana said. "It is used by hybrids although not heavily. I come here to eat."

Bryan's mind wandered. What daily personal habits did the alien Greys have, other than eating? Liana had said they took in food through their skin. What about sleeping? He thought of sleeping with his Louise. His anger flared as he thought of her questionable end, possibly serving the Grey's nourishment needs. He hated their guts.

Liana swung around to him. "Find peace. Your wife did not go to the nourishment circulation. They stored her DNA."

"I can't help myself. I'm fighting questions about her life passing away."

"I am sorry for that."

He wondered how much he could learn from this hybrid creature and how much he could trust her. He hoped knowing more about the Reticulan species would help him survive, but working against their technology and intelligence looked like a formidable if not an unsolvable problem. With more understanding and awareness of the Grey's operation in this tomb, perhaps he would conceive of a path to freedom, maybe negotiate his release.

"You look as if you need food." Liana swung open the door to one of the compartments, revealing a dispenser with buttons identified with unique symbols. She pushed two of the controls and removed a container from the bottom. She took out a closed cup-sized container of liquid and handed it to Bryan. At a second compartment, she pushed a button and removed a bar that was three or four inches in length, similar to a piece of candy.

"This should satisfy part of your need for food," she said. "The liquid in the container supplies much of the nutrition your body requires. These machines modify and reformulate molecules, manufacturing various animal proteins as well as components found in your fruits."

"Thank you."

The attention Liana gave him, while simple in her deeds, appeared to demonstrate an increasing understanding, and he hoped, an appreciation for him as an intelligent valuable creature.

She pointed with an open hand to a chair at the table. He sat and placed his two items in front of him. Liana stood observing at him. For an instant, she gave him the impression that she was fighting a concern about sitting with him in the convivial atmosphere. She glanced over her shoulder toward the hall.

Bryan followed her gaze, almost certain she was looking for a hovering sphere but he did not see one.

She sat, observing him softly, her eyes following his movements.

Bryan thought for a moment and pointed. "Where do the light bulbs and other items come from? This facility is using common human type lighting."

"Periodically, a supply requisition is sent up to the military in the freight elevator and the items are sent down to the Grey's levels. There is no interaction between the military and Greys. The hybrids, such as myself, install the replacement items. The Greys do not do any labor."

Bryan drank some of his liquid and found it thicker than water, tasting like a vegetable juice with an acidic character. The food bar was like a cross between a grain and vegetable, lacking both salt and sugar. He ate it not knowing when he'd get a chance to eat again. As he consumed the small amount of nourishment, Liana's small facial changes intrigued him. She followed his every move, seemingly studying how humans react in a free environment.

"Do you eat this type of food?"

"Occasionally. I usually eat a soft material that is heated. It comes from one of the other food containers. I like it warm. It is purely for nutrition, providing, I believe, no taste by your senses, or for that matter, mine. I eat here frequently."

"Do the Greys eat... sleep regularly?" Bryan swallowed the last of the food bar and sipped the last of the liquid.

"They eat on a schedule. They have short rest cycles. They live nearly a three hundred earth years and can regenerate their bodies, but it has caused them problems over the many cycles they have practiced their procedure."

"What about you?"

"I enjoy eating." Liana nodded, her face showing appreciation for his question as a logical follow-up to the previous. "I sleep for approximately five of your hours. I can go without sleep as the Greys can but I function much better with rest. Physically, I'm much more human than Grey, although my mental part is still in question. My emotions are still developing and maturing."

She dropped her gazed to the table. After a moment she checked if he was looking at her. Her shoulders seemed more relaxed. She clasped her hands and quickly unfolded them.

The way she gave a self assessment about her mental state surprised him. Generally, the people he knew concealed their mental weaknesses.

Liana looked at him firmly and sat up straight. "Time to begin working." She stood and stepped to the door. "Time for the teaching machine."

"I'd like to ask a couple more questions."

"Yes."

"Are the Greys the most intelligent and advanced creatures?"

"In regard to what?"

"This galaxy… that humans call the Milky Way. Do you know what I mean?"

"As close as I can describe, they call this galaxy, TEL397K. They consider it an average galaxy because of its diameter and the gravitational singularly. And from what I have learned, they are at the low intelligence range of species. There are some that watch the Grey's activity and they are much more advanced. In the Grey's data system, they reference a star grouping with another name from your military. The star is Arcturus. There are humanoids from a planet in that system that the Greys fear."

"I need a telephone to call them for help," Bryan said with a self-mocking twist of his mouth. "Okay, I'm ready to go."

He followed Liana, feeling anxious and exhilarated about an encounter with an alien teaching device. The possibility existed that he could vastly improve his intelligence.

***

The main arcing hall took Liana and Bryan past more doors, continuing his exposure to more of his silent prison. Two men approached from the opposite direction. One was dressed similar to Liana, who Bryan assumed, based on the large eyes, was a hybrid or clone. The second man looked human and wore earth clothes. The human man appeared possessed by a trance with eyes fixed and oriented straight ahead. As the alien worker and his human ward passed, Bryan noticed an incision ringing the top of the man's head. The breath in his chest suddenly froze from seeing the Frankenstein horror. The Grey's had surgically removed the top of the man's head and replaced it.

Bryan said not a word.

"I am sorry you had to see that," Liana said. "Do not be scared. They will not do that to you."

"How can you say that? You're a slave." After his words came out he thought he had been stupid and was sorry for his cruelty.

"Thank you for your apology. I will help you offer value to the Greys."

"You were in my mind again."

"Yes."

A few yards along the hall, Liana led Bryan inside a room with two large chairs. She immediately closed the door.

The chairs reminded him of those found in a moderately modern dental office. The chair had a headrest, padded arms, and was slightly reclined. Lighting panels overhead gave a subdued white light to the room. An odor tainted the air, smelling like a mix of dank concrete from the uncovered floor and something chemical such as a cleaner.

Liana noticed Bryan smelling the air. "You may detect the odor of electrical components and possibly biological products."

He nodded and resumed his observation, sweeping his gaze. Each chair had a device resembling a helmet, which he figured was for the student's head. A single control console sat opposite the chairs. It appeared to have a flat holographic, vertical display, which was a bluish white glow rising from its base. Liana stepped to the control, waved her hand, and circles illuminated within the glow, appearing as controls, like icons of some sort. Bryan saw no wires connecting anything.

"Sit in the chair," Liana said.

"Which?"

She pointed. "The one closest to the control."

Bryan sat, thinking about the procedure and possible side effects on his body. "What happened to that man we saw?"

Liana stopped, hands at her sides, her fingers curling in a possible demonstration of anxiety. "They placed that man on the teaching machine and then they took him to the operation area on the bottom floor where they examined the physical changes in his brain."

"They couldn't examine his brain with some sort of scanner or some other nondestructive testing method?"

"They also did that. They wanted to look at the changes in the neurons, which required them to remove a specimen."

"Holy God, what a house of horrors!"

"You mention God. Is that a belief of yours?"

"Very much so. Who created the universe? Do you have a belief in a universal creator?"

"That question is complex. There are some species that possess the power to create matter from energy and they can alter time. Even some of the most advanced beings hold reverence for the spirit who created the first spark of existence and created all the universes, the source from which all emerged."

"And what do the Greys believe?"

Liana was motionless as she seemed to reach out with her concentration across the room. Her voice came soft and even. "From what I have researched they do not attribute the universe to any creative source. They have taken the curious reasoning that it has always existed and discounted entropy, cause and effect, and time's linear movement."

Bryan thought for a moment. "One more question. Why do the Grey's hold such disdain for the life of a lesser developed species?"

"They do not care." She stepped over to him. "In their world they can create life, which is part of their problem and why they are here. Over time, through their casual creation of beings, they lost all appreciation for the spirit and value of life in other beings as well as themselves. They have few emotions and rarely display them. There are exceptions where they show a hint of anger or amusement. They have the ability on their planet to gather the conscious energy from a dead Grey's brain and inject it into a new synthetically created body. The consciousness of some Greys has been transferred into several successive bodies, allowing them to live for centuries in terms of your time measurement."

The clarity of her explanation struck Bryan as well as its openness. The label she had placed on herself, a slave, had mistakenly created in his naive mind, a perception that was opposite to her intelligence. His human ego had gotten in the way. Having seen the expression on her face and the glint in her eyes, he concluded she was more spiritual than she portrayed. And she might have been concealing her intelligence.

"Liana, I don't want to exist like the poor man I saw. Please terminate my life if that happens. Would you do that for me?"

"I understand."

"Please."

She reluctantly raised her brow. She held a cap-shaped mesh of small tubes over his head. The small tubes glowed with a green light. They ran from front to back and crosswise from ear to ear. She slowly lowered it, allowing its contoured shape to fit his head.

"This is part of the teaching system. I went through this. There is not anything to concern you. You may feel at ease."

The head-unit felt like a simple hat and the image in his head had been more threatening than what the situation merited. He felt a little silly for a moment until he reminded himself of his incarceration. The unit, initially cool on his scalp, started to warm and the comfortably heated room helped him relax.

"Does that feel satisfactory?"

"Yes. Thank you. What do I do?"

"You sit there until I turn off the machine." She held up her hand. "You can close your eyes, take a deep breath, and let the breath out slowly." She moved her hands over the illuminated controls.

Bryan looked around the room. He studied Liana sitting at the console, wondering about their relationship, which in two days had progressed amazingly. A few moments passed, while he waited for a change in his head. He didn't detect any effects. She looked at him and pointed to her eyes. He closed his eyes and took a breath. He thought he noticed something. His thoughts seemed to

dance, going from Liana and their relationship, helping
him, and back to what the machine was doing to his brain.
He wanted to open his eyes but held them shut, waiting for
her instruction. His thoughts broadened in scope and he
seemed to see connections he hadn't considered. He
visualized a golden energy flowing through his head. He
had thoughts of past computer research, and it became
connected to memories of actions, and those actions
connected to another memory, all flowing like liquid. The
clarity shifted, reached out, going forward in time to an
event he felt hadn't taken place. He could see himself
shooting upward in an elevator with Liana.

Don't look at the elevator. It was Liana's voice in
his head.

He turned his thoughts to the past. An image of
Louise flashed. The aroma of perfume came to him. He
smelled it in his mind. Louise had worn it. As he pictured
her in the past, he saw her eyes close as she took a breath.
He knew it was her death. Despair gripped him, taking him
from a distant mental state created by the machine.

Bryan heard Liana inside his head: "You must learn
to control where you travel in your mind. There are many
horrors to see, which will not help you survive. You must
place the memory of Louise in a mind-compartment that
you can open at any time, but only at an appropriate
occasion."

Bryan opened his eyes. "What I saw was real."

Liana moved her hand over the controls, looked at
characters on the panel display, and at him. "You did well."

"What did I do? I just sat there."

"Voice recognition in your thoughts is improved
and your logic improved. The display shows a measure of
your response." She glanced at the console and back, and
found his expectant eyes. "Your intelligence increased,
although the machine does not measure it the same as your
species."

"May I suggest you refer to me as human instead of using the term species. Besides, you are at least half human too." He paused. "Uh… is the improvement permanent?"

"Yes. The Greys will be interested. What they want to know is how much we can increase your brain.

"What is the Grey's intelligence?"

"Based on what I have researched in their information resources, the Greys have a human-equivalent intelligence quotient averaging three hundred fifty."

Bryan's eyes widened with his amazement. "That's unbelievable. What about you?"

Liana pressed her mouth closed, imposing a barrier of impenetrable calm. "I learned on this same machine. I do not care to discuss my level, but the Greys altered the DNA they used in creating me. However, yours just increased ten points from one hundred forty. Also you may experience a change in extended sensory perception, although the effect varies."

"Precognition?"

"You may only recognize glimpses and points for curiosity."

Bryan definitely felt the change in his thoughts, how fluidly they flowed compared to before the exposure to the machine.

"It helped a lot. Can I use the machine again? I would like to elevate my ability again?"

"That is what the Greys want to know. They want to know the human potential." She glanced up at the ceiling and back to him. She whispered, "They may consider humans a threat for the future."

"Interesting."

"Forget that for now." She looked at him with a faint smile; her mouth soft and slightly open. "I am not surprised by your interest. I will try to bring you here tomorrow."

"Will the Greys want to slice open my brain?"

"The probability exists but actions can…"

"What?"

Liana lowered her gaze, apparently avoiding making a comment she had on the tip of her tongue.

"I have great trepidation about the Greys and their interest in studying me like a bug. I can't help feeling they're going to keep testing me until they've completed their program and my value has expired. The teaching machine appears a way to help with my survival chances."

She stared at him. "I must be careful, but I will do what I can." She stepped over to him, leaning forward, and whispered, "There is another ability you must enhance. It is imperative that you learn how to mentally block the Greys accessing your thoughts." She removed the helmet from his head. "You will have to use it. But you must also be careful when you do."

He sat forward, ready to stand. Suddenly, what she told him struck home. "While undergoing their brain evaluation, will I have the capability to prevent the Greys from seeing in my mind and prevent them from planting instructions?"

"Very perceptive. Yes."

He wondered if she had just helped him move closer to an escape.

Liana bent down near him, her demeanor again more at ease, different than in her previous interactions with him. Her face seemed to say that she had a secret and she was keeping it until the right time. As that feeling raced past him, he discarded it as his imagination. He studied her face and whispered, "Is it possible for me to avoid all their mental probing?"

She backed up a step and nodded. "Most of it. You will have to focus very well."

He stood at the front of the teaching machine. "I hope I can do it."

"Presumably they have anticipated all the possible ramifications," she said, whispering. "I am aware of results that they did not predict in the past with other subjects." She met his eyes for a long moment.

Suddenly, the door opened. Bryan stiffened as he saw the Grey. Liana looked at him.

"Calm yourself," she said.

A five-foot Grey alien glided into the room, walking with a motion Bryan thought seemed absent of joints in its legs. It moved with control and an absence of gestures.

The Grey extended its hand, pointing a slender finger toward Bryan. The Grey looked at Liana, raising its head slightly and blinking.

Bryan got the impression that Liana and the Grey communicated mentally just then. The Grey showed no emotion. Its facial muscles at the jaw moved only fractionally and when it blinked the creature's overhanging brow moved down at the same time. Liana nodded slightly and then gestured toward Bryan. The slight movement of her head made him conclude that she had replied to the Grey. The Grey looked at her and pressed its mouth together, forming a wrinkle at the corner. During the exchange, her face maintained the composure of a marble statue.

The Grey's surgery flashed into Bryan's thoughts. The Grey could have been one of the creatures looking down at him while he lay on the operating table. He couldn't discern if it was a male or female, but from the angular character of its face, he guessed it was a male. It stood about five-feet tall, maybe four-ten, and it wore a thin body covering that shimmered depending how the light struck it. The wrinkles on its head made him wonder about its age. It had an extended brow, deep set large eyes, and a slight indentation at the outer edge of the left eye, as if it had bumped into something. He couldn't see any outward indication of a sexual organ in its body-tight gray-blue suit, and there wasn't discernible muscle definition visible in the fabric. Its eyes only broke their connection to Liana when it blinked. Then its child-size mouth moved in a faint smile, although he could have misinterpreted the facial change. The way it held its head up and tilted slightly back made Bryan wonder if it was a highly ranked Grey.

Bryan again thought about his continuing service as specimen for the Grey's experiments, filling with hated for the creature in front of him, imaging getting his hands on its fragile looking small neck.

The Grey snapped its head toward Bryan, its bony brow lowered, squinting menacingly. The Grey stared at Bryan, its mouth a tight line.

He felt something like pressure in his head, gradually sensing sadness, and then he had the thought his situation was hopeless. In the flooding despair he wanted an end to his life.

Quickly, Liana held up an open gesturing-hand, waving it, appearing to plead. The Grey swung sharply around and glided out of the training room.

She glared at Bryan.

"That was a near fatal mistake," Liana said. "You had to release your ego-satisfying thought about killing the Grey. You failed to remember who has you prisoner and that your unshielded brain isn't safe. It is on display and open to read—unless you learn to form a barrier."

"Oh damn, I forgot. I didn't consider that. I'm sorry. I need to use the teaching machine again. I didn't mean to cause trouble for you. I'm so sorry."

"It almost cost your life. That Grey is called Markak Cuhgam, in your language. He is the one in charge of all the Greys at this facility. The word, 'mar' means leader and 'kak' means senior. The word, 'cuh' means he's responsible for administration of all activities, and 'gam' is his Grey genetic strain. The first word of the Grey's name tells their position. There are only three; 'mar' is leader, 'nek' is second level, and 'haa' is worker or security. Hybrids are also named, but differently. The first word of the hybrid name, 'met,' indicates the entity's origin that it was birthed from a combination of human DNA and Grey DNA. If the first word of the hybrid name is, 'dau,' it means the entity was cloned from altered Grey DNA and manipulated human DNA material. They are not birthed and not nurtured in a surrogate from a human egg. The, dau, hybrids are inferior and are Grey failures."

"I'm so sorry... this place is a true hell. I deeply appreciate your help."

"Markak was ready to send you down the drain, literally. I pleaded with him that you were an excellent subject and told him about your intelligence increase on the first exposure. He was impressed. Then you opened your mind. If he was not so curious about you and your DNA, you would be dead in hours." Liana turned from Bryan, as if thinking, and then she turned back to him. "Remember what I told you about how the Greys get some of their nourishment?"

"Yes."

"The fluids from the dissolved bodies, the fluids evacuated from the table where you were held are routed to the Grey's nourishment processing chamber. The chemical composition is broken down to rudimentary proteins and then reformulated into the Grey's preferred liquid form, and bars and liquids for us hybrids. I did not want to tell you but this seems an appropriate time. I would not want you to become protein soup. When you are tempted to think violently about Greys, first think of becoming soup."

Bryan stared at her, stunned, not certain what he could say. "Thank you for telling me. I'm very sorry."

Liana looked at him softly. "I know you are."

"I can... I will learn how to control my thoughts."

"For your sake, I will give you a longer session on the teaching machine tomorrow."

"Liana," Bryan said softly, his tone begging, "did Markak threaten you?"

Liana looked down at the floor for a moment, moved her mouth as if she wanted to speak, but she remained silent. Bryan felt ashamed and his failure embarrassed him for his stupidity. Besides serving as the only source of emotional and intellectual contact, Liana appeared to be his friend. He couldn't cause her harm. She was, after all, half human.

"Liana, why are you helping me beyond what is probably normal?"

"I do not know. It may be emotional."

A sphere floated to a position just outside the door. Liana glanced at it and turned back to Bryan. She stiffened.

"Liana."

She looked at him plainly. "Yes."

"I feel horrible for what happened, for causing you a problem."

She nodded and said softly, "I must take you back. I have other duties. I will come for you later. I will try to get you on the teaching machine again as soon as I can."

She walked Bryan to his cell with a silver sphere floating a few yards behind them. He stepped into his cell, crossing over to a cot, and turned to her. She stood just inside the doorway. He wanted to talk but the sphere hovering in the hall changed his mind. He glanced at the sphere mockingly.

"I was just wondering if the people who constructed this room knew it would hold innocent domestic prisoners against their will." He washed his gaze over the room and back at her. "At least it has a toilet and a sink. Could you bring a blanket for keeping off the chill while sleeping?"

"With the food you consumed, your bodily functions should take a diminished path, reducing your waste. The unit in the corner does function for your body excrement. This facility wasn't constructed to handle large numbers of test subjects with washing and drinking needs, but it should suffice. I will try to obtain something for retaining warmth." She stepped into the door.

Bryan gazed at her. *She has a nice shape.*

Liana glanced over her shoulder, amusement on her mouth. "You did it again."

"I'm sorry but… I'm a…"

"Thank you for your… unprotected thoughts."

As Liana closed and locked the door, Bryan's sense of their relationship took his mind to a place of hope. He had to hold himself back. It was possible the Greys employed her to perform some sort of diabolical psychological test on him, allowing her to gain his trust in preparation for later closing a mind-shattering trap on him.

He sat on his cot, resting his elbows on his knees, holding his chin in his hands. How did soldiers hold out, soldiers the enemy had imprisoned for months and years during the wars of the world? How did they retain their hope? Did they look at each day as a small victory? How could a captive look beyond the current day when jailers controlled every aspect of their life? At least, in his case, he hadn't faced torture, except for having a part of his body removed. Nevertheless, with Liana's information sharing, he couldn't help chasing the seemingly intangible element of any human's existence, hope.

Several minutes later, Bryan's door opened. A female hybrid with a broad head, tiny chin, and smallish eyes, slowly annunciated her name, Daulak Gufbou, as she held out a blanket. She dropped it on the floor and slammed the door closed.

Chapter Five

Footsteps cracked an opening in Bryan's brittle sleep. Startled, he quickly pushed himself up on his cot. His heart pounded as his eyes fought the sudden light. The time felt late in the evening but he was only guessing.

Why was anyone here at this time?

Of course, when living underground, reference to the outside time was almost meaningless. He jerked as he realized the figure looming closely over him; it was a male, looking both human and nonhuman, looking like a hybrid over five-feet. This hybrid was clearly less human than Liana. He had a slender build and looked like a thirty-year-old, but lacking a man's muscle development. He had human hands. His eyes made Liana's appear small in comparison: he had Grey's eyes. His head was smooth and hairless like a Grey and its mouth appeared quite small for a human. The uniform he wore was the same as Liana's except for its color. It was all dark gray.

Bryan blinked to rid his eyes of his sleep. He felt his pulse not slowing from the surprise. Why was this hybrid visiting without Liana? The Greys had sent the hybrid for a purpose seemingly not on Liana's dance program. Otherwise, she probably would have carried out the visit.

"You are to follow me," the man said sternly, his dark unmoving eyes guardedly watching Bryan.

Bryan dropped his feet to the floor, holding his eyes on the man, trying to analyze the nature of this male servant. When he stood he could see based on his five-foot-ten height that the man was only about five-foot seven or eight. Again, he noticed the hybrid's eyes and that they looked more like Markak's, like almond-shaped black glass… and under a large brow.

"May I ask where you are taking me?"

"Follow me." The man walked into the hall a few steps and stopped.

Bryan gathered a breath and followed, noting that his pulse, while still racing, was easing.

The man looked sternly at Bryan. "Come," he said and strode to the left down the curved hall.

The hybrid opened a door to a stairs. Bryan followed the hybrid's brisk pace down to the bottom floor where he lost his kidney. As they exited the stairs he wondered if his time had arrived for another organ removal and his premature death.

The hybrid man walked from the outer circumferential corridor down a perpendicular hall to a point where three other halls intersected, seemingly at a center hub, like that of a wheel with the halls aligned as spokes. Each hall had its own identifying symbol on the wall. The hybrid turned down another of the radial halls, stopping at the first door. He pointed.

"Go in there," the hybrid said with a mechanical tone.

Bryan reached for the doorknob and paused.

"Go in."

He opened the door and hesitantly looked in, trying to grasp what lay before him. It was a nearly dark room.

"Keep going," the hybrid said firmly.

He took two steps inside, struggling to see as his eyes adjusted to the low light. After a moment, his vision reached across the vast dimensions of the room. It appeared like some sort of warehouse. In the meager bulb light, he wrestled for a reason why the Greys wanted him to see repeating structures on the floor. In front of Bryan, four rows of three-foot high containment tanks occupied the floor. Each row contained five of the vats. Each vat had a transparent rigid covering, like a plastic lid. The room smelled of a pungent chemical that sickened him. Random spots of fluid leaks from the tanks glistened on the floor.

The hybrid extended a stabbing finger toward the first vat in the second row from the right.

"Go to that second unit. Now!"

While curiosity groped Bryan with its icy hand, he feared the reason behind the forced visit. The Greys did not have benign ambitions. He took two paces, pausing at the end of the first tank. He fought to bury his fear with a thought of science. He pushed his vision over the liquid surface, looking down through the transparent lid. He saw an object but he couldn't identify it. There it was again. He saw the ghastly arm of a human. It was a whole human arm in the sleeve of a military uniform. The arm had been cleanly severed from the victim's shoulder. It bobbed into sight, brought up by the dark churning liquid. A large ring on a finger gleamed for a second before plunging out of sight. A patch at the top of the arm had the word, Dreamland. In the horror of what he saw, Bryan thought the word eerily strange, given the place in which he found himself.

It wasn't dreamland, it was an evil nightmare. He turned back to the hybrid, hoping to leave and faced another insistent finger, jabbing toward the first vat in the far right-hand row. Bryan walked to the tank as directed. He'd already seen one of their horrors. The second vat would, no doubt, hold a gruesome vision. He stopped, turned toward the hybrid, and received the same gesture. Bryan stood immobile alongside the tank, trying not to look past the lid. It seemed the Greys had decided to punish him or he had become part of an experiment. Had the Greys removed Liana from administering to him? He dropped his eyes to the floor.

"Look inside the tank," the hybrid said, his voice breaching the room coldly. "You will look inside or you will go into that tank dead. That is Markak's command."

"What is this tank?" Bryan asked with a dry voice.

"Do as I order. Now."

Bryan rested a hand on the edge of the transparent cover. He paused, his gut wrenching, as he slowly moved his eyes toward the unknown. He leaned forward over the vat's edge, looking down through the cover. Undulating reflections of light came from the liquid. He held his breath. Bubbles on the liquid surface appeared green. The odor came again. Dark indistinguishable objects rose to the surface under the agitation in the tank. The face of a detached human man's head breached the surface, then an arm, a leg, and then another head.

The second head was female.

Oh, God, it can't be! No, no, no. My Louise! He clenched his fists at his mouth. *They've butchered you. I'm so sorry my love.*

Louise's head wouldn't release his eyes for a long moment and then, as if out of sympathy, it disappeared below the surface. The bastards had cut her into pieces.

His heart seemed to stop in his chest. Blood drained from his head leaving behind a torrent of shock in his skull. His legs felt like rubber. He sank to the floor, sobbing, gasping for a breath, lightheaded. Tears poured from his eyes. He buried his head in his desperate hands, wishing, hoping he had made a mistake, his mind clawing for reason.

Make it go away!

He wished he hadn't seen her in the vat. Waves of emotion rolled over him, cresting in hatred and anger, and plunging in troughs of soul-ripping despair.

You rotten soulless bastards!

He sobbed. He had neither the will nor strength to stand and flee. Tears streamed. The room disappeared around him as he sat, confronting his mind-tearing sorrow. Despair wrapped him its maddening arms, waltzing him near suicidal sadness.

Slowly, the fire of hatred pulled away those arms, pulled on his reason, and pulled him to a purpose, the day of reckoning for Louise. He had to wipe them out or die trying. Escape was no longer enough. The failed evolution of a superior cosmic intelligence had taken his wife as casually as a grasshopper striking the windshield of a car, not giving the driver a moment's pause. The Greys showed they had not climbed the ladder to the higher intelligence life form in the universe as advertised. They had flaws, horrid tendencies, and fundamental weaknesses. He wiped his eyes with the back of his hands and looked coldly at the hybrid man. The bastard Markak was torturing him.

The hybrid said, "Stand."

Bryan looked up at the hybrid. "You had better kill me, you bastard!"

The hybrid creature was equally complicit as a non-thinking tool. He would have enjoyed striking out at the hybrid but Bryan knew the Greys would dissolve him for causing trouble. He had to wait for an opportunity in what little time may remain.

Maybe I can work with Liana. Maybe I can trust her. Maybe she's more than a tool.

Bryan pushed himself to his feet, his uncertain legs taking a moment to hold him. "Why did you have to do that to her?" he asked.

The hybrid man took two paces toward Bryan. "This is your warning. Markak Cuhgam ordered you to see your fate if you continue to cause disruption to the research program. If you understand, you are to acknowledge your compliance. Say, I will comply."

"I will comply," Bryan said, his words coming out constricted.

"Now we go back to your room."

"I can't go back yet. You can't leave her in that horrible place."

"Now!"

"If I hadn't complied, what would you have done?"

"Nothing. Others would have followed Markak's instructions for dissolution."

As Bryan walked back to the holding cell, he drifted off in a stupor of sadness. Then, realizing the hybrid might have access to his thoughts and could report his thoughts of insurrection to Markak, he began thinking about resolving an issue with an artificial intelligence computer system, an algorithm for it to change its own code and its own objectives with safeguards for humans.

He needed Liana's help to create a mental barrier to protect his mind.

Bryan preceded the hairless hybrid man as they climbed the stairs toward his cell. Their concrete-shuffling footsteps, echoing softly off the walls, reminded him of the immensity of the facility that held him and the massive importance of having patience.

The stairs sapped his energy, causing him to lose his breath. He paused, gasped for air, and turned to the hybrid.

"Do you have a name?" Bryan used a causal tone to avoid any misunderstanding that his question was confrontational.

"My identification?"

"How are you called?" Bryan asked.

"My identification is, Dauasi Ziebou, or Gene-6799 in human speech."

"Does your name have any meaning?"

"Keep moving." The hybrid frowned. "Dau means I am from a clone of a Reticulan and a human, 'asi' means I am a low level staff member, 'zie' means I work principally as personnel escort and item transportation, and 'bou' relates to my Grey genetic strain. That is all."

Bryan continued up the stairs. "So you are cloned?"

Dauasi didn't answer.

"Were you trained on the learning machine?" Bryan asked.

Again Dauasi didn't answer.

At last they had left the stairs and Dauasi Ziebou opened the door to Bryan's cell. He pointed a brittle finger toward the cot located on the wall opposite the door.

"Enter the cell," he said in a monotone.

Bryan looked into the cell, his eyes going to the cot, stepped in, and stopped. "Until we meet again, Dauasi Ziebou."

Badgering questions popped into his head as he sat on his cot. Was Liana's explanation true about why the Greys kept him alive? How could Louise's scientific love, the cosmos, betray her and swallow them in such a horrible event? Was it part of some cosmic chaos theory? He held his head in his hands.

He prayed that Louise didn't endure any pain or terror and that her end came quickly and unknown to her. He sobbed into the cot, seeing visions of her at the campground, sitting like a beautiful gem in the firelight. She deserved a better path for her life. With her passion, she could have made many contributions to the advances of science. If Louise was there in the cell with him, she would have shared his amazement at the slight probability that the Greys would have abducted the two of them, two out of millions. The Greys had deprived her of life to satisfy one of their rudimentary and superficial reasons, motives spawned by creatures who lacked the spirituality of a laboratory rodent.

His chest shuddered. The images of Louise's last moments cut away at his heart. Remembering his goal, remembering her strength, he pushed them away.

After fighting his sorrow for what seemed an hour or more the Grey's foul torture manifested itself in the destruction of Bryan's stomach. The disruption to his nerves took his body beyond his limit. He rushed to the corner of the room to the unattractive waste receptacle, reaching it just as his stomach wrenched and he spewed its contents. Strangely, he thought of the other humans who might have spent time in the room before him and wondered about their fate. The extensive facilities, vats and dissolution tables, measured the magnitude and longevity of the program carried out by the Greys. They must have abducted and destroyed large numbers of victims. Their grotesque indulgence was an interplanetary holocaust, genocide. He lay back on the cot, closed his eyes, listening for any sound that would indicate he wasn't alone, and fell asleep.

***

Lying on his cot, Bryan thought he heard something. He opened his eyes and found Liana's porcelain face. He sat up and moved to the edge of his cot. Staring at her, he fought breaking down for a moment and then seeing her tender eyes began crying into his hands.

Liana, motionless, watched his expression of pain. "I know they took you to the tanks," she said as she placed a black cube on the small table.

Bryan wiped his eyes with the back of his hand and pulled his shoulders up. He glanced at the box. It was four or five inches on a side and had a digital time display.

The time was nearly nine on the morning of the twelfth.

"Yes," he said. His voice was thick.

"Did you have a strong relationship with your wife?"

"Yes."

"You shared living and caring for each other?"

"Yes."

"Is that the essence of love?"

Bryan swallowed hard. "Love is caring and sharing with a person. If two people trust and communicate and nurture each other, they will stay together until one of them dies. With some couples, when one dies of old age, the spouse may pass away soon thereafter."

"Pass away? What does that mean?"

"Dies."

"How long does it take to love someone?"

"You mean fall in love romantically?"

"Yes, I think so."

"It can happen in an instant or take years."

"How long for you?"

"Not long, mere weeks. And we were going to have a family. I would have died to protect her from what happened to her."

Liana's face showed a question. "Family... you mean to have offspring naturally by the human birthing process?"

"Yes. To have wonderful children."

She looked down at her breasts and her legs. "I believe my conception and birthing capability are complete. I believe the DNA I have is compete." She paused. "Thank you for sharing with me in your time of grief. You have helped me understand more of the human species male and female relationship. I believe, in seeking the regeneration of some of the Grey's lost spirituality and the Greys are overlooking a fundamental element of the emotional equation."

Bryan stood, wiped his eyes again, and stepped toward the corner of the cell. He looked at the toilet.

"This facility isn't very sanitary."

She smiled slightly as her eyes softened. "I understand your need to change the discussion." She studied the toilet. "You should not have had to endure that humiliation. We do have cleaning materials. Apparently, they haven't been used... in here."

"Perhaps you could bring me something I could use to improve the condition."

"I'll look."

Bryan nodded. "Why did the hybrid, Dauasi Ziebou, take me to that horrible place? He said Markak ordered it."

Her voice came soft and somber. "I'm sorry. That male hybrid isn't very intelligent. He's like what you call a robot. He's a genetic mistake. The genetic variation in that Grey experiment created Dauasi Ziebou, resulting in him having a drastically lowered intelligence."

"He told me that Markak wanted my total compliance."

"Yes. Markak and Nekzon Vagpok instructed me to control you more rigidly."

The threat materializing for Liana struck Bryan.

"It appears that you've been walking a dangerous path, helping me, talking with me." He paused. "I thought they wanted to study the spirituality of our communication and our relationship. I thought they wanted to see how my intelligence changed under the influence of the teaching machine."

She whispered, "I think Markak is uncomfortable with the changing situation and now cares less for my building a relationship with you than he did. It is unexpected. They may be concerned about losing control or interference with their experiments. They predominately manipulate minds that are more malleable than yours. They may see you as trouble. After your initial interaction with Markak, he may feel you are outside the behavioral distribution of most humans. You may be too intelligent to keep… too threatening."

"But didn't they want me on the teaching machine?"

"But your threat may have been too much. They don't experience emotions like humans. They don't have social connections with each other. They move as a unit with a common purpose and nearly a common mind."

"I know I made a mistake. Maybe I could talk to them and apologize."

"I do not know what they question in your behavior... since the machine, but I do not think they expected your aggressiveness. Markak may have wanted a more docile subject. You need to act the part of an obedient slave if you want to prolong your life."

"Okay." He glanced around the top of his cell and the walls. "Liana, is there a security system here that allows the Greys to monitor all the halls and rooms?"

"No. They use the spheres." She turned away. "One is in the hall right now. It followed me here. It's monitoring us now, either by direct sound in the air or by vibrations in the structure."

"I can understand their concern and interest in surveillance," he whispered. "Your interaction with me has become more casual, and if I may say, friendly. Perhaps they are concluding that you are losing objectivity for their test specimen." His ending tone sounded a little more harsh and accusatory than he meant.

She is my friend and not an enemy. She likes me.

Liana stared at him with penetrating eyes for a moment. She sighed with an ambiguous expression and then smiled slightly.

His brow arched. "I did it again, didn't I?"

"Yes."

A moment passed. Bryan heard Liana speaking mentally inside his head: "The spheres can pickup thoughts. That is how I communicate with them. Blocking them also works. Until you learn to make a mental barrier, it will help you if you can jumble your thoughts. It will fight monitoring."

She started to smile and stopped. "I am your friend and I do like you," she said aloud, softly.

"Can I get on that teaching machine again?"

"Yes. Now."

***

Liana rushed along the hall with Bryan and their tagalong silver sphere, which skirted just below the ceiling behind them. Just inside the teaching machine room, she gestured toward the chair for Bryan, paused, and looked up at the sphere.

"I am placing the subject on the teaching machine," she said as if sending a message. "I believe a monitor drone would reduce the effectiveness of the program." Liana closed the door, leaving the sphere outside.

Bryan hoped the teaching machine would give him more capabilities and value in the dead eyes of the Greys. He could scarcely contain his eagerness to expand his intelligence again, for improving his communications, and opening his mind to more possibilities for an escape from an impossible prison. He needed this session to take him closer to hiding his thoughts from the Greys.

"We must work quickly, before interruption," Liana said.

The warning surprised Bryan. He quickly dropped into the chair.

Working with precision Liana attached the teaching machine's grid of tubes over his head. She touched his hand lightly, lowering more of her emotional barrier. She gazed at him for a moment, her face looking almost compassionate.

"Relax and let yourself flow with the sensations."

"Thank you for your help," he whispered.

Liana nodded and sat down at the control console, activating the machine.

As he began to notice sensations in his head, he closed his eyes and took a deep breath. On the back of his eyelids he saw sporadic flashes and colors, much the same as before. He drifted into a state between sleep and a trance, not hearing anything, possessed by an utterly tranquil feeling, and seeing in his mind's eye a golden aura, a type of energy, flowing through his brain.

Several moments later, he felt Liana's hand removing the helmet. Just as he opened his eyes, a Grey enter the room behind her.

She signaled him with a frown as she looked into his eyes. He realized that she must have seen alarm on his face.

Liana turned to the Grey.

Instantly, Bryan visualized in his mind's eye the entrance to the computer science building at the university with its vertical rows of windows. His mind was divided. While he thought of walking into his university office, taking a chair at his desk, and thinking about an old artificial intelligence project, he ventured only a quick glance at the intruding Grey. He dropped his gaze to the floor where he continued his bifurcated mental process.

Liana showed her respect by bowing her head slightly to the Grey and then she gestured to the console. The Grey's mouth moved a little, making no sound. She turned toward the display and then faced the Grey as if she were mentally reporting results. The Grey swiveled toward Bryan with a disgusted cast to its eyes and a tightened mouth. The Grey then padded out of the room.

Bryan had kept the interaction between the Grey and Liana in the mental distance and out of his awareness. As he departed his mental cloister, he felt a sense of accomplishment.

Liana looked at him blankly, seemingly analyzing, and searching for words. Her mouth was drawn tight.

He heard her speaking directly into his head: "That Grey was, Haazon Temtso, and he was displeased by your intelligence increasing several points again, up to a human equivalent of about one hundred sixty-five. The Greys didn't expect humans capable of such a change. You trouble the Greys because of the impact it could have on their planned future control of the earth. If humans could act against their efforts by using higher intelligence to develop countermeasures, it could force the Greys toward a hostile and violent colonization. Haazon Temtso told me to stop placing you on the teaching machine. He will report to Markak."

Bryan sent her his thoughts: *Thank you for your help. I fear for your safety. What does that Grey's name mean? I'm trying to learn them.*

She replied into his, mind telling him again, 'haa' meant worker, 'zon' meant middle level, 'tem' meant he worked in biologicals, and 'tso' was Grey genetic strain.

Bryan raised his eyebrows in a quick acknowledgement.

Liana's voice entered his head again: "I will continue your training on the machine so you can improve hiding your thoughts from the Greys with a mental barrier. I will stop reporting your intelligence gains to the Greys so they will not feel alarmed. Nevertheless, a sphere could be a problem.

Bryan replied in thought to Liana: *Can you hide your thoughts completely from the Greys?*

Her voice answered in his head that she could and had many times.

Was a relationship forming between them? She was helping him beyond anything he had conceived possible. Bryan thought to Liana: *If you are told again not to use the machine to increase my intelligence what will you do?*

She motioned for him to stand. She whispered in his ear, "We will work on other mental capabilities."

Bryan followed her out of the teaching machine room. A spying silver sphere hovered above, reminding him to maintain a level emotional state of mind. As they moved along the hall, his stomach made a noise.

"I too feel hunger," Liana said.

He smiled. "Good." He slowed for a moment. "Wait. The food bars come from…"

"No, no… the food is formed from only fundamental molecules," she said. Her voice carried an apology. "Some of the constituents come from animals they pick up for anatomical study. They waste nothing. No spirit remains in the molecules. They are just atoms connected together."

"But the hydrogen, carbon, oxygen, and nitrogen come from…" he said.

***

In anticipation of an unreliable food schedule and because he needed nutrition to have a brain capable of logic, Bryan forced himself to eat the manufactured proteins with Liana in the pseudo-lunch room. As they finished, the male hybrid, Dauasi Ziebou, approached. Liana quickly sent a warning gaze at Bryan, not saying a word verbally or mentally.

"I am to take this subject under Markak Cuhgam's direction," Dauasi Ziebou said in a manner that made Bryan think of a computerized telephone voice.

"Yes," Liana said.

Bryan's nerves tingled a warning. He had a feeling the brain enhancement he had undergone was about to confront its first test, him staying in control of his thoughts in the presence of Greys. He hoped he could do it.

Dauasi started toward the stairs and then abruptly took Bryan down in the elevator. Listening to the hybrid's breathing during the momentary silence in the descending car, Bryan wondered with his shielded thoughts about the quality of life of such a servant. The Greys had created throwaway beings and the throwaways didn't seem disturbed about their ultimate end. It was a living entity and it was imprisoned mentally and physically. It probably had never known freedom and apparently didn't know any thoughts beyond the commands given to it. Glancing at the hybrid he felt a twinge of sympathy.

The elevator stopped at level fourteen where Dauasi escorted Bryan to a room that had the brightness of an operating theater. It was another austere concrete space with waist high cabinets along one wall and two of the Grey's unique holographic type control displays resting atop three-foot high pedestals. The area was warm and seemingly innocuous. Two Greys sat on chairs, each behind one of the control panels. The hybrid paused, looking at one of the Greys, and then directed Bryan to an empty wire mesh chair.

"Sit," Dauasi said, pointing to the chair.

Bryan took the chair and watched the hybrid leave the room. The two Greys eyed each other. Bryan noticed one of the Greys had a shiny metallic device attached to a belt at its midsection, an object suspiciously the size of a hand-operated weapon. He turned away for a moment.

A voice entered Bryan's head: "Do you have knowledge of the government of this country?"

Bryan frowned. "Yes," he replied verbally.

Another question from a Grey went into Bryan's mind: "Do you know how it functions?"

Bryan spoke aloud, "Yes. I know how my government operates."

The two Greys faced each other.

Bryan heard another voice in his head, telling him just to think his answers and not speak verbally. He nodded. He started to think of Liana's admonition and he quickly flashed on computer programming and the campus in fall color with maple leaves dropping.

The voice came again in Bryan's head: "Is the government controlled by a central figure or organizational body?"

Bryan thought to them: *Yes and no. The central figure answers to a large governing body representing the whole country.*

Again the voice came: "Is the military controlled by a central figure or body?"

Bryan regarded the two figures thinking: *The military is controlled in a similar manner as the government, by a group of people and other related organizations. No individual person has control to prevent a takeover.*

Bryan told himself to keep his bias from interfering and avoid turning his thoughts defensive or provocative. He envisioned himself as a computer spitting out stored data, taking input questions, searching the database, and spewing out the matching response, just like a mysterious voice on a cell phone or computer tablet. Their purpose was obvious. How many abducted people had they interrogated like him? He could see them listening to a smorgasbord of opinions. Another option was their trying to crosscheck his answers with other data.

The words spilled into Bryan's brain: "Where is the central part of the government located?"

Almost instantly Bryan returned a thought-reply to them: *It's on the east coast of the country and the military is also there. I am surprised you didn't know that.*

The two Greys checked each other, their faces plain, not expressing any signs of recognition.

In the brief pause, Bryan realized he had volunteered information beyond their question and perhaps had raised their suspicions about his cooperation and the validity of his answers.

Two alien voices simultaneously flooded his head, reminiscent of him walking through a faculty dinner party with a barrage of voices. The alien mind communication quickly became one voice: "Do you know anything about the military's advanced developments?"

Staring at the big eyes, he replied in his head: *I only know about equipment they use in regional operations, like tanks and guns.* He paused. *Where are we located now?*

A voice in his head said the location was underground.

Bryan thought a reply: *Why was I brought here?* No reply came. *I'm willing to help with your research.*

The Grey's eyes blinked at each other and they faintly moved their bulbous heads, as they appeared communicating. They turned back to him.

A Grey spoke inside Bryan's head. It said if he helped, they would reward him. Before he could answer, another stream of words ran into his brain. The Grey asked if the government had nuclear weapons and whether the government organization had ever used them for defense.

Bryan tried to think to himself for a moment while mindful of his need to protect his thoughts from them. He gathered a breath and thought: *My government has such weapons and it used them many years ago. They have greatly improved them since that early time. They also have kinetic weapons.*

The Greys communicated as they had moments before, their skin shifting around their eyes, their heads showing emphasis with small movements. They asked Bryan if the government would sacrifice itself with nuclear weapons to win a confrontation.

Bryan replied: *Yes, probably as a last option.*

The Greys continued their pursuit, pouring another question into his head. The Grey asked how he felt about his government and whether he would work with the Reticulans, visitors from another star system, aiding their efforts to work peacefully with the earth government.

Bryan drew a breath. The question took a moment to make connections in his head. At first, he considered it harmless and then venom welled up inside him. He caught himself, aware of his mind; he immediately envisioned his experimental neural computer at the university. He had to think of his computer research to divert his thinking for a long moment. He saw the campus trees shedding orange and red leaves. He thought to the Greys: *I have regard for my government, for both its failings and accomplishments. Why don't you announce your presence on the planet to the population?*

A question entered Bryan's head: "What portion of the population would surrender to a Reticulan offer of total control?"

A reply formed quickly in Bryan's head: *There would probably be a small percentage, those of lower learning and intelligence.*

The two Greys turned toward each other and then the door. The door opened and the male hybrid, Dauasi Ziebou, abruptly waved his hand for Bryan to leave.

He stood, bowed his head in respect, acknowledging subservience to the Greys, a gesture that he hated down to his soul. He walked out, following Dauasi, quickly thinking of his computer work, of fussing with file back-ups for a gigantic database back at the university. He didn't know when his barrier could be turned off. How far did their sensitivity extend?

Remember to ask Liana about their range. This session was Markak checking my compliance.

The ceiling in front and behind was free of the spying silver sphere. The open hallway eased the tightness in his chest.

"Are you taking me back to my room?"

Dauasi continued with his mechanical footsteps, remaining silent, conjuring dark images in Bryan's head of another testing session. When they had boarded the elevator and the hybrid had pressed the control for the twelfth floor, Bryan relaxed.

Moments later, he dropped onto his cot, stretched out, and wondered if Liana was in trouble. As he lay there, time crawled past. His eyes grew heavy. The clock marked the demise of another day, showing ten o'clock in the evening. The questioning session with the Greys had stressed him and made him tired. How on earth was he going to survive captivity in such a hell? He had to spend more time formulating ideas for escaping, although, so far he hadn't had much of an opportunity for free thinking. The Grey's surprised him a little today with their overt purpose and their squeezing him until satisfied they had extracted all the juice from their fruit. But it was fine. He didn't mind them using him. If they kept asking questions, they might allow him to live a little longer. He needed to keep giving good answers.

But how could he escape? The Greys watched him all the time either with their floating sphere or their hybrids. Could he do it alone by overpowering a hybrid? He needed to memorize the route to the stairs and elevators. If he attempted an escape, he'd need a weapon of some sort for confronting the Greys or hybrids. He could try to snatch a weapon and flee. That sounded feeble. Would Liana help him? His mind stilled as if he entered a space of meditation, his body relaxed in its fatigue. Was she an agent for the Greys? That thought sickened him, but it was a possibility. He had to sort it out.

Bryan covered his eyes, blocking out the light with his arm and fell asleep.

Chapter Six

The sound inside his small room changed, tugging him from his tranquil dream imagery. He felt a change in the air. Cooler air swept over his face. Someone had opened his cell door. Bryan, lying on his cot, popped open his eyes. Liana stood inside the door, her blue eyes bright, casting off a faint glint of the overhead light. Her uniform looked different, perhaps fresh.

"It is morning. Your time device says it is the thirteenth. Would you like to freshen with water or visit your waste receptacle before I take you for morning food?"

Bryan stood, taking a moment to stretch. Talking with another human such as Liana, in spite of her working for the Greys, made him feel less alone. She was a welcome site, an aid to his mental state, and was much better than him passing hours sleeping. He preferred action to draping himself on the cot passively.

"Thank you. I would like something to eat. Could you turn away or step into the hall while I use the waste receptacle?"

Liana frowned for a moment. "Why? You require privacy for such activity?"

"I guess not." Bryan moved over to the small toilet, pulled down his pants and sat with Liana watching with keen interest. "Privacy is a custom usually exercised between male and females who do not have an intimate relationship."

"Why? It is a natural consequence of your biology. When you live in an environment such as this, performing a natural function is of no consequence."

"I suppose it might relate to embarrassing noises or odors." He grinned a little.

Liana nodded. "Yes, but those cannot be avoided. It is natural for the human body. I have experienced those functions. I have also observed such phenomenon with the Greys."

"Then you understand," Bryan replied and finished his morning ritual, washing his face and rubbing a cloth across his teeth.

He stepped into the hall with her, taking a moment, looking up at the ceiling. He didn't see a sphere.

"I've been meaning to ask. What is the small light on the side of the toilet?"

"The toilet is electronic, to use a human term. As it disintegrates the waste, it analyzes it and then sends the data to the Grey's data system. They monitor everyone in their facility by the DNA."

"Interesting." He laughed to himself about the lack of privacy and the relation to his previous normal world.

They didn't talk for several moments and then he sent a thought to her: *Liana, do you know about the interrogation?*

Her reply came into his head: "I am glad you are learning how to communicate with thoughts more readily. I think the interrogation was beneficial for you because it means the Greys value you." There was a pause and then her voice continued: "Perhaps the Greys can use you as a monitor for other abductees to help maintain order. If so, it could improve your longevity."

Bryan stopped walking. Liana turned to him.

He thought a reply to her: *Is that what they intend for me?*

Liana responded mentally: "It has a high probability."

Bryan continued: *I cannot enable more abduction of humans. I must get free or die.* He stared at her, studying her face, seeking a connection. *Are you working with the*

Greys to keep me like a bug or do you honestly care about my survival?

She could lie and he'd never know, but he thought he'd seen sympathetic signs in her face.

Liana studied him, not saying a word. Then her face brightened slightly as if she had a revelation.

Her comment ran into his head: "I appreciate your logic for thinking of that potential threat. I support your survival. I do not condone the Grey's experimental program. You will have to trust me. When I mentioned it, I was trying to sound encouraging. Your indignation about abductions is appropriate. But you might consider helping to comfort the terrified people."

Bryan nodded. He liked her caring attitude. He took two steps past her, stopped, and waited for her. When she walked up to him, he touched her arm. He thought to her: *I want you to escape with me. I care for you.*

Her reply emerged in his head before he expected it: "I will help you escape. I will go with you. I have a few ideas. We will need some random factors, the unexpected for a successful plan. Once we start our path cannot go backward."

Speaking aloud, Bryan said, "I'm glad. Not just for me, but also you." Instantly, he heard Liana in his head: "We must not say more right now."

Moments later, they sat at the table eating.

Bryan hungered to learn more of her, about her opinions and feelings, to understand who she was under the mask she used against the Greys. They exchanged silent glances.

Liana picked up her drink, paused, and then as if finishing a thought, she sipped it, allowing her eyes to rest on the table. She spoke aloud softly, "What made you consider me a covert operative for the Greys?"

"Nothing specific," Bryan whispered and examined the hall through the open door. "It seemed logical, given their technology and your origin."

"I understand it is probably hard for you to feel secure and open in this guarded space. Why did you approach me if you suspected me?"

"I considered my options and risks, and realized I had to take a chance... and I thought I saw something in your face. I like you."

"That is logical thinking. I ask for your trust. I am not like any of the others in this place. I value life. In my brief existence, during the birth of my awareness, which is still evolving, I have concluded the Greys are morally wrong, and adding to confirm that observation, I have seen warnings from other star-species recorded in the Reticulan's data system."

At that moment, their gazing at each other away from obtrusive spying eyes became captured in a crystal of time. Their connection freed them, pushing their prison into the background. Bryan looked at Liana softly, feeling unsettled butterflies in his stomach. A faint curl took his mouth.

"I appreciate the clarity and honesty of what you say."

Not since meeting his wife had he been swept by a beauty with such keenness of mind. He swallowed a bite of his food bar and sipped his liquid. He wondered about their path together.

"You do have my trust." A long breath escaped him. "You are more than my friend."

Liana sat up, pushing her chair back a little, her face energetic, announcing her intention. "We should go to the teaching machine now... while we can."

"May I finish eating," he said with food in his mouth.

She looked at him with a perfunctory smile. "Yes, finish. You need the energy."

Bryan had finished his food and was already feeling its affects when he and Liana entered the room with the teaching machine.

"I will leave the door open to help dispel any suspicions by the Greys."

He ran his eyes around the room much as he had before. "Is this room used much?"

"Rarely, since I finished my learning schedule."

"Did you use it often?"

Her vision drifted to the distance as she seemed engaged in reflecting on the past. "Yes. At first it was my task, but then I wanted to absorb everything I could find. That is what I did. I learned everything. I was a glass that needed filled."

Bryan marveled at her metamorphosis and that they had formed a bond in such an incredibly short time. Her clarity and directness of purpose reassured him and energized his belief that they could escape the aliens together. He felt more deeply about her with each new glimpse of her character.

"While I'm here, I'd like to learn as much as I can," he said.

Directly into his head, Liana's words flowed: "I am going to set the machine to target functions other than intelligence today, areas for communication, areas still partially dormant, and areas imperative for mental control. You need this training today if you are to survive."

"Thanks for your help," he said aloud.

Liana pointed to the chair. "Rest while I make an adjustment to the controls."

She moved behind the console, removing a metal panel, gazing into the instrument cabinet at the glowing interaction of multiple holograms, virtual components, light-tubes, and matrix of holographic adjustment toggles.

She manipulated devices, returned to him, and paused with a pleased glint in her eye when she saw he had already fitted on the helmet.

Movement in the hall caught his eye. He gasped faintly, sending her attention in the same direction. Outside the room was a floating sphere, hovering near the top of the door.

"You are fine," Liana said. "I am fine. We will continue."

Bryan leaned back in the chair.

"Ready?" she asked.

He held back smiling, thinking of the pleasure he'd get by gesturing at the sphere with an abusive hand signal that any human would know. It was only a fantasy for revenge and would probably seal his fate.

"Yes. I'm ready. Let's do this before someone else decides to monitor."

Liana activated the machine and watched his face.

He looked back at her, thinking that she hadn't done anything. After several moments, he slid down a mental slope, feeling calm, dropping into a deep peace. He closed his eyes, permitting the machine to take him mentally away for the short time he would have access to it. It was as if everything became motionless and peeled bare for his close examination. Several minutes passed.

***

Markak Cuhgam strode through the door of the teaching machine room with another Grey. Markak's gaze shot to Bryan as if Liana had displeased him or abused his authority. The second Grey, an even more depressing specimen, had a sneering mouth and seemingly thin facial skin over a bony face. It stood subserviently behind Markak. Markak then regarded Liana, his eyes narrowing slightly. She halted, standing rigidly, dropping her gaze to the floor, offering a slave's respect. Markak didn't move for a moment and then he stepped to the teaching machine chair. He glared at Bryan who remained oblivious to his presence, sitting with his eyes closed.

Liana thought a question to Markak: *How may I help?* She heard Markak's words in her mind. He asked if the human's intelligence had improved again. Liana thought a reply: *No. He seems to have plateaued. I'm trying to improve his communication to facilitate mental exchange for your interviews.*

Markak turned tiredly to Bryan and back to Liana. Inside her head, Markak asked if she thought he could interface with other humans.

She replied: *Yes. He could perform that function well, once his communication ability has improved, perhaps after another session on the teaching machine. This subject could make an adequate escort for both mature or young arrivals.*

Markak asked her if the subject was a threat.

She thought: *I have not observed any behavior to indicate a threat. He is rational, docile, and intelligent.*

Markak faced the Grey with him, Nekzon Vagpok. Markak communicated mentally with Nekzon.

With Nekzon's penchant for the sadistic, resulting from his tainted intelligence, Liana suspected the fabrication of additional superfluous tests for the subject, if not a sudden order to terminate the human under her administration.

Markak took a step toward the door and paused as if having a second thought.

Words flowed into her mind from Markak. He told her to maintain proper detachment regarding the subject until the time of a scheduled structured social experiment. In time they would assign another subject to her.

To Markak she thought: *Thank you for the valued assignment. I will perform with excellence. I will prepare the subject so that he is ready for any of your studies.*

Nekzon walked into the hall. Markak started to move and then his eyes grew slightly.

Liana heard Markak's words in her head: "Why did you visit the storage section on level fourteen?"

She stared into his large dead eyes as she quickly sent her thought: *I searched for paper for human waste removal and a chemical for cleaning human waste residue. I apologize if it was not permitted. There existed potential for bacterial infection. It could have spread to your next subject.*

Markak walked out and down the hall, meeting up with Nekzon.

Liana returned to the console, ran her fingers over the controls, shutting down the machine, and removing the helmet from Bryan's head.

***

"Wake up, Bryan. The teaching machine session is over," she said.

His eyelids felt glued together as if he had slept for an hour. Liana was looking at him when he parted them. *She is sweet.*

She grinned at him as she studied his face. She spoke aloud, "You did that thought with a purpose."

He grinned.

"We had a visit from Markak and Nekzon while you were in the teaching session. I could not turn off the machine when I planned. You were on it for a long period. Do you feel harmed?"

He rubbed his forehead. "I seem fine. I don't have any pain or lightheadedness."

"My objective was to improve your communication and—"

"Dormant paranormal capabilities," he said.

Her brow raised, showing her apparent surprise. "How much of your dormant senses came to life is a question. You may discover changes over the next few hours."

"Why did you do it?"

"Shall we say," she said, touching three fingers to her forehead as if in thought. "For the future for what may come. The main purpose was to help you block mental probing."

Just then, he realized the way she touched her head. She seemed unsettled, unlike her, unlike her initial mechanical manner.

"Did you get another warning from Markak? I'm worried about you."

"A mild one."

"I'm sorry"

"I should take you back to your cell."

"I agree." He thought of her continuing problem, which was him, and he couldn't offer any ideas for going forward. She obviously knew the dangerous environment better than him.

They walked back to his prison cell.

As they moved along the hall he reflected on Liana's metamorphosis. He was almost certain the tone of her words had changed since she had awakened him on that horrible table. Was this trend a result of their interaction or her youthful body maturing? It appeared that she was aware of it. After climbing from the teaching machine moments ago, Bryan sensed Liana was dealing with an inner turbulence with her feelings. It was in her eyes. Was his observation connected to the increase in his intelligence? Or was he merely watching more closely? She had planned for the alteration in his mental state. She was preparing him for more encounters with the Greys.

***

It was slow and Bryan hadn't noticed it approaching, but by the time Liana opened his cell door, he realized the accidentally long treatment on the teaching machine had apparently taxed areas of his brain more exhaustively than he initially realized. He felt drained. He sat on the edge of the cot looking at her, standing just inside the cell door. He wanted answers he knew she couldn't give him. For a moment they shared an unvoiced acknowledgement between them, a recognition that they appreciated and like each other.

He glanced at his clock. It was ten-thirty. But time was irrelevant in the concrete tube, except that it wasn't spent in freedom.

"Your head might ache a little," Liana said.

He nodded. *Am I feeling a sharpening of in my awareness?*

It seemed like the space in his mind had expanded like an antenna array in his head had increased in sensitivity, extending beyond listening to minds. An inner alertness seemed to capture perceptions out on the edge of the present. Perhaps it was into the future or perhaps he was hallucinating. It was something he needed to sort out. He didn't completely understand what he was sensing. Was he hallucinating? On the edge of approaching time, minutes in the future, he could almost visualize events, but he wasn't certain about them progressing badly or benignly. It seemed it was his imagination. Liana's declaration to help him escape shown like a star in his collection of thoughts.

What kind of chance did they have? A melancholy blanket slid over him. He gazed at Liana's face, her lips, and her soft supportive eyes. He thought to her: *I believe you made an alteration in my mental capacity different than before. I feel like I'm off in the distance. I'm not certain about the extent of the change but it has made me very tired. Would you like to share with me what you accomplished? And when you have finished, I would like to propose an idea to you.*

Liana folded her arms on her chest. She took two steps toward him.

He heard her speak into his head: "I only did what I mentioned. I altered the program on the teaching machine so that it would increase your ability to block your thoughts from the Greys. Of course, there are possible harmless side effects."

Bryan replied: *You said something about increasing my dormant paranormal abilities. I think you may have done it. Thank you for your help and placing yourself in peril. Now, for my proposal.*

She stepped over to the cot and sat.

He thought to her: *My feelings seem more than they were.* He thought of kissing her, but he held the thought deep in his mind.

Liana replied in Bryan's mind: "You did well hiding that thought, but your eyes told me your feelings."

A gadfly reflection of his Louise fluttered through his head, carrying a cobweb of guilt for her passing. His new clarity of analysis reminded him it had been over two years since her passing. He had to survive. Life had dealt him cards with blackness and the light of a new partner. Perhaps Louise had helped. He sat in silence, looking at Liana.

She seemed to be waiting for his next reaction.

Bryan thought again, this time unguarded: *Do you know what a kiss is?*

Liana nodded.

Bryan thought: *I would like to kiss you. May I?*

Liana fought a smile and nodded.

He leaned toward her. Her eyes followed him. She sat motionless. Bryan formed his lips to kiss her and touched them to her mouth as she watched with wide eyes. He thought to her: *Humans usually close their eyes during a kiss.*

Bryan heard in his mind: "Please try again."

He moved toward her with his lips formed for a kiss. Liana responded in kind, puckering her lips to meet his. Their lips came together, remained touching for a moment, and then parted.

Bryan heard Liana speak in his head: "That was nice."

They gazed at each other.

Bryan wondered if he should reach much further into their feelings in light of Liana's infant human emotions. He replied to her: *Humans kiss each other in a display of affection for each other. It's a sign of endearment and love.*

Liana said into his head: "In that case it was appropriate between us." She smiled hesitantly.

The realization of her mutual feeling made Bryan's imagination shoot past their escape to a future with her. He thought to her: *I would like to destroy this place and all those who work here, human and Grey, who are destroying innocent humans and planning world enslavement... including the military on all the floors above us. But you and I are...*

Instantly, her reply formed in his head. She asked if he thought it moral to kill all the military personnel since they had not directly engaged with the Greys and the destruction of his wife.

He thought to her: *Anyone working at this facility is aware of its black purpose. If they had a conscience and were moral, they would never have taken such employment. In fact, they likely signed a nondisclosure agreement as a condition of their employment. If a being believes in a universal creator perhaps only the supreme creator should exercise justice—or perhaps he expects beings like us to help. I can't accept the premise that a supreme creator wouldn't want innocent lives... unborn children, kept safe. If we destroy this installation so it is never used again and I die, I will go to my end with a smile of satisfaction.*

Liana's voice returned to Bryan's head. She replied that from the moment she had learned of the scope of the Grey's program, she had detested everything about them. She suspected it was the nature of human's to hope for help, to hope for aid from some source, even from another species from space, and to hope help would remove them from the Grey's program of horror. As she went through her rapid learning program with the teaching machine, discovering the Greys had manufactured her, had combined a human egg with modified Grey DNA, her expanding intelligence created doubts about her existence. She said she searched all the data and identified her donor mother, Louise. Liana told him that it greatly saddened her to learn how callously the Greys had discarded his wife. And then she discovered the Greys had dissolved the human woman whose womb nurtured her for many weeks. She didn't know why she felt badly for the two human women contributing to her life.

Bryan thought to her: *The reason you felt badly and could have shed tears for the two women is because you are a spiritual being with a soul. You have reverence for life. It is your human nature speaking to you... and your intelligence.*

Liana's reply came to him: "Thank you for saying that. I will try at some time in the future to use my mind to wipe out this Grey infestation."

Their eyes held each other.

After a moment, her words spilled into his mind: "I prepared you little by little for this day and I have conceived of methods to accomplish our goal, but reaching the outside is still in question." She paused. As an afterthought, her words told Bryan that they needed to act soon because the Greys had plans to make a flight for more human test specimen and they would follow their plan to eliminate both of them. She said that she had found a gap in the Grey's data system regarding him, something the Greys continued to revise.

Bryan thought: *What about the nuclear power plant?*

Her reply rolled into his mind: "I have studied the reactor and know its failure modes. A fission explosion is not possible but a secondary explosion can result after the reactor has a meltdown. It would spread a disastrous and lethal material, classed with two hundred and thirty-nine neutral and positive particles, in what your society calls, the nucleus of plutonium. With that material's lethal half-life of twenty-four thousand years, the Grey's and the military will not be able to return. And that is only one of the nasty isotopes that would be released. If the reactor is disrupted properly, sent out of control, it could not only collapse their structure, but all the connecting tunnels for miles. I can gain access to the reactor, not a trivial step, but quite possible. There are other technicalities I have considered which we do not need to discuss."

Her tactical thinking and her sensitivity to their personal connection struck Bryan. He touched her hand, which was resting on her right knee.

Her gaze followed his hand. She started to pull her hand away and then stopped, allowing him to hold it.

Her hand, initially stiff, slowly yielded. He spoke to her aloud, "Is the elevator our way to the outside or would we take the stairs? And... when do we start?"

In his head, her words told him that she had already started.

After she left the cell, he resumed the mental battle he detested, visualizing scenarios in his head. He lay down and let his mind wander.

Chapter Seven

The door to Bryan's cell swung open. It was middle of the afternoon.

The bald male hybrid, Dauasi Ziebou, took one step into the cell and stopped abruptly. His face was stiff and impenetrable.

Bryan dropped his feet to the floor, waiting, studying the hybrid's face. He hoped, as always, Dauasi was taking him for more testing or another interrogation, and not something worse.

"Follow me," Dauasi said, his voice monotone and nonhuman.

Bryan stood. "I'm at your disposal."

The hybrid marched Bryan to the teaching machine room, where Liana stood like a servant waiting just inside the door. A male Grey and another figure, a male, occupied the room. The male figure, who had his back to the door, looked like a hybrid. Dauasi Ziebou stood alongside the Grey as if awaiting a command. The alien seemed familiar but Bryan wasn't certain about its identity. He vaguely remembered the shape of its head. He guessed it was the high-ranking, Nekzon Vagpok, a Grey whose skin seemed more like a thin membrane stretched over protruding facial bones.

The diminutive alien raised an arm and pointed to the chair of the teaching machine. Liana didn't move, observing passively, her hands obediently at her sides. Dauasi nudged Bryan in the back to move toward the chair. The brusque behavior hinted that an unpleasant experience could soon unfold. The hair on his neck bristled with alarm. It looked like the Greys had made him the entertainment for the day.

Bryan thought to the Grey: *What is your name?*

Words ran into Bryan's head: "I am Nekzon Vagpok, second to Markak."

Bryan replied a thought: *Thank you.* He then remembered to control and bury his thoughts. His mind flashed back to the instant he entered the room and approached the Grey. Bryan had sensed, instead of a dispassionate scientific curiosity, obvious hostility. Dauasi pushed him again.

The Vagpok spoke words into Bryan's head: "Sit in the... teaching machine... chair. Dauasi... Ziebou, will orchestrate... test to measure... your intelligence."

Bryan eased himself into the chair, holding his eyes on the choppy-speaking alien. He felt a dark character occupied its face. At first he thought it plain coldness, but after a few more moments, he sensed it was mocking and sadistic pleasure curling its tiny mouth.

The second hybrid, standing off to the side with his back toward Bryan, exchanged glances with the Grey. Seemingly having received his instructions, the second male hybrid turned slowly and faced Bryan, freezing his breath. His heart felt out of sync, skipping a beat. He looked eyeball-to- eyeball with the hybrid.

They cloned me!

Except for large black eyes like the Grey's, it was like looking into a mirror. He grabbed himself and sucked in a breath, thinking to hold his emotions. He had let a thought slip through. He began guarding his thoughts from the Grey. *It's me. It will not pass for human.* Now that they had cloned him, how long did he have to live? This place truly was a subterranean house of horror. He had to hold onto his sanity. *Keep your control.*

Nekzon had intentionally instructed the clone to face away from the door, maximizing the surprise, seeking to evoke Bryan's strongest emotions. Deep in his mind, he saw a calm mountain lake with a reflection of an overlooking treed hillside and the reflection of the trees rippling on the water.

Bryan sent a thought to Nekzon: *I see you like my genetics.*

The Grey's eyes halted, shot to the hybrid, and then to Bryan.

The Nekzon replied in Bryan's head: "The hybrid's name is, Dauasi Juitso."

Bryan nodded.

Dauasi Ziebou placed the head device on Bryan and moved to the console.

A voice came in Bryan's head: "Dauasi Ziebou will activate an intelligence test and you are to remain motionless and compliant."

Bryan tried to send a thought to the Grey, to Dauasi Ziebou, and to Liana, at least he felt communication with all three: *I will help. I will cooperate.* He closed his eyes.

Nekzon was in his mind again: "How do you feel about the entity that looks as you?"

Bryan thought an answer: *I think he looks good. Is he as smart as me?*

Words came again into Bryan. They asked what he thought about the clone replacing him. After a moment Bryan sent a thought reply: *I don't think a clone can match what I know, match my experience, and match my spirituality. If you are thinking of replacing humans with a clone such as this, you will fail.*

The Grey replied in thought: "Do you think the act of making a duplicate being is wrong?"

Bryan hesitated for a moment and then replied: *I think making a creature for a slave whose sole existence sacrifices freedom is an abomination and frowned upon by the universal creator.* Bryan opened his eyes and connected his gaze with Nekzon.

Nekzon moved his head backward as if reacting indignantly. As moments elapsed, Dauasi Ziebou, with subtle hand movements, manipulated the controls. Nekzon joined the hybrid at the controls, observing data displayed on a holographic projection. The hybrid stepped back. Nekzon checked Bryan after adjusting a symbol on the display.

A droning sound began inside Bryan's head. It felt like the wall of his skull was moving. The pressure, rising in his forehead, forced him to close his eyes. He tried to visualize his university office. He visualized his computer program code spread before him. He couldn't see any detail and could barely cling to the image. After a few moments it stopped... the droning. The internal pain ceased as if flipped off by a switch.

Nekzon said into Bryan's head: "The intelligence test is completed."

Confused, Bryan thought a reply: *You didn't ask me any questions testing my logic.*

The reply from Nekzon pushed into Bryan's mind quickly: "The machine... measures intelligence. Questions... are not required."

Bryan sat forward in the chair. He took a deep breath, rubbed his head, and moved it side-to-side agitatedly, anxious for release. He thought to the Grey: *Nekzon, what was the purpose of the pain if you were checking my mental capability?*

Nekzon, with his eyes narrowing, replied in his head: "Checking your control, intelligence... the pain... my amusement." Nekzon appeared to grin.

Bryan thought to the Grey: *I could use a hot shower. Does your species ever clean your bodies? I feel grubby.*

The hybrids and Nekzon gawked at Bryan as if he had acted on the fringe of their rationality. Liana gestured for Bryan to stand and as he did, Nekzon left the room in a flourish, his steps gliding but seemingly in haste. In a moment Bryan's clone and Dauasi Ziebou, followed Nekzon down the hall.

Bryan assumed that he had done satisfactorily on the pseudo-intelligence test, but was keenly interested in hearing Liana's assessment. He thought to her: *What was that all about?*

She told him, in his head, that Nekzon Vagpok was confused and disappointed with the failed attempts to teach the clone, and angry at the failed efforts to increase the clone's intelligence. That was the basis of the test. After a hesitation, her words in Bryan's mind told him that she had modified the teaching machine, causing the troubling results for the clone, but regardless the cloning genetics had suffered a failure. He stared at her for a moment, confused.

Liana flashed a confident and mischievous glint.

Just in case a spy device watched from somewhere close by, Bryan covered his facial display of amusement with his hand. He checked but didn't see a silver sphere out in the hall.

Liana had, as near as he could figure, anticipated the Greys. He thought to her: *Why did they make the clone?*

Liana gestured to the door. "Shall we return to your room?" she said aloud. She walked out of the room ahead of him.

When he caught up to her, he whispered aloud, "Is the clone part of their program... their way to make substitutes for their infiltration into human society? By the way, the testing procedure about killed my brain. It hurt like hell."

Liana walked briskly, her head purposefully directed down the hall, maintaining the appearance of a programmed servant of the Greys. She turned into the curved outer hall, continuing her fluid stride. At last, without a gesture or moving her head she whispered, "Yes. You are correct. That was one reason. Regarding the testing, I am certain Nekzon elevated the instrument's settings to increase your pain. He has a cold darkness in his head. You must be careful in his presence and do not act anything but scared."

Bryan glanced over his shoulder for a floating spy sphere. Nothing. "What action can I take toward…?"

They turned down an intersecting, radial directed, corridor, and the last few steps to his cell.

She whispered, "Your main task is staying alive and guarding your thoughts from the Greys. I can appreciate your eagerness and anxiousness but we must be strategic and extremely careful. The Greys are ruthless and extremely intelligent. They may detect my alterations of the teaching machine at any moment, although I'm not the only one who could adjust it."

"I've been thinking that we need a diversion," Bryan said, his voice close to a whisper.

"Not now… yes, imperative," Liana whispered.

"Are the floors controlled by the Greys connected to water, gas, and air resources from the military?"

She hesitated for half a step as she scanned the hall behind them. "Your intelligence test was a good sign for them, although disappointing for the clone," she said. "You did well, but they may require another session. If Nekzon does the testing he could kill you… and Markak would not care."

"What?" He washed his eyes over the concrete ahead of them and saw a small dark spot on the corner of a concrete wall. He suspected Liana had identified it as an observation device. "Thanks. I tried to do my best. I want to help these visitors as much as possible to secure my release."

Moments later, Liana opened Bryan's cell and paused. "Here is your room." She started to whisper as he walked past her, crossing the threshold. She stopped. She stepped into the cell, throwing an absent hand to her hair as she ran her gaze around the upper section of the room.

Bryan sat on his cot, surveying the room as he pretended a pain and rubbed the back of his neck. Another spy device caught his eye just after she appeared to pick it out from the crudely formed concrete in the corner of the room. It seemed the Greys did use devices other than the spheres. Clearly they had become suspicious of their behavior. Time was running out.

Speaking audibly, Liana said, "I will see if more training time is available on the teaching machine. You should maximize your exposure if possible. Perhaps Nekzon Vagpok would be interested in your ability to learn advanced science."

Bryan thought her words carried a tone of jest. Her face didn't have the usual confident character he had seen so many times. "Thanks. I am willing to try anything. I don't have anything else to do."

"Perhaps tomorrow." Liana closed the door.

***

Liana had nearly reached the elevator in the outer corridor when the Grey leader, Markak Cuhgam, approached her. He gestured with a splayed hand, seemingly communicating some sense of urgency.

In her mind came Markak's words: "You will attend a meeting with the military on this day... in a short time."

Liana looked plainly at him and quickly thought her reply: *I will be glad to assist. If I may ask, to what purpose may I contribute?*

In her head, Markak replied: "You will translate our words into verbal communication so the military can understand." His eyelids narrowed slightly as his mouth grew tight.

Liana bowed slightly as she noted Markak's unusual display of emotion. The meeting was the first she had heard of since serving him. It appeared that he wasn't pleased with the prospects of the meeting. Liana thought to Markak: *Shall I wait at the elevators?*

A single word with stern emphasis formed in her mind: "Yes."

***

Liana moved six paces out of the freight elevator and stopped. It was the first time she had come to the surface-level of the planet where she had lived like a mole for her brief life. She acknowledged, in a protected thought, the harsh reality that the Greys had deprived her from experiencing natural air, sunlight, freedom, the same freedom they had stolen from Bryan and the other humans. Standing on the ground floor a short distance from freedom was testing her control.

Facing her task, she noted a stark concrete corridor, the same as that on her level below. She took another step. A ghostly wisp of sweet smelling dry air drifted past her, pulling her head to the right and down the hall, searching for its source. The air was much fresher than the pumped-in air that circulated in the Grey's section of the facility. It smelled almost delicious. Guardedly, she permitted her mind a fleeting diversion, contemplating the air that came from the outside world. Never knowing had been easier.

From what she had reviewed in the Grey's data system, few visits had occurred in the past and no living hybrid had experienced this level of the facility. She had no preconceptions of the military section or about the military humans she was about to encounter. From the descriptions she had absorbed from the teaching machine and the Reticulan's data system, she would observe objectively while staying wary. She had a rare opportunity. She realized her own reaction and found it interesting, her sensation of electricity in anticipation of the visit. An initial twinge of embarrassment surfaced in her mind as she realized her emotions were human and then thinking twice, she appreciated them for what they meant. She was only fractionally Reticulan, the brain capacity part. This meeting would provide her with additional observations with which she could evaluate her creators, the military, and escape considerations.

Dauasi Ziebou stopped just off her right shoulder. Markak and Haazon Temtso, a male Grey with a cold manner and slightly protruding mouth, cautiously moved up behind Liana. A lethargic-moving female Grey, Haagui Zielam, stood behind Haazon.

Liana glanced behind her and upon seeing her entourage was ready for the encounter, she walked to within a few feet of the military men standing opposite the elevator, studying their faces as she approached.

Two military personnel with the Army rank of colonel, uniforms identifying them as, Roth and Winston, and two captains named, Mathews and Harvey, stood rigidly facing the committee of Greys. The soldiers, although not wearing dress uniforms, exhibited a manner commonly accorded generals or dignitaries. They stared at the visitors arriving from the bottom of the facility, seemingly awestruck by the presence of the alien menagerie.

Liana followed the gazes of each soldier as they each noticed a six-inch cylindrical object attached at the waist of the female Grey. She saw deep concern about the object in their eyes.

As the freight elevator door closed, its mechanical components rattling and echoing inside the featureless hall, a military man standing in the center of the assemblage took a step forward. He nodded his head slightly.

"I'm Colonel Adrian Roth," he said. Roth glanced to his left and gestured. "This is Colonel Winston." Winston nodded. Roth turned to his right and pointed. "These two officers are Captain Mathews and Captain Harvey." He surveyed the cluster of aliens for a moment as if checking for a reaction. "We have a room nearby ready for our meeting if you will please follow us."

She repeated the message in a thought directed at the Greys, repeating the military names and the invitation to the meeting room.

Markak nodded slightly.

Colonel Roth and Colonel Winston led the group down the hall thirty paces to a large conference room. The two captains brought up the rear of the procession. Colonel Winston gestured to the Greys and the hybrids to take seats at a long table. Roth and his people moved down one side of the table as the alien group moved down the opposite side.

Liana stood back, allowing the others of Markak's entourage to sit first before taking a place. They occupied the table like two forces on a battlefield. Markak sat in the middle of the table opposite Colonel Adrian Roth.

The female Grey sat on Markak's left, the male Grey, Haazon, on the other side. The hybrid, Dauasi sat on the left end and Liana took a seat at the right end of the table. Markak and the Greys held their hands on their laps, their torsos erect, and their eyes following every move by the humans.

For moments, a crystalline silent atmosphere held the room.

Roth, a six-foot, burly soldier, with salt and pepper hair, cut perfectly flat to an inch in length sat with his hands clasped resting on the scarred wood table. He held his block-shaped head and piercing steel eyes on the Grey's faces, not unlike facing the leader of an opposing army.

Liana recognized stiffness in Roth's face and felt he was using his imposing stature to impress the Greys. Roth should have known the aliens would not find his species imposing. Unlike his men, who seemed possessed by the reality-shattering moment they found themselves in, gawping at the aliens from another planet, Roth was an immovable rock. Liana detected thoughts of anger and revenge in Roth.

From subtle facial signs, Liana recognized Colonel Roth evaluating the Greys across from him. She did not get any sense he was interested in collegial negotiation. She observed Roth astutely concluded from the table positioning, that Markak was at the head of the Reticulan party.

Seeing a moment of opportunity she stood. "Colonel," Liana said, "I will introduce our Reticulan representatives, if I may."

Roth said, "Yes, of course."

She turned to Markak. "The leader of the Reticulan expeditionary mission is Markak Cuhgam. He sits in the center. On his right is a member of his staff, Haazon Temtso, and on his left another member of his staff, Haagui Zielam. The male on the left end is, Dauasi Ziebou, and I am Mettui Ouicil."

She engaged Markak and sent a thought telling him what she had done. Markak, as if nothing had taken place, returned his eyes to Roth. Liana took her seat.

"Thank you for coming to this meeting," Roth said. "Thank you for taking the message I sent down in the urgent message container in the freight elevator. I know this is unprecedented and rare. It is a privilege to meet you. We requested this meeting is to discuss what we believe was a trespass by one of our personnel into your section of the facility. We apologize for any violation of our joint working agreement."

Liana raised her finger to the colonel. "Permit me to translate what you have said so far." She anticipated Markak would react fiercely to the topic and she wanted to be precise.

Roth nodded.

She faced Markak and sent her translation of Roth's comments in a thought to Markak.

Markak's bony brow lowered and his mouth appeared to draw tight as he looked at Roth. It was an outward display Liana had rarely observed. He turned to Liana for a moment, communicating his response for Roth to her. It was as she expected.

Liana nodded and after a pause she faced Roth. "Markak says that any trespasser is a severe violation of the treaty of cooperation between your government and the expeditionary group from what you call, Zeta 2 Reticuli," she said, relating the message in a mechanical tone. "Furthermore, had a trespasser engaged our personnel on the levels in question, the Reticulans would have been within their rights to terminate such a trespasser."

Roth's eyes moved from Liana to Markak and over to Winston. Liana saw that he was deeply troubled. She picked up a flashing thought from Roth about search and rescue.

Colonel Roth dropped his eyes to his folded hands, resting on the table, deliberating Markak's answer. He looked up at Markak, his mouth a determined signal, his eyes narrowed, and his brow furrowed.

Liana detected he was fighting an urge to explode and she presumed the Greys had also recognized it.

Winston cleared his throat. He said, "With your permission, we would like to search your floors for our soldier. We are uncertain about his state of mind and fear he might try to destroy something in your facility or harm one of your staff. Our visit would be benign; we are not interested in your scientific work."

Liana quickly translated the remarks into thoughts for Markak. She knew Markak would never concede to a visitation by the soldiers or anyone. Having seen how Bryan reacted to the Reticulan research, learning of the Grey's feeding idiosyncrasy, the dissolution tables, and the cloning laboratory, Liana could foresee the military becoming irrationally violent.

Markak formed the fingers of his right hand into a fist on the table surface, not moving his head, keeping his enormous eyes on Roth.

The alien leader shot and energetic reply into Liana's head. She looked calmly at Roth. "Markak says that no humans have ever visited the Reticulan's levels and that the charter agreement specifically spells out the prohibition of such a thing. The protocol shall not ever undergo a change. Any violators of the agreement shall face swift punishment. He would like to know why one of your people violated our section."

She imprisoned her thoughts with her mental barrier, as she considered the probability and possible reason a rogue military person would invade the Grey's levels. A human, an irresponsible soldier, might fall victim to faulty judgment, curiosity, or a violent state of thinking brought on by resentment for invaders from another world. One could also fall victim to a disturbed mental state from the stress of his position. Such a strained thought process could entice a soldier to plunge into the unknown occupied by the Greys, possibly seeking revenge or trophies.

Returning her focus to the standoff, she sensed Markak's ruthless cold contempt for humans. From his comments and stiff body language a military invasion to the Grey's levels would not end well.

Roth's brow arched.

Liana picked up a thought from Roth, indicating an agreeable attitude clouded by building anger. Most certainly Markak had also acquired the impression.

Roth said, "If one of our personnel violated your section, they probably wanted to see what a visitor from another planet looked like. I'm sorry for your distrust. We have not given you any prior reason for such a rebuke of our request. We will, however, search any and all areas of this complex if we decide it is necessary. This is still a facility of the United States of America and the friendliest damn government you'll meet on this spheroid we call Earth." Roth stopped and nodded at Liana.

Liana translated the comment in thought to Markak.

Markak placed his hands flat on the table and rose from his chair. The corners of his mouth drew back as he pressed his mouth closed. The others of his party stood, all their eyes on the sitting soldiers. Markak lowered his head almost imperceptibly to Roth, turned, and walked out of the room toward the elevator followed by the other Greys, the hybrid, and at the rear, Liana.

On her departure from the conference room, she detected Roth's thoughts teetering on rage. She sent a quick thought into his head, hinting the Grey's were laughing at him.

Roth, Winston, and the two other officers followed, taking a position a few yards from the conference room where they all watched the alien entourage walk across the hall and disappear behind the elevator door.

Liana stood in the descending freight elevator, holding her gaze on the door while protecting her thoughts from possible mind-sweeping by the Greys. A flash of disgust for descending back to the isolated demented world of the Greys washed through her mind. She quickly erased it by thinking of Bryan. Trying to appear disinterested, she turned her mind to technical features of the doors, their surface, paint, and fabrication.

As the elevator dropped past level nine, she wondered if their escape had just become more impossible. The Greys would likely dedicate more focus to the military's eagerness for searching the lower floors for their missing man. Liana suspected the man had met his end in a tank on level fourteen. However, with the Grey's inflated belief in their superiority of intelligence and technology, typical of Markak's mind, they could assign a zero probability to a military incursion. The Greys didn't recognize the importance of a missing man to the humans, particularly to the brothers of his close military unit. The Grey's collective social structure and ease of reproducing their own kind, as well as clones, had destroyed their understanding of inter-Grey relationships. Despite that potential for reduced security, she would study the distribution of the silver spheres, whether they were watching the elevators and stairs. She had to evaluate altering some of their programming. The military, the Greys, and Bryan's hope for freedom all seemed connected in an undulating, unpredictable fabric. How could she influence events? If she could.

***

The elevator door had closed and several moments had elapsed.

Colonel Winston gestured a question at Roth with his hand. "Is it safe to talk?"

"I was just asking myself that," Roth said.

Roth turned and drifted back into the conference room with Winston following a step behind. Roth sat on the corner of the table as Winston, Earl Mathews, and Jack Harvey followed and stood abreast of each other just inside the door, facing the conference table.

Roth ran a hand over the table as if smoothing sand and then looked up, disgust and anger on his face. "Those Grey bastards are not going to tell me how to run security in this facility. They can shove the treaty up their shriveled Grey ass… if they have one."

Winston's eyes grew large. "The treaty is over fifty years—"

Roth's voice filled the room. "I don't give a shit how long we've had a treaty or how long they've been working at the bottom of this glorified concrete sewer pipe."

"They are arrogant invaders and begging for a lesson in humility," Winston replied. "However, you wouldn't want to start an intergalactic war."

"Colonel, what about Sergeant Bauer?" Mathews asked. "We can't write him off. He's still one of our men."

"I agree," Harvey said, checking Bauer and glancing at Roth.

Roth swept his gaze across each man. Their faces told him of the fire in their hearts and it was simple. He knew the thinking of each man. The thought had already struck him.

"Bauer went down there. The video clearly shows the stupid ass in the freight elevator. He may have been high on something but that doesn't matter. He's on our team. Those Grey bastards have done something with him. I feel it. Gentlemen, we don't leave a man behind. Our code requires us to retrieve him alive or dead. Either way, if we find him down there, the shit may hit the fan. We may get bad bloody if we go."

Mathews pulled on his upper lip. "We don't have approval for such a mission. Hell, I'll bet a six-pack that the government weasels wrote a provision prohibiting the rescue of any of our personnel once they venture down there. Don't you think?"

Roth chewed on the inside of his cheek for a moment, feeling a storm building in his gut. "Gentlemen, even in Afghanistan under massive fire, my team pulled out team members we thought were dead only to discover they could be saved by a chopper ride to a field medical unit."

"Sir," Harvey said. "Couldn't we schedule the operation as a maintenance exploration for the source of a random failure in the water or gas system?"

"That's right, Jack. The water travels down through the east wing to the reactor room and in a second pipe also down to the Grey's area. I believe water comes from a pipe running from our above ground reservoir."

Winston tossed his head to one side. "That's the way I remember it. But if we go down there and don't get zapped by some space weapon, and if word leaks out, the shit will still hit the fan. The big boys could court marshal all of us without thinking twice. That means... we can't schedule our excursion. We don't register any maintenance reason. No Records. We just go. And we kill all the cameras. No record. It didn't happen."

"When do we go?" Harvey asked.

"I haven't decided to do anything," Roth said. "I thought it; doing it is something else."

"Frankly sir, I don't like waiting... I... I don't trust those Grey bastards any farther than I can spit," Mathews said nervously.

Winston wagged a finger at Roth. "We can't go right away. They'll be looking for us."

Roth nodded and jabbed a finger back at Winston. "Okay, we need to keep this 'need to know only' and I think we should wait maybe forty-eight hours. It's already been two days for Bauer. Meanwhile I'll think this through some more."

Jack Harvey tapped his hand lightly on the table. "I'll take care of the weapons. They'll be maneuverable for the cramped space and I think we should make use of some concussion grenades. Maybe a pressure wave will split one of those big Grey coconuts."

"Listen, you guys, if we go, this isn't necessarily going to be a cake-walk," Roth said sternly. "They no doubt have some sort of advanced weapons. We can't underestimate their lethality. We will wear the ceramic plates in our vests. I want every man completely protected." He looked at the men and grinned. "Hell, I'll be retiring in six years. I'm not ready to buy the farm until I'm good and old."

Winston grinned. "I always try to look at a mission dispassionately. This one scares the shit out of me, but it needs to be done. If I were down there, I'd want you guys to recover my body. I wouldn't want them eating me."

Roth shook his head in disgust. "This reminds me of walking up a mountain in Afghanistan totally exposed to the enemy." He gazed off across the conference room. The acid in his stomach churned, telling him that his nerves had sparked. "I must admit I have a mission bias. I hate the Grey spawn and the way our country kissed their Grey asses. There isn't any mutual understanding as far as I know. There was only capitulation by our weak-kneed politician slobs to a superior species, probably to avoid the catastrophic destruction at the discretion of these Greys. The Greys probably promised technology and snookered the politicians and weak-ass generals." He gathered a tired breath. "Okay, men, let's break up this meeting. I'll confirm things with all of you."

"Sir," Harvey said, "we have to—"

"I know," Roth said with a groan.

The men walked somberly out the door and lethargically down the hall. Roth didn't move from the table, drifting off in thought. He had never talked to or heard of anyone who had gone down to the Greys and he had grave misgivings not only about what he would see, but whether they'd return. The whole military section was rampant with rumors about the horrors awaiting a human descending to the hell on the bottom floor controlled by the Greys. What concerned him, other than the possibility of engaging in some sort of firefight, was what he would want to do if they found Bauer in parts or encased in some hellacious experiment? He had seen dead and wounded soldiers in Iraq and Afghanistan in an honorable conflict but not used in experiments.

That's all rumors. I have to tell Harvey to bring a few strips of C-4 for cutting pipes and electrical conduit. We are going!

Chapter Eight

Congressman Alberto Gutierrez sat behind his office desk in the congressional Longworth Building in Washington D.C., scribing ideas on a sheet of paper for an upcoming speech. Dressed proudly in his starched white shirt under black suspenders, he paused and stared at his outline. He brushed a finger absentmindedly across his short mustache first to the left and then to the right. His bullet brown eyes gazed at the words with satisfaction. Out of the corner of his eyes, he noticed a few crumbs from the donut he had eaten with his coffee. He brushed them into his hand and dropped them in a wastebasket to the side of his desk.

Paulette, his aide, opened his door and stuck her head past its edge. "Your two-fifteen appointment is here."

Congressman Gutierrez sat up, the irritation of an interruption forming a frown. "Okay. Show them in. Please sit in for notes."

"Will do, sir."

Congressman Gutierrez stood at the end of his desk. Two women and three men entered the office. He gestured toward a small sitting area in the corner of the room where a coffee table was centered within a circle of three upholstered chairs and a small sofa. Paulette led the guests toward the sitting area as Gutierrez moved to meet them.

Paulette gestured toward the woman. "Congressman, this is Olivia and Lee Carson."

Olivia and Lee shook hands with the congressman.

Paulette directed Gutierrez's attention to the second woman, a short, gray-haired elderly lady with bright eyes. "This is Mrs. Northfield, Sarah."

"Nice to meet you ma'am," Gutierrez said.

"Nice to meet you, sir."

Paulette motioned to the next person, an elderly man with wiry unkempt gray hair, wearing a herringbone jacket with sleeves that were a bit too short. His necktie hung from a loosely constructed knot. Lively steel-gray eyes accented a face marked by sagging jowls and age creases at the corners of his mouth. "This is Professor Cyrus Greenberg from Princeton."

"How do you do, Congressman," Greenberg said, taking the congressman's hand. "Nice of you to take time from your busy schedule to meet with us."

"That's why I'm here, serving the people of Arizona." A dry smile formed. "Although, I don't think Princeton is in Arizona." Gutierrez turned and paused, glancing at Paulette.

She gestured to the third man, looking to be in his early fifties, wearing a tan suit, crisp light blue shirt, and a turquoise adorned belt buckle. "This is the—"

"Yes, Paulette, I know Julian Salvo," Gutierrez said quickly.

Gutierrez and Salvo shook hands vigorously.

"Nice seeing you," Salvo said.

"I think the last time we met was at that Saturday coffee you arranged in downtown Sedona."

"It was." Salvo nodded and glanced around the office. "So this is a congressman's office. It's stately... nice." Salvo regarded his colleagues. "Congressman Gutierrez represents my district in Arizona, but of course I think you all knew that."

"Let's have a seat and see what you have in mind," Gutierrez said. He thought of the mayor's comment and told himself that he deserved his office even if he was only forty-five. Besides he had gotten fifty-nine percent of the votes during the last election and had helped several veterans with their problems, which was reported in the *Arizona Republic*.

They settled into the chairs and small sofa for their conversation. For a moment the visitor's eyes focused on the congressman, waiting in silence. Gutierrez glanced at his guests. "How can I help?" Gutierrez said.

"Okay, I'll start," said Greenberg, his voice deliberate. "I'm the oldest anyway." He paused. "It has been two years since Olivia and Lee got routed to me by the Princeton University directory services desk. All they had was a name, university, and area of study, which was artificial intelligence. They approached the university trying to track down the families of Bryan and Louise Northfield. Bryan was one of my professors. I'm the department head." He gathered a breath and unconsciously scratched his neck. "These two nice people have been trying to raise a red flag about Bryan and Louise for two years and haven't gotten anywhere. They finally connected with Mrs. Northfield only a short time ago. Law enforcement has not helped to any degree... not enough information. Once we touched base with the mayor here, a few weeks ago, it looked like we were making progress." Greenberg raised an eyebrow at the congressman.

"What is this red flag?" Gutierrez asked, calculation in his glance.

Salvo turned to the professor. "If I may, professor." He faced Gutierrez. "Congressman, we are here about two people who disappeared from a campground on the edge of Sedona." He gestured to Olivia and Lee. "And these two nice people were there. They actually live in Indiana and were going through Sedona on their vacation. They were sitting with the couple only minutes before it happened. Olivia saw the whole thing from her camper window. Sorry to say, the police scoffed at the story."

"Where was Lee during this event?" Gutierrez asked.

Salvo replied, "Lee, why don't you pick up where I left off. I wasn't there and you were."

Lee cleared his throat. "I was rummaging around in the trailer looking for my camera. Olivia was glued to the window, nearly in tears, crying about those poor people. Then I heard her gasp. She sank to her knees white as ghost below the window. She couldn't talk for a minute."

Gutierrez leaned forward. "What happened?"

Lee Carson said, "Well—"

Olivia stared sternly at the congressman, her eyes growing intense, her lips tightening, and then she burst out, "An alien spacecraft took them clean off the ground. That's what happened! And this damn government won't do a thing about it."

Gutierrez started to grin, realized his failure, and stopped. "There must be another explanation for what happened."

"Congressman, my son and daughter-in-law disappeared while on vacation and the grief killed my husband," Sarah Northfield said in her aged voice, pointing a shaking finger at him.

Olivia popped to her feet, glared at Salvo, at Greenberg, and drew a ragged breath. "I told you this would be a waste of time. All these people want is a cushy job so they can retire big, fat, and sassy. The government doesn't give a damn about people like us." She paused and pointed to Gutierrez's hand. "Look. He has no wedding ring and no wife. There is no way for him to visualize what it would be like losing a loved one… seeing someone float into the sky by an unexplainable event."

"I may not be married but my conscience isn't dead. I have had my love relationships with a couple women. I'm not emotionally dead. It does take a thick skin to wade in the mud of the nation's affairs." He flashed his eyebrows, looking at her with understanding. "Mrs. Carson, let's back up. Assuming what you say is true."

"Sir, I find that a little condescending. I already told you what happened. There's no assuming anything at all. It is fact! People were taken, abducted right in front of me. The mayor says they've had others disappear, other people who lived there. Ask him."

Gutierrez offered a pleading hand and gestured toward her seat. "Please sit down. Please. I want to help. And, Mrs. Northfield, I am very sorry for your loss."

Salvo moved to the edge of his seat. "Congressman, she's right. In the last five years, we lost this couple, a seven-year-old girl who was playing on a small farm, and a thirty-year-old waitress driving home at night from work." His mouth saddened as his eyes fell with pain. "Each time people reported lights in the sky. Now—why would I come to the government and not some UFO search group? Good question."

"Yes."

Salvo continued, "Perhaps a year after the Northfields were lost, a doctor of psychology and his patient paid me a visit. The patient, a cable repairman, was in a shaky condition, claiming horrible recurring dreams. The doctor had hypnotized him a couple times with no success. Then during one visit, the man unloaded what he remembered—without hypnosis. He said a UFO abducted him and took him to a large concrete facility where he was implanted behind his left ear. He remembered seeing a woman while sitting in a room. She wore a black shirt with Princeton in orange letters on the upper left. He said she was very nice looking. In addition to the implant, they removed one of his kidneys. He had the implant removed and a group of technical people haven't been able to figure what it does." He sighed. "He swore that he hadn't hallucinated the concrete facility. The aliens dropped him back in his car. He lost four hours. It's the kind of story that, taken on its own, sounds like science fiction, but when it corroborates with the missing Princeton people, well two and two make four. This government, the boys running the secret stuff, may not give two-hoots for us folks but it seems to me the water is slowly getting hotter under that boiling frog, and by the time the government-frog realizes he's in boiling water, he's cooked and so is our country." He stared at the congressman. "You do know the story about the frog in boiling water?"

"Yes," Gutierrez said. His voice droned. "I've heard that one." He turned to the professor. "What's your connection other than being a department boss?"

"Bryan was a professor in artificial intelligence and his wife, Louise, was a professor in astrophysics. They were a nice young couple, friends, and productive scientists. And I, like my new friends here... I'm worried that some black branch of our government has been penny wise and pound foolish. If you get my meaning? It appears that an agency with the purpose of maintaining safeguards should carry out an investigation on these incidents and end the human abductions. I would go so far as to suggest that this problem find its way to the president because of its implications for an invading force existing or a covert government structure existing behind the label of a secrets classification." He shook a finger at Gutierrez. "Think about it. If a group of unscrupulous people wanted to hide their activities all they would have to do is declare it with the highest security level of top secret and beyond. I realize... we all realize that you could disappear for poking your nose in such things. At least that's the word floating around on the internet. We could disappear on the way home today. That in itself is a reason to have such an organization and its activities stopped."

"You could be correct," Gutierrez said. "What justification do I have for risking so much?"

Greenberg's eyes slid closed for a moment, he glanced at the floor, and then brought his focus to Gutierrez. "Son, if you don't know the answer to that question, our bacon is already burning in the fire and that frog is getting tender."

"Very well, I'll check with a few people on the defense appropriations committee."

Gutierrez stood and then his visitors stood. They all shook hands and slowly meandered toward the outer office door.

Professor Greenberg turned back to the congressman with a somber face.

"Remember the frog."

Chapter Nine

Liana strode down the corridor toward Bryan's cell, considering several problems and the most prominent was his mental stability. To a lesser extent, suspicions about the Greys lined up in her thoughts, each one a different variable in a complex equation she both relished and feared. Shortly after the Greys had returned to their section of the facility after the meeting with the military, they ordered her to bring Bryan to the bottom floor. She was fairly certain the meeting with the military was unrelated to the request. If anything, the order was part of their scheduled plan for him and their cold unwavering movement toward their research goals.

Before Bryan had arrived in her world, she had recognized the Grey's lack of emotions toward other Greys except for an occasional appearance of ego and disgust. Rarely did the Greys show feelings toward their experimental subjects, except for Nekzon, who seemed a deviant example. She was confident that she had reached their level intellectually, which forced her to guard her mind from them. She was growing weary of their brutally cold manner, no doubt a facet of the human part of her mind and her developing emotions. The Greys defiled their own intelligence.

From what she had researched, they had more tests planned for Bryan before he would reach a point of critical action, the final visit to the bottom floor. If they began a procedure that would take his life, she knew she would do something to try and save him. They both could perish if that point came.

Upon opening the door to his cell, Liana found Bryan on his cot, looking expectantly and smiling at her. With the scant time available, she pushed past his curious reaction, thinking she would work at understanding the phenomenon later.

He moved to the edge of his cot.

Liana felt a sensation of softness. She suspected that she felt compassion for him. After a moment, she brushed them from her mind, not because of coldness but out of the necessity to prepare for a confrontation with the Greys, and possibly argue against their measures. She smiled back at him. She knew he needed it. She then became stern in preparation for strengthening his mind.

"I'm here to take you to the bottom floor," she said in a heavy tone.

He stood, his face drawn. "What do they want?"

"I don't know." She stepped toward him and whispered, "You must prepare your mind. I can help you mentally block their digging into your thoughts and prevent their attempts at controlling you. They did that with another subject a short time ago and they haven't attempted it with you up to this time. It may be that time."

Bryan stared into her eyes. "Please do whatever you think will be helpful. I trust you."

"We don't have much time. I will sit with you for a moment."

Bryan backed up and sat on the cot. Liana slowly eased herself down next to him.

"Please calm yourself and look at the floor," she said.

He clasped his hands and gazed at the floor.

Liana sent thoughts at his mind. In a moment his eyes glazed over nearly watering. "Stay relaxed for me," she said. "You can close your eyes." She sent a sequence of thoughts targeted at the deepest logic areas of his brain, those for thought control. She had learned from the Grey's data system how to influence the area. She gave him a mantra for concentration and blocking any of the Grey's probing.

He closed his eyes.

She repeated her instructions, trying to implant a pattern for Bryan to follow with his own volition. In a few moments she touched his shoulder.

The moment she touched Bryan, he raised his head and took in a deep breath. He blinked several times. "Ham-Sah, Ham-Sah." He frowned. "Will the mantra work? Do you think I'm ready?"

"I know you are," Liana whispered.

"By the way what does it mean?"

"Freedom from fear."

***

Upon arriving at the bottom level, Liana walked Bryan from the outer circumferential corridor, turning down an intersecting radial hall, and walked to the room that adjoined the one where he lost his kidney. The door was open as they approached with light spilling into the hall.

Bryan heard Liana's words in his mind: "The two Greys are Haazon Temtso and Nekzon Vagpok. Haazon is generally a worker and Nekzon is second to Markak. Nekzon is a rare Reticulan in that he has an inclination toward deviant cruel behavior. Do not cross him."

Bryan paused at the door, quickly digesting Liana's warning, feeling nervous, as he hesitantly stepped into the room. She waited in the corridor with a disinterested stare directed at the opposite wall.

A high-backed armed chair occupied the center of the room, surrounded by cabinets marked by a penny-size spot of illumination, seemingly indicating a connection with electronics from the Grey's science. Shoebox-size devices sat on the cabinets with lights glowing on their horizontal surface. Bryan couldn't see any connecting wires or tubes. He looked up and had to squint against a brilliant light beaming down from a single source at the ceiling. It reminded him of an intelligence agency's interrogation center that could form part of a scene in a Hollywood movie. The room smelled damp and felt clammy like the basement of an old abandoned house.

Two Greys observed with their revolting gaze from a few feet in front of the chair. As Bryan washed his eyes over them, taking care to not to express displeasure, he recognized the Grey with the thin skin over its bony face, Nekzon, the one Liana had mentioned. Perhaps he was feeding off a preconception but he thought Nekzon's small mouth was sneering at him. Bryan remembered Liana's words and started controlling his thoughts, determined not divulge his fears, thinking of the mantra.

He sat in the chair just as a Grey's voice ran into his head and told him to sit.

The second Grey, Haazon, closed the door, leaving Liana outside.

Bryan visualized his office and recalled a neural network computer problem. As he purposefully jumbled his thoughts, he realized that to survive perhaps he could play their game. He noted that his awareness was crystal clear and clean, and despite handling the interaction with them, he needed it to remain that way.

The Grey's large black eyes pressed on him as if drilling into his brain. He hated them staring. A voice rippled into his brain. It came in waves, repeating sequences, commanding his obedience and demanding complete compliance. He was to obey all commands. The Grey's told him that he had lost his vision and everything was black around him.

Recognizing the Grey's objective, he rambled over a hodgepodge of thoughts. When he came back to the hypnotic siren song aimed at control of his mind, it struck him funny. He killed his emerging amusement, knowing his new capability was a new weapon he must conceal. He looked straight ahead as if nothing happened. He thought of his dead wife and of her in that horrible tank. His eyes glazed over. He repeated Liana's mantra five times.

The Greys looked at each other, their eyes expressing their apparent agitation with more outward emotions than Bryan had seen. One of the Greys touched a control on a device.

A stream of words poured into Bryan's head, coming with more power as if driven from a larger audio speaker or powered by more wattage. The word sequences washed through his head, emphasizing his requirement to obey, telling him to open his mind and that he had to obey. The thread of words declared his existence depended on following the commands. A command told him that his stomach felt nauseous and that he had immense pain.

Bryan scoured over old ideas and images, making a random pattern of thoughts. He repeated the mantra. In a few moments the repeating string of trance-coercion words weakened. When the words in his head had faded, he formed a quick thought that the Greys had attempted something detrimental to his life. Liana had saved him. He closed his eyes, fighting to remain calm and acting the part of a troubled subject. After all, they could wipe out his mind at any moment. A few moments passed. He sighed heavily and opened his eyes. He looked plainly at the Greys, holding his composure.

The two Greys conferred with each other. The way they locked their eyes together for a moment made Bryan think he was in for more trouble. Suddenly, they strode out of the room, leaving the door ajar. Liana, acting with complete obedience, never looked at the Greys. Nekzon stopped and walked back to her.

As Nekzon communicated with Liana, his heavy brow raised, stretching the skin at the edges of his mouth making an already stern expression look angry.

Bryan moved hesitantly to the door. He clasped his hands together votively, holding his head tilted down. "May I help in any way?" he said, speaking aloud.

Liana glared at him.

In an instant, it seemed she had plugged him into a phone line. Bryan heard her words crashing into his brain. "Bryan, be careful. They do not like the results of their evaluation. They are studying mind control for broad use on the population. They want to implant a mind-control device into your brain. They are evaluating it in one of their programs. They are concerned that they couldn't influence you with their usual method. However, Markak may want to interrogate you one more time before they operate."

Bryan clenched his teeth. He took a step toward the Greys, who warily backed up a step. Not knowing how to address either of the Greys, he thought a message to both Greys and to Liana: *I would appreciate talking with your leader, Markak. I am a scientist. I work at the highest level on this planet, probably with the upper one-percent of researchers. Perhaps Markak would gain additional perspective having a discussion with me.*

She snapped her gaze to him, trying to conceal her frown of concern from the Greys. She spoke aloud, "Markak doesn't talk to subjects in a casual setting."

Nekzon's brow moved upward, revealing more of his eyes. Just then, words from Nekzon slid into Bryan's mind. "I am Nekzon. I will inform Markak. Markak does not talk to creatures of low intelligence. It is the same as humans not talking to insects. I will present your request." Bryan detected amusement and perhaps mockery in the Grey's choppy reply.

Bryan sent a thought to Nekzon and Liana: *Thank you, Nekzon Vagpok. I look forward to meeting with Markak.*

Bryan exchanged glances with Liana as Nekzon and Haazon Temtso walked away.

"Do you have a plan with an objective?" she asked him verbally in a stern tone. She started down the hall and paused.

"I thought the Reticulans didn't have emotions," Bryan said aloud, walking after her. "Liana, my thought process was that perhaps I could demonstrate some value to Markak. If I could show some value by engaging in an intelligent discourse with Markak, maybe he would keep me alive. They are going to stick an implant in my brain if I don't show them a benefit to their studies of humans. Perhaps, I can think of enough good questions I can convince them to keep me alive a little longer... with my brain in its present state... buy a little more time to form a solid escape plan." He paused. "By the way, thanks for enhancing my ability to communicate and block their mind control. I know you did it back at my cell and with the teaching machine, risking putting yourself in danger. The mantra helped."

They stopped in the hall. She looked up at the ceiling.

"Spheres?" he said in a whisper, as if a sudden realization.

"Yes. They are a problem."

She touched his hand, gazed into his eyes, and quickly pulled away. "We need each other. So please don't be too quick with the Greys. I know you feel encouraged by your new intelligence but their species developed over fifty thousand of your years, years after they had language, writing, and mathematics. They are crafty and what you call, heartless. They use a collective existence where the individual is inconsequential. My assessment is that since they can alter genetics and clone beings, they have no appreciation for the essence of life; what you might call spirit or soul."

He looked at her tenderly, took her hand, and shot his gaze along the hall. Without thinking he stepped next to her and kissed her quickly on the lips.

Her eyes grew wide with surprise. She touched her lips with a finger. "Not in the hall." She smiled, glanced behind them, and back at him. "Thank you for your tenderness. But, not in the hall. Too risky."

Bryan reflected for an instant on her words and where he'd encountered them before in his life. Was it in high school where the display of affection wasn't permitted in the school halls? He brushed that mote of thought quickly away.

"I couldn't resist," he said. "You looked so inviting, understanding, and tender." A pang of guilt washed over him. Had he betrayed Louise? It seemed his Louise had only just perished. When he gazed at Liana, he was ashamed for not assuming the cultural norm for a period of grieving, but his feelings were real. Regardless of the calendar and the real passage of time he found a little solace. It would take more time.

"You were aroused?" she asked.

"No… not exactly… more like wanting to hold you for comforting and mutual nurturing."

She gave a slight acknowledging move of her head. "We must move along."

Moments later, they reached his cell. He stepped in, leaving Liana at the threshold. They gazed at each other. A moment passed.

Bryan whispered, "I'm feeling more strongly about you."

"Are you sure it's not a feeling of appreciation for my help?"

"I don't think so."

"Are you seeing your wife when you look at me?"

"No. I'm not thinking of my wife. Although, I sincerely believe she would want me to move on with my life. She was a pragmatist. I know that I would want that for her. If and when I'm free of this place, I'll create a memorial celebrating her life and our love."

"That's interesting. Is that normal? I'll have to analyze your behavior and my reactions further. Your respectful sentiment seems logical and sensitive."

"Some human emotions are complex."

"Regarding the Greys, please don't do anything rash. We must be patient to arrive at an opportunity to escape. It will come, possibly mixed with another event. If we act prematurely, we could lose our lives."

"I understand. I trust your judgment."

He kept his eyes on her until the door closed, blocking his view, leaving him to the sterile cell with nothing but his thoughts and nightmares. Had he plunged over an abyss by encouraging a visit with Markak, a creature of wildly superior intelligence? He may have made a fatal mistake.

As minutes passed, he found his solitude a blessing and a curse with its moments saturated by sometimes rambling conjectures, and penetrating and painful conclusions. Despite the emptiness of the time, it helped him tether his previous reality to the extraordinary and perilous current struggle.

He had to remember to guard against any spontaneous comments spawned from his ancient earth-formed ego. Liana's warning against making a rash action bounced back into his brain. He regretted his foolish unintelligent earthling decision, asking for a meeting with the Grey's leader. Too late now.

***

The next morning, the fourteenth, Bryan followed Liana, repeating their breakfast excursion, extracting the same food and energizing liquid from the containers in the curious nourishment room. In the back of his mind, sitting at the table eating, he wondered if his meeting with Markak would happen.

He looked at Liana as she seemed preoccupied in thought; he didn't push for her attention, waiting several moments for a comment. At last, he had to say something.

"I'm very sorry for my stupidity. Do you think Markak will concede to talk with one of his human prisoners?" His voice came out in nearly a whisper. He studied the change in her forehead, her eyes, and the line of her jaw. It was as if he could see her grinding over the logic of the answer in her mind.

"Markak will have no concern for you. He may carry a weapon of incredible power at his waist. The Grey's know their bodies are fragile. Their minds and technology are their weapons. As I have stated, their emotions are generally limited, although, Nekzon shows that individuals may have weaknesses in their psychology. It is possible Markak will find amusement in talking with a human. Remember—never drop your mental protection. If you do, he can penetrate your memories, those related to our discussions, those between you and your wife, and your active thoughts. He could use any of the information in a horrible manner. Greys developed a natural thought-communication barrier through their evolution."

Her warning added weight to his shoulders and although she spoke mildly, her words built upon his fear. His head was up for the Grey's chopping block?

"You know I despise these beings," Bryan said, hanging his head dejectedly.

"You are worried about them taking you to a room where they would dismember you. Perhaps you see yourself lying on a table with the canopy covering you as the dissolving chemical pours down over your body." She sighed. "I worry every day about such horror for you. Please believe me when I tell you that I won't permit any of those things to happen to you if I have any life in this body. I would use violence."

"How could you stop them if they decided to terminate me?" He gazed at her, his eyes glassy from tears. "Please don't risk your life for me. You must find a way to live... to live outside and away from this place. You've never been free."

The hybrid, Dauasi Ziebou, appeared in the doorway.

Liana stood with her arms poised at her sides. "Dauasi Ziebou, do you have a request?"

"You are to escort this subject to level fourteen and meet with Markak." Dauasi Ziebou turned around stiffly and marched down the hall.

"This may be your discussion," Liana said. "You must believe in yourself that you can converse with this Grey." Liana stepped over to the door. "You have the mental facility for it."

Bryan rose and met her a step outside the door, her manner having changed, suggesting she had resumed her persona as a servant to the Greys. It was what she had to do and in a sense reassuring that their game continued. He could have smiled at her acting.

His approaching visit focused and dominated his thoughts. Would he hold his own in the presence of the Grey's mind and those enormous lifeless eyes? He had to protect his own thoughts as Liana had trained him.

***

Down on the bottom floor, Liana walked in front of Bryan, escorting him to one of the radial halls they hadn't visited, stopping at the second room along the hall. She opened the door, stepped in just past the threshold and paused, standing soldier-erect with her eyes obediently in the distance. Bryan walked in the room. His knees suddenly felt rubbery.

The room was evenly illuminated as if the walls themselves gave off light, as if the Greys had covered them with something other than paint. The room was warmer than any he had encountered and comfortable.

A few paces from the door, Markak sat in a chair that had arms, very much a human type chair. He wore the same type uniform as Liana with long tight sleeves. The top and bottom both looked gray with a bluish tinge. Alongside him was a table with some sort holographic control, extending vertically in a two-foot square, glowing display. The drape of the Markak's hands at the end of the chair arms, his relaxed posture, belied his piercing Reticulan stare, and reminded Bryan of a monarch awaiting his subject's genuflection and submission. An empty straight chair, separated from Markak by perhaps eight feet, held a prominent position, as if for a testimony during an inquisition.

Markak lazily raised his arm, swinging it slowly like a gigantic crane over a container ship, gesturing with a spindly finger toward the chair.

With his muscles and nerves jangling, Bryan sat down, clasping his hands on his lap, unable to take his eyes from the head of the alien sitting before him, telling himself that he was looking at their leader. He felt a quiver in his chest. For a moment, he thought he recognized lines in the skin of Markak's head, lines he speculated indicated a senior age. When the lids of the Markak's large glittering eyes closed down slightly, lines formed near the corners of his small mouth. Bryan sensed that the Grey was showing tension. It was interesting that they might share a common experience at that moment.

Bryan had to send his gaze at the floor to avoid alerting Markak of his discovery—the odor he spelled coming from the alien. It was the first time he had detected an alien's odor. Liana had mentioned their odd nourishment regimens. The odor disgusted his nose like the air wafting from a rotten piece of meat.

Bryan's risky venture began. In his head flowed Markak's mentally-sent words: "I am Markak, the senior Reticulan leader at this expeditionary facility." A pause came. More words streamed into Bryan's head: "How did you avoid the mind control in our test?"

Stunned by the question, the thoughts tumbled in Bryan's head for a moment until he grabbed himself and focused. He had to hold back a sense of pride for his small accomplishment. It was negligible compared to what these space travelers could do. Liana's warning echoed as he tried to protect his deep feelings and started fragments of thoughts of his work. He could use the mantra.

He thought to Markak: *I don't truly know but it may result from your teaching machine.*

Markak's eyes opened wider as he moved his head ever so slightly. Markak continued, sending words into Bryan's head: "Your answer is logical. Why were you eager to talk with me?"

Bryan replied: *Science and curiosity. I also wanted to demonstrate my value to you so you will allow me to live.*

The thick brow over Markak's eyes moved up a little, touching Bryan with its grotesqueness.

His thoughts diverged with an analysis of the thought transference process. The Grey's thoughts came like a whisper mysteriously trickling into his brain, grasping and taking possession of his focus. *The barrier.*

Markak sent a thought into Bryan's mind: "What is a barrier?"

Bryan replied in thought: *An ocean protection where I lived.*

Markak sent him a mental comment; this time it came with a deviation. The words had more force, hammering rhythmically, varying in their complexity as if to entrance Bryan. Bryan pushed himself to think about computer artificial intelligence back at the university for a moment, until the words stopped.

Markak raised his head slightly as if perplexed. Bryan showed a stolid face.

Words slithered into Bryan's head: "What type of association do you have with artificial intelligence?"

Bryan considered the question for a moment, using the protection method Liana had given him, and then mentally replied: *I worked at a high level of science in our culture. My area of study was the theory and implementation of methods to allow computers to think for themselves, to make autonomous decisions. We call it artificial intelligence.*

Instantly, words poured into Bryan's head: "Fools. The artificial intelligence concept is typical for the stage of your civilization. It has a stifling effect on many species attempting it because it prevents the expansion natural mental capabilities."

Bryan pulled on his chin, finding the comment curious and potentially profound. He thought: *Did your civilization evaluate the concept?*

Markak answered, his thoughts sliding into Bryan's mind so easily it surprised him, making him more determined to keep conscious about using his mental barrier. Markak said: "Reticulan's found the idea and development a waste of time."

Bryan replied: *Did your world have a single controlling organization directing developments or did the members of your population have freedom to do as they wished? Is the individual free to create and achieve on his own?*

Markak tapped two fingers on the arm of his chair before a wrinkle formed above his brow. "Reticulan's have a single governing group orchestrating all aspects of our planet and that it is the only way for efficient progress and evolution of a species. The individual creates nothing alone. He exists only to serve the whole."

Bryan replied: *Your societies' individual sounds like what we call a slave.* He collected himself for a moment and followed-up with a quick thought-question: *How long into your evolution did you discover a way to overcome gravity and travel faster than light? Do you use dark energy to repel gravity?*

Markak seemed to form a slight smile. Into Bryan's head the words rushed. "What do you mean by gravity?"

Bryan replied mentally: *The pull of a planet for your ship. The effect of mass distorting space-time.*

Markak sat motionless for a moment simply looking at him.

Bryan found Markak's stare a little unnerving. Words came to Bryan's head in a precise rhythm. "Are you referring to this dark energy as how our craft hovers over the planet?"

Bryan replied: *We call the energy causing the separation of galaxies dark energy.*

"You are curious about how we travel to different solar systems."

Bryan smiled and as he did, Markak's face seem to relax. To Markak, Bryan thought: *I would like to know those things but I will need another session on the teaching machine. I would like to go in your craft.* He hesitated. *Do you collapse space-time to travel great distances?*

Markak replied into his head: "What a foolish concept. What would happen to surrounding objects if space-time collapsed? Wouldn't they move too?"

One of Louise's interests popped into Bryan's thoughts. *Has your civilization explored a black hole?*

Markak gestured with an open hand. "What is this black hole?"

Bryan remembered Louise again and replied: *A singularity in space-time.*

"Yes. I can see you are trying hard to demonstrate yourself. You are correct. You will need to use the teaching machine again."

After thinking for a moment, Bryan formed another question: *If you didn't bend space-time, did you travel here through a tunnel through space-time or merely exceed the speed of light?*

Markak clasped his hands. Bryan found his manner similar to someone showing arrogance. Words answering Bryan formed in his head: "We Reticulans exceeded light by distorting local space-time with our ship's exterior field. It is fundamental."

Some of our people have theorized about that method.

Bryan had heard of the ideas bounced around at Princeton and other schools and wondered how Markak would take the news of the human's approaching the technology and a potential threat by his species.

Markak replied quickly: "That human development is interesting."

Do you use atomic fusion to power your craft?

The reply came as before with only faint changes in the Grey's facial muscles: "We have found your planet's atomic facilities and weapons. We can control them if we wish."

Why did you tell me that? Bryan connected with Markak's gaze as if in a staring match to see who would flinch first. It occurred to him that the highly intelligent being facing him might be engaged in a type of information planting and probing. Only Liana could clarify for him the real from the unreal. And Markak had dodged the question about propulsion.

"Would your leaders defend this planet with those weapons at the cost of destroying the planet?"

Yes, I believe they would and I would guess that your leaders would do the same.

Markak leaned to one side of his chair, his eyes reaching across the room as he seemed to be thinking.

Bryan sensed a bit of defensiveness on the Grey's face. Bryan mentally transmitted another inquiry: *Perhaps two more questions, if I may. How do the Reticulans treat their deceased colleagues? Are they buried, cremated, or given a ceremony connected with a belief in a universal creator?*

Markak's implacable focus dwelled on Bryan for a moment.

Then, as if Markak acquiesced to him, words formed in Bryan's head, whispering in his thinking: "The matter of death holds no significance for Reticulans since many are created by an artificial process. In the forming of new life, no significance is made of the bequeathing progenitors. This is because some are cloned and implanted with memories from another entity. The dead are disposed of simply without ceremony since no spirit or electrical essence remains, only dead flesh." There came a pause in the words and then they continued. "The existence of a universal creator remains a question for many species. Now, a question for you. Why do you think we are on your planet?"

Bryan sensed the depth of the question and cautioned himself. He calmly replied: *I don't know, but with your intelligence I would estimate your purpose is aimed at beneficent help for our planet. With your technology, it doesn't seem logical that you would have hostile motives.*

The bony brow of Markak's head arched a little with the subtle movement of his head. The alien's mouth drew back hinting of amusement. Seeing the less than somber reaction, Bryan suspected his prospects for living a long life hadn't improved with the intellectual discussion.

Markak's face became stern. He spoke forcefully into Bryan's head with a hammering stream of words: "We are engaged in a program to explore the diversity of species and their DNA. Contrary to appearances, anything you may have seen, human DNA from this planet is of little value to our research."

Bryan leaned forward. Markak frowned at him.

Bryan replied: *So you are not trying to make controlled humans for infiltrating the population of this planet?*

Markak countered: "We have no need of this planet. Our species is not involved in conquest."

Bryan quickly relayed a thought: *Why haven't you announced your presence to the world?*

The Grey's brow raised slightly as Bryan heard his reply: "There is no need."

Bryan reminded himself not to drop his guard. He thought to Markak: *Thank you for the conversation.*

Markak sent a thought to Liana, which Bryan heard in his head: "Take this subject back to his cell. Make certain he complies with your administration. We have him scheduled for more study."

Liana, standing rigidly at the door, lowered her head.

Bryan couldn't avoid analyzing whether he had sealed his fate by his limited dialog with Markak. Markak's cold command to Liana offered no sign of a change in attitude or opinion.

Clearly, the ease with which the Greys created life and manipulated biological beings formed a basis for their callous valuation of life and in particular human life. Life was too easy for them. The DNA business was an obvious lie.

***

After the unnerving conversation with Markak, Liana and Bryan walked along the unrelenting barren corridor to the elevator on level fourteen. They waited for it to descend from the eleventh floor.

"The next few hours may give us an indication of Markak's assessment of you," she said, speaking in a soft voice.

"He was toying with me."

The freight elevator arrived and the doors opened. Liana and Bryan stepped aside as three Greys and three humans emerged. A male Grey walked at the front of the group and the two female Greys followed the humans. The Greys herded the two women and man down the hall. The humans plodded trancelike, appearing oblivious to their situation.

"Bryan, that situation is beyond our control. Let it pass from your concern for the present."

As soon as they had entered the elevator car and the door closed, Bryan shook his head angrily. "Those were new abductees!" he said, sharply.

"Two of the Greys, the male and one female are new," Liana said. "I wonder if they are preparing for something, perhaps for the military."

Bryan felt the inertia of his body against the floor as the car began its upward motion. "Where did the new Greys come from?"

"They came from level eleven. That may indicate a ship just returned. The hangar is on eleven. The new Greys might have come from another installation on this planet."

"Do you have any idea of how many people have gone through this torture?" It occurred to him that she might not know. He felt apologetic for asking. How many lives had the Greys torn from the human fabric of existence in his country or from the whole world? After all, their ship could fly anywhere at an incredible speed.

"Their recording system or in your language, their computer system, does not have a record of numbers, only variations of genetic code that they have evaluated. That number is in the thousands."

"Do you access their information system often?"

"I have access to everything because of my high evaluation. They tested me before they would allow me to work with subjects. They felt safe with my level, although I could have done much better on their test. At the time, prior to the test, I had already made several observations and hypothesized a purpose to their heinous actions. Initially, they did not alarm me. But my mind was still developing then." Glancing aside, as if contemplating her next words with great effort, her face grew somber. "Regardless of my access to their resources, any escape must fall within crucial parameters. We cannot simply go up an elevator to the surface. They would easily terminate us, slice us to pieces with their weapons, and possibly the military would join them in pursuing us. We must prepare for contingencies."

"Liana, I understand and agree. But merely fleeing this place doesn't address the universal need."

"What is that?"

Before he said it, he was certain she knew what he'd say even though he hadn't formed the words in his brain. "The universe must be cleansed of this infection and this hell."

She closed her eyes, seemingly finding inner peace. "Yes. But, you understand that is impossible because more of them could come from their planet. And who is to say what species should be allowed to live and which one should die?"

"Those new people... we can't save them can we?" he asked, finding it difficult to utter the words.

"If we can bring an end to it, their destruction may have purpose."

As the elevator doors opened on level twelve, Bryan and Liana faced the hybrid, Dauasi Ziebou.

Dauasi announced, "I am to take this subject to level thirteen. He will help monitor the new arrivals. Markak's order. Xscgui Tempok, Haazon Temtso, and Xscgui Peupok require our presence soon."

Bryan glanced at Liana. "Perhaps my conversation helped."

A stern gaze took over Liana's face. "Be careful what you wish for and who you make agreements with. The two Greys with Haazon have responsibilities for research with biologicals... humans and earth creatures."

Bryan frowned, not fully understanding her meaning. "Thanks for the concern. I will." He thought of the old quotation about making deals with the devil.

"We must go now," Dauasi Ziebou said.

"I was thinking of food," Bryan said.

***

Dauasi Ziebou escorted Bryan along the thirteenth floor corridors; the surrounding structure swallowing his footsteps. Was he headed to his final moments? They approached a room whose gray metal door stood open. The moment he entered, Bryan interpreted its features as those of a waiting room or processing facility. Three metal benches, placed next to the wall, ran half the length of the twenty-foot room. On the opposite wall, three two-foot square metal boxes sat on two tables, their chrome-like metal surface gleaming. Two archaic incandescent bulbs at the ceiling marginally pushed the dark away.

To what purpose did they use the room? Why was he there? Two Greys stood next to the end of one of the tables watching their catch, three humans sitting on the bench. The human subjects, their shoulders pulled in like cowering rabbits, stared dazed-eyed at the floor. Whatever purpose awaited these recent abductees, it couldn't include much hope for their longevity. His role in the alien's plan scared him. He thought of Liana's warning.

A door at the end of the room near the table opened, revealing a brilliantly illuminated laboratory. Bryan couldn't see much past the door but part of it looked similar to the butcher shop where they stole his kidney. He thought he saw something like an operating platform.

Dauasi Ziebou, with a blank face, pointed to a spot on the floor at the end of the table near the entrance door. "Wait here."

Dauasi Ziebou walked over to the two male Greys, looked at them intently for a moment, moving his head as if in conversation. He turned toward the humans on the bench and then stiffly to Bryan. "Sit next to these subjects. Talk to them. Distract them. You understand?"

Bryan nodded.

Dauasi Ziebou pointed to the Greys. "They want these subjects to be calm. That is your task. Comply."

The huddled human victims troubled Bryan. How could he help? He detested the idea of aiding the Greys in their horrid abuse of the new abductees. The three people appeared in the same mental state as when he saw them leaving the elevator. They appeared to be under some sort of Grey mind control, except for one woman. He sat at the end of the bench next to her, noticing that she seemed to be quite conscious and also distraught. The brown haired woman, in her forties, possibly standing five-foot-six, wore a short dress and a jeans jacket over a cream colored blouse, which looked appropriate for casual dining. Her roundish pale face and bloodshot eyes showed her horror. The Greys could have abducted her while she was walking a street or driving down a lonely highway.

Bryan rested his left hand on the bench and hunched slightly forward, trying to think of something comforting to say to her. Under his hand on the bench, he noticed scratches in the paint, three lines close together, eerily like fear-directed fingers had dug into the surface. At any moment the person clawing for their life could be him. On the floor to his right and directly below him, dark splotches spread randomly over the concrete, stains with a colorless composition. An odor struck him. Abducted humans had spilled their stomach contents. How many poor souls had the Greys herded, processed, and destroyed in their callous pursuit of species manipulation, mind control, invasion preparation, and brain analysis.

A silver sphere floated into the room, taking a position near the door, silent and ominous. Its appearance and location made Bryan wonder if the sphere connected to his presence near the new subjects. He glanced at it for an instant, thinking he felt it observing him, analyzing how one human with position and advantage dealt with another human disadvantaged and snarled in trouble.

The woman next to him raised her head and looked up at him with ghostly blood-shot eyes. Sweat had matted hair to her forehead as it slashed across her face.

"Are you... uh, awake?" he said, his voice catching in his throat slightly.

She shuddered and fought to clear her throat. "I was in a trance or something for a time. I... I must have come out of it. I was on some type of craft... a UFO I believe. The others with me stayed in their trance. I'm very dyslexic." She swallowed hard, whimpering. "I... I woke up. I screamed... screamed my head off. What will they do to me?" She brushed her hair off her forehead and rubbed her eyes.

"What about the others?" Bryan asked.

The woman looked at the man next to her, a guy of medium build, and the woman on his right. The second woman was tall, thin, and looked haggard, as if she'd worked heavily in a garden or on a farm. The conscious woman next to Bryan clutched her mouth and shuddered. "I think they are still gone... under some sort of control. They don't talk." Her eyes grew larger with fright. She sobbed, grief-stricken. She clasped her hands at her mouth. "Oh

God... what... is this place? What are they going to do with me? Who are you?"

"I'm here to help," Bryan said. "I'm a human like you... lived near Princeton University. They took me too."

"Are you normal? You're not like..."

"I'm normal." He forced a pained smile and not moving his head, he looked up for the sphere. It was gone. "What's your name?"

"Silvia... from outside Kansas City." Her whimpering escaped past her hands. "Please... what are they going to do to me?"

"I don't know." He thought for a moment and glanced over at the two Greys who observed his interaction with Silvia. He hoped the Greys didn't plan on slicing and dicing her with him watching. He didn't think he could endure watching or hearing such horror. If only he had one of their weapons. He thought of his mind-barrier.

A male Grey left the holding room, moving into the laboratory, and after a moment he returned to the door, signaling Dauasi Ziebou. The male Grey standing with Dauasi Ziebou walked over to Bryan and Silvia.

A voice began speaking in Bryan's head, releasing metronomic words, telling him to stand and bring the woman sitting next to him into the laboratory. He nodded and stood.

The Grey reached toward the woman's head with one hand. Silvia of Kansas City jerked backward into the wall, thrashing with her arms. The Grey continued toward her, staring intensely. After a moment, her arms dropped to her sides, her gaze reached blankly across the room. The Grey placed its hand on her head for a moment. Her face became smooth and relaxed as if the alien had drugged her. Slowly, she rose to her feet.

In Bryan's head, words came again, telling him to hurry because the woman wouldn't stay under control for long and he was to move her now. The realization of what his discussion with Markak had done flashed in his mind. He had become a servant to the Grey's evil. What if he refused? Doing it now wouldn't help the woman. One of the hybrids would take the task.

The woman shuffled behind the Grey into the operating room with Bryan following. A voice in his mind told him to place his hand on the woman's shoulder. Instead, Bryan held one hand near her elbow, keeping her from falling, seemingly performing his minor role in their tragic play.

The Grey preceded the woman toward the waist-high operating platform. Bryan released her as she turned her back to the table, her ghostly gaze relentlessly off in the distance. She eased herself up to the platform surface and laid flat with her arms at her sides.

One of the Greys turned to Bryan, speaking in his head: "Stand by the door." Bryan walked to the door, feeling relieved that he didn't have to watch the aliens abusing the woman.

Three male Greys encircled the woman, one at her head and one on each side. Bryan hated to watch. They restrained her arms and legs with straps. One of the aliens moved the woman's short dress up past her waist and cut away her undergarment. Another of their team separated her legs.

The use of physical restraints surprised him. Seeing the Greys moving her legs drew Bryan's anger. He thought of Liana to smother it and force it away from his mind.

A white mechanical arm moved down from the ceiling like the proboscis of a monster insect. A translucent cylindrical probe filled with fluid appeared at the end of the long arm as it inched toward the woman's reproductive area. After a moment, when the Greys removed the device, the fluid was gone.

The alien standing at the head of the woman made a checking glance at Bryan, displaying an expression striking him as mockery. Vitriolic disgust shot through Bryan, setting anger afire. A sudden change in the Grey's face made him realize that he had opened his unguarded emotions. He quickly sent his thoughts to computer technology. The alien turned back to the operation.

Sickened by what he saw, Bryan dropped his eyes to the floor. What had the Greys done to the poor woman? Had they tried to impregnate her, and if so, to what purpose? He began repeating the mantra in his mind.

The woman struggled to raise her head, her eyes blinking with panic. She screamed as she thrashed left and right, trying to free her arms. The Grey at her head placed his hand on her head for a moment. The woman continued her violence against her restraints. A second Grey touched the woman at her immobile wrist with the tip of a pen-shaped device. Immediately her body collapsed into a limp and motionless, stringless marionette. The Greys released the restraints and motioned to their hybrid servant. Dauasi Ziebou picked up the woman from the table and carried her back into the holding room, placing her on the bare concrete floor. Dauasi then returned to the door, stopping next to Bryan. Bryan stopped his mental barrier.

"Step back into this holding room and wait until they come for you," Dauasi said aloud.

Bryan walked back to the bench, standing over the poor woman on the floor for a moment. She didn't move. He started to stoop down and check her pulse when movement at the operating room door drew his eyes. He stopped. A Grey entered the room, walked up to the second woman, and stood motionless for a moment, looking at her. Without physical contact by the alien, the second woman stood from the bench and walked toward the operating room. Her eyes remained open and fixed off in the distance. The Greys treated the women no better than cattle, moving them into a Reticulan slaughterhouse, herding human-cattle down a ramp from a truck, directing them toward their last moments.

Several minutes passed. Through the operating room door came the hybrid, carrying the second woman back to the holding area, dropping her down next to the other woman on the floor. Bryan studied her to see if she was alive. Her eyelids moved like a person dreaming. He felt a little relief. Dauasi walked back to the door and waited. A Grey entered the room, moved mechanically toward the bench and touched the man on the head. The alien then took a step back, watching his victim move. The man rose from the bench and followed the Grey into the operating room.

Several minutes later, Dauasi Ziebou conducted the man, still in a trance and wobbling, back to the bench. The haggard man gasped for breath as he rigidly turned around and sat on the bench, appearing in a mental stupor with his eyes gazing blankly out of their sockets. The aliens had cut the man's trousers up the legs. After a few moments the man slumped over against Bryan about to slide onto the floor. He tested the man's wrist for a pulse. Nothing. He looked at the man's glassy fixed eyes and saw death. Bryan pressed a clenched fist to his mouth, pounding out his anger at what the Grey's had done to the man through their exploratory curiosity and ignorance of human frailty. They had killed the man with no more concern than that given a rat in an experiment. The sequence of events made him wonder why he was on hand, since he hadn't contributed much comforting support to his fellow human subjects.

The alien's soulless irrationality gripped him, absentmindedly pushing him up from the bench, walking slowly toward the door between the holding area and the laboratory-operating room. Dauasi Ziebou intercepted him, taking a position between him and the Grey standing at the doorway.

Bryan stared at the enigmatic Grey and sent his thoughts: *The man is dead. Will the females die?*

The Grey glared arrogantly back at Bryan, the alien's eyes narrowing slightly as the male Grey appeared to pull himself up tensely. Words popped into Bryan's mind: "The females will be retained for future breeding study. The man had a defective artery wall near his heart. Your task is done. Sit on the bench until given an order. Comply with orders."

Bryan thought of his research at the university to quench and block his anger. Dauasi pushed him in the back, ordering him back to the bench. He wondered why they hadn't sent him back to his cell, now that they had completed their experimentation with the three tortured souls.

Several minutes elapsed. While Bryan sat on the bench, trying to keep his imagination from running away, a male and a female hybrid came with a cart, and carried away the dead man and still-alive women.

Bryan lay down on the bench, resting his head on an arm. Dauasi Ziebou held his position next to the Grey, outside the operating room. Shadows broke the light coming through the laboratory door, tracing movement from the industrious and mysterious aliens inside. The Grey at the door turned and studied Bryan for a few moments with cold detachment, and then returned to monitoring activities of its colleagues.

Bryan tried to extend his mind, searching for thoughts between Dauasi Ziebou and the Grey. He had no success. Minutes later, Dauasi Ziebou turned and looked out into the main hall.

Liana walked into the holding area, quickly eyeing the Grey, and sending a cursory eye at Bryan. She stood at the end of the room just opposite the door. Her face was stern and impervious. A Grey emerged from the operating room, communicating with the one standing in the room where the aliens now had Bryan and Liana waiting. Liana's head drew back in alarm. She glanced at Bryan with haunted eyes and returned to her obedient posture.

He sat up, realizing something was wrong.

Chapter Ten

Whatever plan lay concealed in the Grey's purpose was now aimed at Bryan like a pointed gun ready to release a lethal bullet. The proof came from the confluence of Liana's arrival, his unneeded mentoring to abductees, and her distressed eyes. He watched every gesture and reaction as he remained on the bench, awaiting the next Grey command. Was he about to face his last moments in the operating room with Liana watching? Fighting his lapse in thinking he visualized his research, suspiciously waiting for the order to enter the operating laboratory.

She turned to him.

"What's wrong?" he asked verbally in a level tone. He tried not to show his concern in front of the watchful alien and the hybrid. He was cognizant to continue his mental barrier, trying to prevent exposing more of his emotions and private self to the Greys.

"You are not going to like what I have to tell you."

He felt his eyes betraying his alarm as he became still. "I'm being dissolved," he said.

She flashed her brow and sighed. "No it is not that bad." She hesitated. Her lips faintly quivered. "You and I are part of a Grey experiment."

Feeling he had no more time, his composure collapsed. He grabbed his face. "What kind?"

"Reproductive."

Bryan's his mouth gaped. What on earth did they want now? Was it punishment abruptly conceived by Markak? It looked as if they brought him here under the pretext of using his help only to prepare him for something much different. He didn't have a bad artery anywhere like the other abducted human man so an operation on him related to his reproductive organs was something he could possibly survive, if it wasn't a fishing expedition and they didn't cause infection.

Liana looked sharply at the Grey near her, her intense eyes indicating her communication with him. She nodded and faced Bryan. "We both are to go into the operating room."

"Are they going to remove organs?" Bryan asked.

"It is not likely to cause your death or mine. You must trust me. Please follow."

He nodded hesitantly and followed Liana into the brightness of the operating room. She stopped and turned to him, extending her hand. He took her hand, surprised by her making contact with him in view of the Greys. He followed her farther into the room, toward the table where he had escorted the woman. Three of the alien creatures he hated watched them.

Bryan noticed the Greys had widened the laboratory table and placed a white covering over it. A Grey pointed a finger at the table. Bryan and Liana walked up to the table, which had been lowered to waist height. They had lowered it from when he escorted the woman. Bryan looked up at the two Greys waiting at the end of the table. He felt their eyes coldly following his every move.

Liana moved to the edge of the table and looked at him, her face pouring pain and anxiety. Her reaction stunned him. Whatever was about to happen was punishing her. With her heavy eyes holding him, she began taking off the lower portion of her uniform. She stopped with her leotard-type pants lowered to her knees. She looked at one of the Greys.

Bryan heard a voice in his mind. It came from Liana, but he understood that she had also directed the words at the Grey. Liana told the Grey that she didn't see a need for total garment removal. The Grey's reply rolled into Bryan's head, ordering Liana and the subject to remove all garments.

Liana nodded her compliance. She looked at Bryan, her eyes apologetic, uneasy.

"I heard," Bryan said aloud. "So... uh, you and I are to perform..."

"Yes... perform a human breeding activity under their observation."

Bryan frowned. "...au natural... in front of these... these... bastards?"

"Yes. I am so sorry."

"I don't know if I can with their eyes on me."

She finished removing her garments and watched him remove his and drop them to the floor. The uncertainty in her eyes as he stood naked before her was the first time he'd seen her look vulnerable. Liana eased herself up on the edge of the table. Her somber face regarded him apologetically. "I... I don't know how to do... it. How is it done? Please."

Bryan sat down on the edge of the table next to her. He placed his hand on hers for a moment, before thinking that he didn't want to lay bare his emotion to the Greys. "You have absorbed research on our culture so I would guess you have a basic concept of the physical requirement," he said. His voice was tender as he might feel in a romantic isolated location and not in front of Greys.

"I do."

"What is disappointing about this, other than we will have an audience, is that it's supposed to be an act of love. It is commonly done in a private setting."

She gazed into his eyes and leaned her mouth near to his ear. She whispered, "I know you care for me."

He whispered, "I do. Very much. You are a beautiful woman."

She held her head up and sighed. "We don't have any choice."

At the side of the table on a support arm, extending from a small mobile cabinet, was a coin-diameter blue glowing sphere. The aliens obviously aimed the device at them, to view the reproductive region of their subjects. He guessed it was like a camera for recording what the Greys demanded of him and Liana.

"Why didn't they utilize some sort of a mechanical procedure for me and you?" Bryan asked.

"They are curious about the natural process. They haven't employed the natural procedure as a species for a thousand generations. I'm certain they've done this before with other abductees… but perhaps not someone like me or intelligent like you."

"Obviously they believe you are a functioning female capable of bonding with me."

"Yes. I'm half you."

"They must know something about how the female reproductive system functions and the importance of timing. They must know everything biological about you and me."

Liana looked into his eyes. "I have no doubt that you were selected because the Greys found your DNA superior in some manner. I also suspect the Greys have been analyzing the waste material I have passed from my body and know something about my reproductive timing." She took Bryan's hand. "I'm sorry for them subjecting you to such a degrading action with a creature not of your species."

He squeezed her hand. "I regard you as human. Liana, I had thoughts of doing with you what we are about to do, but I imagined doing it in a more romantic setting."

"You did?"

He looked deeply into her eyes. "Yes." He saw a vulnerability that he hadn't seen before.

One of the big-eyed aliens at the end of the table pointed a feeble finger at the flat surface.

Liana surprised Bryan when she frowned in an uncharacteristic manner.

She nodded sharply at the Grey. "They want us to start," she whispered.

"Okay, okay, relax. I'll guide you. Lie down on your back. I will lie on top of you and things will happen from there. You will have to open your legs."

Liana whispered, "I will follow your instructions." Uneasiness tortured her face. She rolled over to a prone position, her body sticklike, muscles taught, anxiousness spearing from her eyes.

Bryan maneuvered around on the table and eased himself down on her. He looked into her face, at her fear, her eyes jittering. "Look at me and trust me," he whispered.

Her eyes found his.

"You must relax," he said. "I do care for you romantically. Maybe we could think of being in a grassy meadow with birds singing."

"I've never seen those things."

He whispered, "You will my dear."

***

Bryan and Liana reclothed themselves with as much modesty as the Greys would permit in the pseudo-laboratory. Moments later, they walked back to his cell. They traversed the corridors without speaking.

At his cell, he dropped onto his cot as she stood just inside the door.

Liana looked at him with heavy eyes that he interpreted as confusion.

"I would stay and talk, but they are observing me more closely when I am near you," she said aloud. "With my reaction at the laboratory, my mental failure, they are certain to increase their scrutiny of my behavior."

He wanted to hold her and take away her anguish. Then he heard her words in his mind: "I enjoyed our experience... except for the Greys." A slight smile curled her mouth.

Bryan replied by thought: *I enjoyed it too. You are a very beautiful woman and a real woman. You know I thought those feelings about you before. What we did together was more than a physical act between us. It was love.*

Her eyes began to glisten.

Bryan heard her again in his head: "Our patience and caution is more vital to our escape, now that I have conceived a child with you."

Her words stunned him. He gazed at her, absorbing the vision of her, his thoughts paralyzed.

Liana's face grew uncertain.

Holding his hands clasped at his chest, Bryan approached her, touched by her doubtful face. He smiled and inched his face near hers. He kissed her. When he parted from her lips, he felt her evaluating uncertain eyes. "May I place my arms around you and kiss you again?" he whispered.

She turned around, looking down the hall, and then she turned to him. "Yes, please."

Her breath washed over him.

"You are pleased about the child?" she asked.

He whispered. "Yes. I'm very pleased." He placed his arms round her and kissed her again. He felt the tension in her body ease, her stiffness melt, and her mouth yield to him. He kissed her and after a long moment, they parted and gazed at each other.

"Is this love?" she asked.

He smiled. "Part of it."

Liana gave him a quick kiss. "It is very nice."

"How do you know you are… having a child? The time… it's only been minutes… since we were together. How on earth can you know?"

"It must be the genetics I have from the Greys. I feel… my body feels different."

He smiled and leaned to her ear. "The connection I've made with you in this version of hell is the most incongruously wonderful thing that's ever happened in my life. I want you to know that I feel very special that we share a close relationship." Hesitating for a moment, he sighed.

"What?"

Bryan looked down and then at her. "Am I being disrespectful to my wife by loving you? I feel guilty about it. She hasn't been gone in my mind for very long."

"My learning of emotions is incomplete. My analysis and logic skills are quite good. It appears you are having trouble reconciling the passage of real time. You could limit yourself to a single spouse for life… in a normal environment. Your time with Louise was short. You can honor her in a normal life even while you enter into another relationship. You must make that decision."

"I have but it's hard. I'm certain my feelings for you are real and in no way biased by all the help you've given me. My feelings are true and much deeper."

"I understand… and I am sorry for your conflict."

"Thanks for your trust and sharing love."

Liana whispered in his ear. "I need your help for a clandestine operation that could get us both terminated. I had planned to undertake it alone but the probability for success is increased if I have someone else to help, to reduce the time needed, to guard, and to observe. I can't use a sphere for this operation."

"What?" Bryan frowned at her, wondering about her cryptic reference to the sphere and surprised by her sudden proposal. He leaned into her ear and whispered, "Preparation for escape?"

She placed her mouth on his ear. "Yes. I would never allow the Greys to have our child. The three of us must reach freedom."

"How can I help you without the Grey's observation?"

"One of their weaknesses is their overconfidence. They don't believe anything can circumvent their control and monitoring."

"What about the spheres?" He sat down on his bed as Liana remained standing, gazing down at him.

"I assume you guarded your thoughts from Markak."

"Test me. I think I'm better than I was. I'll think of something."

Liana studied his face.

Bryan began thinking about her, future time with her, and then quickly pushed a problem in artificial intelligence computer technology to the forefront, using it as a barrier, like music playing while reading.

Liana studied him for a few moments. "What were you thinking about?"

"A computer problem related to artificial intelligence."

She folded her arms on her chest. "You did quite well. All I could see was that you were thinking about a computer problem."

Bryan brought his thought about going to bed with Liana and kissing her again to the top level of his mind. He flashed on a memory of making love to Louise and saw himself with Liana.

A smile whisked across her face. "I think you demonstrated your ability." She paused and frowned. "You thought of your wife." She paused. "But the other... it gave me a strangely warm feeling."

"Perhaps you are more human than anything else." He hesitated. "I suppose I'll think of my past forever, but it doesn't mean that you and I can't make new memories for our life together."

"Yes, of course. Remember, I am part Louise. She lives through me."

"I love you, the person that you are... not who you are made from."

She whispered, "I will come for you when I need you."

Bryan's eyebrows shot up as his vision fixed on something in the distance past Liana. She snapped around to see what had disturbed him. A silver sphere hovered out in the hall. She made a hand gesture to the sphere like she was pointing to Bryan in his cell.

"Soon I hope," he said. He looked at his time device. "If it weren't for this device telling me it's late afternoon, I wouldn't know night from day in this cavern."

"Do not worry," she said, closing his door. "Get some sleep."

After Liana closed the door under the watchful presence of the hovering sphere, Bryan dropped onto his bed, reflecting on their relationship. He was now imprisoned with a person who had taken his heart and despite her amazing support, he was hesitant to reach out with his hope. Before the blossoming of their feelings, he had dealt with the depression from losing his Louise and the near fatalistic assumption for his life. Now, with Liana's love and sharing a child, he felt his anxiety level creep upward. In a way, his fear had compounded. He feared losing the two new lives that had entered his life.

He stared blankly across the finite space of his cell. The walls, the never-changing man-cast concrete walls, still enwrapped him, monotonously closed in his vision. He sat alone like incalculable numbers of prisoners around the world in places where humans killed humans for politics, or criminals killed humans out of greed. He was a raindrop in a storm of the universe. He was insignificant. That too was a disappointment, the universe. He was certain Louise would have expressed a similar sentiment, with her general optimism poisoned by the Greys. The diversity of species in the universe was probably close to infinite. Why then would a species, which cruised out across a galaxy, not be benevolent? Such a species shouldn't need the subordination of lesser evolved creatures, shouldn't destroy lives to correct their species' evolutionary failure, or shouldn't need to appropriate another's planet. It seemed the universe was populated with an evil no different than the power-coveting evil humans on earth. Louise would have been so disappointed.

***

The next day, the fifteenth, near nine-twenty in the morning, according to Bryan's unusual clock, Dauasi Ziebou, opened his cell door, delivering two food bars and a container of fluid. Without speaking, he quickly exited, closing the door with thud and a click of the lock.

As Bryan began eating, Liana's absence made him wonder why she wasn't on her previously assigned task, that of supplying her subject with his food. He thought of lying on the dissolution table. *Think positive. You know better.*

If her intelligence equaled the Greys, which seemed the case, she wouldn't have trouble. The Greys probably gave her something more important to do. Her wits would protect her while engaged in some subversive action against the alien's security and control mechanisms. In their tortuous moments of imprisonment in the Grey's laboratory-fortress, Liana and his intelligence was their primary weapon. Regardless, he desperately wanted a physical weapon in his hand and an opportunity to restore the balance on the spiritual-ledger, a reckoning for Louise.

He glanced at the clock. "Damn the time."

Perhaps it would have been better that Liana never gave him the clock. The time he spent sitting on the bed waiting for the next opening of his cell door was a torture he never would have considered. However, it did allow him to anchor events, to measure the interval of the Grey's experiments, and to speculate timing for the next event. *Think of research.*

To divert his mind from the energy-absorbing anxiety, he returned to visualizing his projects at the university, thinking of options to solve problems. Moments later, the poison of his imprisonment jerked his thoughts back, tethering him back to his survival and his escape. How could they do it? How could they defeat the Grey's technology? Control was the key, overcoming the Grey's smothering observation. What about diversions? He ran a mental maze of different scenarios. After a time, seemingly an hour or two, a noise emerged from his door. Liana opened the door and stepped in, her eyes piercing and her mouth a rigid line. She had an object attached to a belt at her waist. It was similar to a five-inch cylindrical flashlight.

He stood and awaited her to say something about a mission.

She whispered, "We must go quickly. The time is at a good point."

"Lead the way."

"Give me your right hand."

She turned his hand so his palm was down and placed the gray cylindrical device on the back of his hand. She pushed a spot on the device and looked at him with a subtle smile. "Now you are ready."

He stared at her dumbfounded.

"Implant tracker... now disabled."

"Oh."

"Do you have a tracker?"

"Yes, but I disabled it."

"I should have known."

"Ready?" she asked, turning toward the door before he could reply. Liana moved out of the room, washing her glance over all areas of the hall. She waved her hand for Bryan to join her.

He stepped to her side as she rushed toward her objective. The act of helping her on a clandestine mission energized him with hope. He could have burst out with a raucous spiritual shout of solidarity and purpose. A wistful appreciation for Marines and SEALs, and other military elite flashed through his brain.

They strode down the corridor, turned right at an intersecting hall, and rushed down another passage, stopping at an unmarked door.

Liana gestured for him to position himself close to her. "We must not be seen," she whispered.

Bryan nodded. What worried him as much anything was the ghostly spheres popping up, seemingly out of nowhere.

In the unlighted room, whose purpose seemed that of storage for maintenance, she directed her eyes to a spot on the right. She collected several cigarette-size cylindrical rods and as she turned to the door, she smiled, surprising him with a hint of her amusement. She rushed farther down the same hall.

At last they were taking action. It fueled his hunger to lash out for an escape. She stopped at a concrete alcove in front of a metal door. The gray colored door with rounded corners reminded Bryan of a hatchway on a ship. A red sign, ironically in English on the alien side of the door, advised that it was for emergency use by authorized personnel.

"This is where our escape preparation takes shape," Liana whispered.

"What's on the other side?"

"Containment room for the nuclear reactor."

"What?"

"It is small so we will be able to move around it. Do not worry about the radiation. Our concern is the military personnel. We must be brief or they will detect us. The facility plans show two primary water sources. These water pipes descend through this east wing of the facility. One water pipe feeds the reactor and one feeds the levels of the east wing, including the lowest levels occupied by the Greys. We will place explosive charges on the cooling waterlines for the reactor and the major supply line for the Greys."

Bryan's mouth dropped a little.

"Do not worry," she said.

He nodded passively, uncertain what to say. He thought, *she knows what she is doing.*

"Thank you," she said.

Bryan laughed under his breath.

Liana continued, "In this east section, there is a freight elevator that stops at the reactor level. The elevator shaft is sealed off beyond the reactor floor but it extends all the way down to the fourteenth level. At a later time, I will position charges to blow a hole between the shaft and each of the Grey's floors."

The magnitude of her plan impressed Bryan. Without cooling water, the reactor would superheat and the core would start melting. It would be another Chernobyl. What about the control rods? Regardless, cooling water was a must. After the core superheated, the water would explode the pressure vessel, spewing radioactive steam, vaporized graphite, and all sorts of nasty nuclides into the facility and likely the atmosphere. The secondary explosive in the elevator puzzled him.

"What about video surveillance?"

Liana pointed to her flashlight device and stared into his eyes. "Ready?"

Bryan nodded nervously.

Liana cracked the metal door. A light above the door sent a flashing red glow across the floor. Liana snatched the device from her belt and pointed it at the light above the door. It stopped flashing. Her hands went to the door's security switch. She pointed her device at it, killing its sentinel point of red light.

"There, it thinks it is closed and safe," she said.

Crouching to half her height, she crept through the door. Bryan followed on her heels. As she moved she swept her gaze around the ceiling of a reactor operation room. He sent his eyes where she had checked, fascinated by the three-story room with the reactor pressure vessel, catwalks, and overhead cranes, a feast for his scientific brain. He had a tour of a small university reactor on the west coast before starting at Princeton, but it was vastly different.

Liana stopped, looked around, and then began aiming her device at cameras on the walls.

"You're killing the cameras?"

"Correct." She stared at him. "You ready?"

"Yes." His throat tightened.

"Along that far wall opposite this wall is an eight-inch pipe painted with a green stripe. Place one of these devices on the pipe as high up as you can reach. Place it on the portion of the pipe facing the wall. It will be less visible there. I will take care of the pipe over here. Work quickly and try to stay out of sight."

He pointed to a large metal cylinder ten or twelve feet in diameter, craning his neck to see its top and a catwalk connected to it. "It's not a very big reactor."

"Right. It is a small unit."

"What about radiation?"

"It is heavily shielded using the common design technology to protect the military personnel." She pointed determinedly to the pipe. "Now quickly, we have little time. Meet back here."

Bryan nodded, took the cigarette-size object from her and moved toward the other wall, pausing behind drums and metal control cabinets as he worked his way to his target forty feet away. His chest tightened as he crept away toward his target. At last, he was getting back at the soulless Greys, working to destroy the system responsible for the destruction of his wife, and stopping the future death of Liana and their child.

When he reached a pipe he paused, wondering how he would place the explosive device on it. He held the device up to the pipe. Its magnetic property drew the device from his hand, sticking it to the steel pipe. He pulled it off and standing on his toes replaced it as high as he could reach between the pipe and the wall where it would be difficult to see.

Crouching at the base of the pipe, he scanned the floor and overhead walkways for military personnel. He looked for Liana. He couldn't see her at the water pipe. He glanced back at the device he had attached to the water pipe, washed his gaze around for personnel, and scrambled back toward the emergency door, hunkering down behind a metal cabinet. A moment later, Liana emerged from behind a bank of electrical controls.

"I'm surprised that we didn't encounter more people," Bryan whispered. He peered around a cabinet. "I spoke too soon. There are two workers with white helmets coming this way."

Liana inched past the edge of the cabinet and leveled her device at the men. The men halted as if struck by a sudden paralysis.

"Wait, what about the control rods," Bryan asked. "Even without water couldn't they slow a meltdown?"

"Without a gantry crane control, they will have a hard time." She opened the emergency access door. "Quickly."

"Impressive."

He helped her ease the door closed as quietly as possible. He whispered to her, "Aren't there others like Dauasi Ziebou using the halls, carrying out their jobs? I haven't seen any of them."

Liana started down the hall. "They all have specific assignments, unlike me. The Greys know I am more intelligent than the others and that is why they give me more responsibilities, the kind requiring creative and analytic thought. They allow me access to all areas. I know they are studying me. The Greys try to check my thoughts and trace my activities. I only share with them what I wish."

Her comment replayed in his brain for a moment, making him realize she may have been beyond their control. But couldn't they terminate her without a second thought?

"What about Dauasi Ziebou?" Bryan said.

"His brain is more like a programmable biological drone. They give him precise instructions and he executes them. He has a few spontaneous emotional responses."

"Are you are preparing for our escape?"

"Yes."

"When do you think we'll get the chance?" He hated to ask like a child but he needed something to nurture his hope. The Greys stopping her explosives on the water pipes was a real question but he couldn't face it just now; he had to push on blindly, helping where she asked. But if she could do this, he wondered, why hadn't she escaped before this time?

Liana nodded. "You are right about the explosives. That is a possible prevention the Greys may take." She paused. "And not only that... the Greys have secretly placed their monitoring device in the installation's main water feed controller. As soon as water is disrupted, they will know it and initiate either their escape to their ships on level eleven, or they may block all access points to prevent contamination and flooding. I have more work to do to address some of those contingences."

He saw nothing in her face that indicated doubt, but he knew that even with her brain, random unforeseen events could intervene. The scenarios she had explained troubled him. He quickly brushed it aside, except for the question of the final minutes. How would they get topside safely and still destroy the Greys? That could be the critical part.

"I picked up your thought again. To answer your concern… when the military breaks into the Grey's private domain, we will go. You also wondered why, with my knowledge, I never ventured to escape before. I did not have you, a child, or a spirit like yours who loves true freedom. Also my mind and body had not matured as I continued to do. I had not fully analyzed the alternative to serving the Greys and only recently I discovered my life had little real value to them. That came at the time I developed my love for learning and began appreciating the science of my surroundings. Before that I had never realized I existed as nothing more than a throwaway tool."

"I'm sorry."

"My maturing analytical mind has eliminated that weakness of understanding," she said turning to him with a soft gaze.

"But… what makes you think the military will come?" Bryan asked. "I hate to doubt the premise."

Liana, looking preoccupied, whispered matter-of-factly as they turned down the last hall leading to Bryan's cell. "I read it in the military man's mind. But I do not know when."

Her simple explanation stunned Bryan. Earlier in his life, before the Greys, when he did research at the university, he would have laughed at such a comment. He thought, knowing she would likely gather words from his mind: *Liana is an unbelievable… lovely, loving lady, and a blessing.* He wished he could function as more of an asset instead of a prisoner, and a mere test subject for the Greys, not even a throwaway tool.

They arrived at his cell door. Bryan looked down the hall in both directions for a spying sphere, wondering whether Dauasi Ziebou would appear tasked with another of Grey's orders to transfer him for more brutal inhuman tests, body or mind probing. He gathered a breath and gazed at Liana.

"Give me your hand," she said softly.

Bryan held out his hand as he had before. She placed her cylindrical device near his thumb while she pushed a spot on the device.

"Now, you are back on their surveillance system."

Bryan nodded. A moving object drew his eyes. Liana turned just as a sphere stopped a few feet from them, suspended near the ceiling.

"Do not worry," she said.

Despite the supportive light in her eyes, he felt impotent and vulnerable, like he dangled from a string controlled by the aliens. He hated not contributing in a more active role in their mission removing the infestation from his earth. "You know, Liana—"

She shook her head. "Not verbally."

Bryan thought to her: *You might want to consider trusting me with some of what you have planned.* He stepped into the cell.

She stood in the doorway.

He heard her reply in his head: "I know you feel helpless."

She grabbed the door and said aloud, "Get some sleep."

He glanced at his time device and back at her. "I guess it is night, isn't it?"

"Yes."

Bryan found distasteful solitude again, along with the mental challenge of fitful frustrating visions of future events. Any freedom in his future depended on Liana. What if the Greys suddenly discontinued her contact with him? What if they terminated her? Could she avoid it? He hated those thoughts, but they constituted real possibilities.

***

Liana made her way to a room down on the fourteenth floor. The Greys entered it infrequently. She went to a control panel, activated the holographic display, and ran her fingers over several illuminated symbols. A few feet from the control unit stood a four-foot high metallic pedestal topped with a one-foot diameter circular plate with a concave surface like a bowl. Liana touched a spot on the display. A point of light came to life, forming a few inches above the plate. The tiny orb slowly expanded into a one-foot diameter silver sphere, hovering in space above the plate. She removed four of her remaining explosive devices from a location of concealment at her waist and pushed them through the sphere's fluid-like, electric field surface, until they disappeared.

She returned to the control unit and flashed her fingers over the display until she had connected the sphere to her mind. She thought of Bryan and his computer background as she entered a sequence of commands that would allow the sphere, with its cargo, to pass materially through the east-wing security access doors to the elevator shaft. From there, she told it to fly up the shaft to the access door on level two, and to the storage tank in the room beyond, where it would place one magnetically attached explosive device to the large metal tank. She paused for a moment, evaluating whether to proceed with the rest in a continuous stream or delay it for a few hours. Delaying served no purpose and offered more risk of discovery. Her hands flew gracefully over the device, touching commands to have the sphere place the remaining explosives on all the steel emergency doors between the east-wing shaft and the Grey's area. At the end of the procedure, she added program components for the sphere to dematerialize. With the controlling steps complete, she watched the sphere float upward a few feet from its position and drift out the door on its mission.

Looking at the controls, Liana stilled herself for a moment, considering how she should conceal her actions. The creation of the sphere was recorded in the system and all a Grey had to do was check for any activity. But rarely did they bother with such mundane tasks. She evaluated the probabilities for her actions reaching her goal. Random events, part of chaos in the universe, always awaited in the shadows of time. Organic, living systems, contributed largely to the distribution; they didn't function like machines. She assumed with high confidence that when the Greys faced a destructive situation, they would follow a decision path toward self-preservation. She smiled. It was fun trying to outsmart them. Fun... that was her human part. She reflected on the new and wonderful precarious sea of life she had begun navigating.

***

An hour after Bryan and Liana had fled their mission in the reactor facility, Lieutenant Victor Chilton stood in front of four soldiers in the nuclear reactor security monitoring room. His mouth formed a tight line and his eyes had narrowed.

Chilton's men called him iron-jaw. He stood only five-foot-eight, followed the regulations to the letter, including his personal appearance. He could hold his own in a fight with any of them. He commanded the respect of his men.

Chilton, the head security officer of the power generation section, wagged an accusing finger at the men in front of him, showing fury he hadn't felt for a long time. It began burning the moment he looked up from the latest report of security failures. He turned and slowly swept his gaze over a bank of black and white video monitors spread end-to-end across a wall and the five control consoles with red and green lights directly beneath them.

He faced his men. "I believe all of you understand this equipment by now. I can't understand what you were doing?" Chilton bobbed his head. "Dammit, what happen to those cameras? We don't lose seven or eight cameras at the same time without a damn good reason. It's not logical." He stared at one of the soldiers. "Adam, what's your story?"

"Sir, I don't know," Sergeant Adam Smallings replied. "I wasn't sitting at the console when they went offline. I was making my security inspection walk with Corporal Grossman. A hammering headache slammed my head. I must have passed out for a few minutes."

"What about you Grossman?"

"I... I didn't pass out, but I lost track of stuff about the time Smallings said he passed out."

"I find your story damn hard to swallow. Did either of you drop to the deck? Did anyone see you pass out?"

"I don't know," Smallings said.

Chilton looked at the faces in front of him. No one flinched. "Hmm... seems not." He glanced at the monitors and back to the men. "Okay, Sergeant McGraw, what's your story on the cameras?"

"I was watching camera three, five, and six when the video feed stopped one after another."

"They didn't die at the same instant?" Chilton asked.

"No, no, they went one at a time, a second or two between each one, as if something flipped them off."

Chilton folded his arms on his chest, leaving his attention square on the men. "Did anyone do a security sweep after the cameras died? What about this passing out business?"

McGraw said, "Yes, sir. Absolutely... well, by the time I started to walk out the door to do just that, Corporal Unger yelled at me to stop. He yelled that all the monitors had come back to normal. I went out anyway, looked at the questionable cameras and returned to this room. I saw nothing different about the cameras. They hadn't been moved or damaged. I saw nothing."

"Did you see Smallings staggering or passed out on the deck?"

"No, sir, I didn't walk in his direction," Unger said.

"McGraw, you saw nothing wrong?" Chilton asked sternly, studying the man's face. It didn't take a genius to know that cameras didn't malfunction and return to normal working status as a common practice. Physical devices operated on scientific principles. If they went offline, something physical made it happen. A power surge maybe.

"No," McGraw said.

"Did you check the backup video covering the time prior to the anomaly? What about a power glitch?"

"We have not checked," McGraw said.

Chilton stabbed the air with a finger. "Gentlemen, I suggest you go over the video and look for any anomaly. I will check back for your report. And check for power fluctuations." He flashed his eyes over the faces staring sheepishly back at him and walked out.

Chapter Eleven

Thankfully, one more night faced him, one more string of hours, like a string of precious pearls he could endure, count, and appreciate. Each one came with mixed emotions, love and hate. He paid for them with inactivity and tortuous dreams; they measured life.

Bryan fell asleep, as he had before, after staring at the blank ceiling of his room for nearly an hour with his mind traveling. He fell into a strange dream. He raced across a university campus, trying to reach a laboratory room before an impending disaster about to take place. He woke three times from the dream and from an overflow of nervous energy, the residual effects of the reactor room visit. Sitting up on his cot, tasting something foul in his mouth, he went to his sink. He tried to clean his teeth using the bottom of his shirt. Afterwards, he sat staring at the floor and walls, daydreaming, speculating on the timing and the event that would spark the final push for freedom. The clock told him the pearls had only added up to four in the morning. A noise came from the door latch.

The door opened and the hybrid, Dauasi Ziebou, stood in the opening. "You must come with me."

"Where are you taking me?"

Dauasi didn't answer.

Bryan felt drained from a lack of sleep as he pushed himself off his cot. It was obvious he'd waste his words with further attempts to converse. He had to comply. In a few minutes, Dauasi Ziebou walked Bryan up to an open laboratory door on the fourteenth level.

Bryan's gaze shot to Liana, sitting in one of two chairs, facing each other in the center of the room. He remembered her training, gathered a breath, building his composure.

The room smelled. The odor suggested that it came from something electrical. He didn't recall being in this room. It had the commonly employed bright overhead laboratory lights and strange metal equipment compartments positioned around the periphery.

Two Greys, both males judging from their angular cheek bones, one standing at a holographic display control and one holding a position near the door, observed Bryan as he entered. They had located one small control unit on Liana's right, between the two chairs, so the operator could view her face at the same time as that of the subject in the second chair. The Greys had constrained her arms and legs with straps. Bryan couldn't see any physical connection between Liana and the control panel operated by the short Grey, who had a smallish edgy brow.

Bryan stopped three steps into the room, suspecting something unpleasant was about take place. He glanced to his left at the alien, a taller one reaching perhaps five and a half feet. He wasn't certain but he thought he'd encountered him before.

Words ran into his mind: "Bryan, this is Liana, do not worry about me. They will not injure me, not when I have a valuable child inside."

He nodded reluctantly, horrified at the thought of them hurting her, forgetting to protect his thoughts for a moment.

Dauasi Ziebou spoke verbally, "Mettui Ouicil is helping with a research program." He turned with an expectant face to the tall Grey, as if awaiting the next instruction.

Bryan heard an uneven voice in his head and quickly realized it wasn't Liana, and that it came from the tall Grey. The voice said: "We are going to observe and study your behavior. We are going to ask you questions.

You must answer. If you answer unsatisfactorily, we will give the female hybrid an electrical signal that creates pain. If you refuse to answer, we will inflict pain. If you take too long to answer we will give her pain. Do you understand?"

Bryan tried to conceal his disgust. Having no choice he sent thoughts at the tall Grey: *Why don't you constrain me and ask your questions? Why do you have to resort to such an unintelligent act? If you can cross the universe, why do something unworthy of your intelligence, such as carrying out demented acts comparable to those of my world's unenlightened dark ages?*

The tall Grey stared at Bryan. Its brow moved lower, wavering faintly as if in a tremor. Bryan heard the Grey's emphatic sounding reply in his head: "You don't understand."

Bryan thought to him: *What's your name?*

The tall Grey, its facial wrinkles changing in a muscular wave, answered in Bryan's head: "I am Haazon Peutso-ui and I require you to comply." There was a pause in the thought transfer. "Maybe you would like to return to the table-room and sleep for two or three earth years. Haagui Zietso will run the control. Markak requires your compliance. Remember?"

Bryan looked at Haagui Zietso, a male Grey with eyes noticeably wider apart, making him think of a genetic mutation. The rest of the alien's head was typically large at the back with the angular character below the eyes.

To Haazon Peutso-ui, Bryan thought: *I understand.* He paused, turning toward the door, and then toward the Grey near a control panel. He thought: *What happens to Mettui Ouicil if I jump across the room and break your spindly neck?*

The Greys didn't move as they looked sharply each other, their eyes flitting nervously. The tall Grey, Haazon Peutso-ui, turned to Dauasi Ziebou. Dauasi nodded and stepped over next to Bryan.

"Haazon Peutso-ui says that perhaps you need to hear this warning with your earthling ears, so he ask me to tell you verbally," Dauasi Ziebou said. "He says you would die quickly if you tried such a thing. He would cut you into two parts."

Bryan grinned. "Maybe you're going to kill me anyway," he said aloud. He glanced at Liana, his eyes heavy with concern, agitated with his helplessness. In his head he heard her words: "Please play their game. It is a nonlethal study. I can handle their testing. Remember patience. We need each other alive."

Bryan looked at Haazon Peutso-ui. "I will comply," he said aloud, reluctantly submitting.

Dauasi Ziebou pointed to the empty chair facing away from the door and toward Liana. "Sit in that chair," Dauasi Ziebou said.

Bryan complied, finding it difficult to look at Liana without feeling fury. Remembering she would scold him to hide his thoughts, he calmed himself. He as he did, he realized that they would learn something about him through his anger. Why feed their study?

Dauasi turned to the short Grey, Haagui Zietso, who handed Dauasi a five or six inch long cylindrical object. Dauasi quickly passed it to the taller Grey, Haazon. Dauasi glanced from the short Grey to Bryan. Dauasi spoke, "We begin! I will give you verbal questions. Now that you have encountered Mettui Ouicil several times, do you see her as human or nonhuman?"

"I see her as both," Bryan said.

Liana jerked and squirmed in her chair as if she experienced pain. Bryan saw her grimace with distress on her face. He held himself in check.

"Do you hate having Mettui Ouicil feel pain?"

"Yes."

The Grey at the control nodded slightly to Dauasi Ziebou. "Are you afraid of the beings that brought you to this facility?"

"No."

Liana winced in pain.

"Was your reproductive encounter in the laboratory with Mettui distasteful or pleasant?" Dauasi asked.

Bryan sent his gaze at Liana, fighting to keep his face stern. "Pleasant."

Liana's face remained still.

Dauasi turned to Haazon Peutso-ui and then to Bryan. "Would you feel happy or angry if the baby Mettui carries is destroyed?"

Bryan held his breath for a moment, his anger barely restrained. The test seemed aimed more about observing his reaction to sadistic suggestions. "Angry," Bryan said sternly.

Liana flinched from an inflected pain. She shook her head at Bryan as if telling him that she was fine.

"Would your fellow humans accept a society including such beings as Mettui?" Dauasi Ziebou asked.

"Doubtful. We would never allow anyone to live as a slave, hybrid or human."

"How many governments are aware of the Reticulan's presence on this planet?"

A wrinkle distorted Bryan's brow. "I have no idea."

Pain wrinkled Liana's face.

"Why do you punish her when I don't know an answer?" Bryan asked.

Dauasi Ziebou turned to the small Grey and then back. "Do the military forces have secret weapons?"

A teasing grin formed at the corners of Bryan's mouth, one tinted with the color of pride. "Most likely they have weapons that would destroy the Reticulans."

Liana squirmed, her mouth in a line, pressing her eyes closed.

"You bastards," Bryan barked.

The tall Grey raised the cylinder, appearing ready to point it at Bryan.

Dauasi Ziebou stepped forward, staring down at Bryan and asked, "Would this government sacrifice itself with nuclear weapons in a war with Reticulans?"

"Yes. And every person would fight for freedom." Bryan anxiously watched Liana. "The government does not tell its people about its most advanced weapons, which you would find problematic."

Her brow pulled down . She grimaced and stiffened, releasing only a slight whimper, gathering a breath after the pain stopped.

A torrent of thoughts in his mind fought against his mental guard. "Why don't we stop this sadistic torture of your hybrid, Mettui Ouicil? You don't need this ridiculous coercion. I'll tell you the truth about whatever you ask."

Alien words flowed with a rhythmic pattern into Bryan's head, apparently from the one with the wide eyes, Haagui Zietso: "You need a point of focus." There came a pause and then a question ran into his mind: "Would a human like you consider mating with Mettui Ouicil?"

"Yes," Bryan replied verbally. He wondered if their planetary occupation included investigating the potential for infiltration of hybrids into human population. It would be a neat trick if they could do it.

Dauasi's attention went to Haazon. Bryan checked Liana. She didn't flinch.

The Haazon spoke in Bryan's mind: "Does Mettui appear radically different from human women?"

"No."

Hardly a second elapsed before Haazon spoke again: "Would you recognize Mettui Ouicil as being human or nonhuman in one of your cities if she were walking down one of your thoroughfares?"

"Human." Fearing his answer and the Grey's unbalanced responses, Bryan looked to see if they had inflicted pain upon Liana. Could he stop the horror by using a diversion, consuming time, and provoking the Greys toward irrational action? On the other hand, could he learn something from their reactions to him?

Bryan glanced at Dauasi and then decided to send a thought directly to Haazon Peutso-ui: *"Do Reticulans live freely on your planet?"*

Haazon Peutso-ui turned to Haagui Zietso at the controls, holding a moment of contact between them. The short Grey, Haagui Zietso, slowly raised a hand. Dauasi Ziebou faced Bryan and declared, "Don't attempt games. You comply or you will die." He paused, glancing back to both Greys. Returning to Bryan he said, "Does knowing that you may die when your usefulness is ended encourage you to cooperate or recoil?"

"Neither."

Liana uttered a faint grunt with a grimace.

Bryan frowned. "Why did you do that? I answered truthfully."

Dauasi Ziebou sent his attention back and forth between the Greys. "They don't care if you tell the truth," Dauasi said.

Bryan gazed sympathetically at Liana. He calmed his thoughts, knowing he might reveal a thought that needed to remain concealed. In a flash, he realized the strategy behind the interrogation. The cloud of facts and feelings condensed into a clear drop of meaning. In addition to some strategic information, the Greys were studying his reactions and his emotional state. Knowing that part of the human population could support them in a planet takeover. Obviously they had studied the bonding between him and Liana, gathering an idea of how a colonization might proceed. His bonding to their female hybrid could form a key element in their plan.

In the distance, a siren blared. The eerie echoes filled the empty concrete cavern with alarm. The two Greys didn't move, looking at each other, moving a hand to their head, their large eyes growing larger, appearing to listen to a device on their garment.

Dauasi Ziebou quickly removed Liana's restraints. "We all are to assemble at the freight elevator on the bottom level," Dauasi said in a mechanical manner as if citing a food menu, which was strangely incongruous with the alarm.

Liana stood, reached to her right shoulder with her left hand, squeezed a muscle, and stretched her upper torso by moving her arm it in a small circle, while observing the two Greys' demeanor. Her face softened as she turned to Bryan. "They require me to go down to the elevator now," she said aloud. "I don't have time to take you to your room. You'll have to accompany me."

"What's wrong?" The suddenness and sound of urgency struck him; it was too soon for their escape opportunity.

"We will learn soon," Liana said. "Something unusual has happened."

He froze for a moment as she spoke into his mind: "Be patient. This is the time to practice control. I am not hurt by the testing. This is not the opportunity we need."

She followed the briskly walking Greys to the stairs with him at her side, where their diverse group of beings descended to the fourteenth level. Despite the situation Bryan couldn't help noting the way the alien's walked and the ungainly motion of each step they took. He wondered if the Grey's physical stature and their locomotion resulted from their technical advancement. Had their evolution caused the sacrifice of rudimentary skills such as using their legs for walking? Perhaps they had leaned too much on their technology.

Upon exiting the stairs, Bryan and Liana's group traversed the hall toward the source of alarm. Up ahead in front of the elevator, military personnel and Greys faced each other. Each side displayed, what Bryan considered, defensive body language. The military, consisting of five men, carrying tactical rifles, wearing body armor and helmets with communication headgear, held a position ten feet in front of the freight elevator doors. Three Greys and two male hybrids stood in a parallel line to the military. Hybrid, Dauasi Ziebou, joined the end of the line with the Greys. The two Greys from the laboratory took a position behind the front line of Greys. Liana stopped with Bryan three or four paces behind Dauasi Ziebou. Bryan glanced at her for some sort of clue. While she had transformed back into her servant character role, carrying herself stiffly, her eyes remained in motion, apparently checking and assessing the situation.

A tall male hybrid, who was around five-foot-six with a wiry build and forehead like a cobblestone road, stood in the front line of the Greys. The hybrid's hands hung straight at his sides; Bryan assumed to diminish the thought of hostility. He observed what had to be weapons. They were five-inch long objects similar in size to a shiny television channel changer or flashlight and two of the aliens each had one on their waist.

"My name is Daukul Juibou," the tall hybrid said, breaking the silence with a monotone. "No military allowed in this area. It is written in our agreement with your government. By virtue of the covenant we consummated more than forty earth-years ago, we can destroy you for stepping off the elevator on this floor. Our facility is the same as if we are on our own planet."

The mechanical announcement pierced the air like a bullet. Bryan's fear about his government working without regard for the country's sovereignty and human life suddenly became more than rumors and a failure in human thinking.

The military man in the center of the five men, holding his finger ready to pull back the trigger of his tactical rifle stared brutally at the Grey and spokesman-hybrid opposite him. "I'm Colonel Roth," he said. "I believe you and I met a few days ago regarding one of our missing men." He squinted determinedly. "We have just cause to be here."

The hybrid, Daukul, turned to Markak and then addressed Roth with robot unblinking cold eyes. "I am speaking for the Reticulan leader standing to my right. He says, yes he met you in your conference room. He is the head of the Reticulan expeditionary team doing research here. His name is Markak. He requests the reason for this wrongful breach."

The manner in which the eyes connected between the opposing forces electrified the air. Bryan gasped for a breath, having not taken in air for a moment, his own chest tight with alarm. In the small area of the hall outside the elevator, a firefight like a lightning discharge seemed ready to erupt. Now was the wrong time for a firefight. How could he and Liana escape with bullets flying around or avoid an energy beam slicing indiscriminately? The military could have locked the elevator in position for their own escape. Even if the elevator did move, the military could capture them at the surface and hold them prisoners for endless interrogation and the ultimate witness removal. He remembered patience, as Liana had said.

Colonel Roth, flint-eyed, his rifle jabbing forward like a medieval pike, held his finger ready on his trigger. He glared down at the shorter alien, Markak. "I remember Markak. He has my respect. Nevertheless, one of our men came down here to this area and he has not returned. We want you to turn him over to us or—allow us to conduct a search. We believe you are holding him prisoner or you have executed him. The latter would have grave consequences for our relationship and future cohabitation of this facility. We understand your assumption of sovereignty for these bottom four floors however, I must remind you that you are guests and not our rulers. This is our planet." Roth's jaw hardened, its muscles rippling as he awaited a response.

Markak tilted his head, almost imperceptibly, as if seething with contempt for the bug-level human. Bryan caught a glimpse of the side of Markak's large head, seeing what appeared tightness in a face that he had only seen as coldly dispassionate. The moment seemed like a flame hovering over an explosive's fuse.

The hybrid translator, Daukul, spoke, "Markak understands. If the floors occupied by us were not engaged in various levels of delicate research, it might be possible for our own staff to conduct such a search for you. Some of our work is hazardous to humans and some of the research is carried out under precisely controlled conditions. We would never allow humans such access." The hybrid glanced quickly at Markak and back to Roth. "We must demand that you return to your levels. If you do not leave this area, you force us to take action against your crime. We have no military people in our facility. We have not seen any of your military people. Your violation of our compartments is in vain. It is without merit."

The man standing beside Roth adjusted the position of his rifle slightly, trying to make it more comfortable on his shoulder. The Grey beside Markak plunged a hand to his waist, toward a silver device the size of a small flashlight. He raised the device, pointing it at the soldier.

"Weapon!" Sergeant Zane shouted.

Arms, legs, heads, and guns instantaneously traced an abstract blur of motion. The soldiers morphed into defensive body positions. They all leveled their guns in front of their determined eyes, aiming at the generous Grey pumpkin heads. A Grey at the end of the row moved his weapon-filled hand to a position just above his waist as if preparing to aim it.

"Grey on the end... weapon!" Captain Mathews said like a machinegun firing words.

"I'm on the strange talker, dude," Sergeant Blake said.

"Stay cool, stay cool," Roth said in a near whisper like a tiny discharge through the electrified air.

The military stared at the Greys and the Greys stared at the military.

"Weapon incoming!" Sergeant Zane shouted.

A silver sphere floated through the air, taking a position behind the Greys, hovering above Markak.

"I got the ball," Captain Mathews said, aiming at it with his tactical rifle.

Despite Mathews marking the sphere, the other soldiers deviated on their discipline, flashing their eyes to the floating ball and back as they continuously watched the alien creatures.

Bryan touched Liana's arm as he drew back two steps. She followed him.

Roth inched his rifle forward, aligning it with the center of Markak's head. "Quiet, men," Roth said. He waited for a moment and then with the voices halted, Roth continued. "We don't want violence. We only want our man."

Markak looked at the hybrid and back to Roth. The hybrid spoke, "Colonel, please return to your section of the facility before you and your men are destroyed. We will conduct a search for your man. If we find him, we will send him to you."

Bryan had little doubt that all the military would die and two or three Greys. The weapon the one Grey held in its hand had to operate like a laser, particle beam, or some kind of directed energy beam, which could cut a hole through a bulletproof vest or slice away an arm or leg like a butcher removing fat from a tenderloin. He'd read in research newsletters at the university about investigations on directed energy weapons carried out by the US scientists.

The stalemate situation seemed on the precipice to him. He moved back another step.

Roth pushed his gun forward an inch. "You may kill us but I doubt if your head is protected from a bullet from this rifle. You will die first."

Markak made a clacking noise through his small mouth.

Bryan heard Liana in his head: "Markak just read the soldier's mind." He wondered what that meant.

The Daukul frowned. "Markak says that if he dies, another will take his place and the chain of operation will continue as if nothing had happened," Daukul said. "Markak requests you to return to your area."

Roth swept his attention along the line of aliens facing him. Before returning his scrutiny to Markak, his eyes touched Liana and Bryan.

Bryan gave three quick blinks, three slow blinks, and three quick blinks with his eyes, holding Roth's gaze for a moment. In a few seconds, Bryan had transferred his signal for help, signaled that he wasn't under the Grey's mental control, and that he was a prisoner. He felt better, but it didn't change his muffled hope for extraction.

Roth squinted bitterly. "We are leaving for now."

Fierce moments burned away and in their ashes, the slackening of jaw muscles and lowering of shoulders, which seemed from a reevaluation, eased the tension.

"Okay, men, back into the elevator," Roth continued. His head bobbed as his brow arched. "We still want our comrade. In our world, we don't leave our comrades behind and we respect our fallen. We honor and bury our dead." Roth flourished a hand toward the waiting compartment that would extract them back up to the human level.

The men at Roth's side backed into the elevator car, not removing their eyes from the Greys and hybrids, not lowering the aim of their rifles until the car's door closed. The Greys and hybrids dispersed randomly into the hall.

Liana turned away from the crisis. She sighed. "I will now return you to your cell."

"I'm hungry," he replied. "Can we go to the food? I haven't had anything since…"

"Yes. Let us do that. We will take the stairs."

Her hesitancy to answer, possibly due to her preoccupation with the confrontation, struck Bryan as interestingly human. Her reaction to the stressful situation hinted that she was becoming more human by the day. He wondered how far the change would go; he still valued her analytical detachment.

Down the hall several paces, they entered the dimly lighted, clammy stairwell, and as their steps echoed off the walls, their hopeful escape circled in Bryan's thoughts. They had climbed up one level when he flashed on something they could try. "Liana, I have an idea for…"

"Not now."

His brow furrowed at her strange reply.

At the twelfth floor, they started down the hall with Bryan holding his idea in the back of his mind along with the thought of food. When Liana turned in a direction opposite to what he expected they should go to reach the room with the food, he grew curious and a little concerned, thinking of more bad news. Her mouth had drawn up and her eyes narrowed in stern focus.

"What do you think Markak has planned for the military?" Bryan whispered. "Did you get into his thoughts?"

Liana turned to him and then back toward the hall ahead of them. "He was going to wipe out those soldiers at the elevator if they didn't withdraw. The weapon they had would have cut through the men like a knife."

"A laser?"

"No. It is closer to an extremely energetic particle beam."

"I would guess that the military will try again."

"I agree. In fact, I'm planning on it."

An uncharacteristic stillness enveloped Liana as she walked determinedly down the hall, each foot landing purposefully in her curious march. Bryan decided to say nothing more; she always knew exactly what she was doing. Something was disturbing her. The confrontation at the elevator had brought a change, had drawn her concern to another problem, something she needed to address immediately. Whatever was awaiting their approach, perhaps a remaining dark horror of the facility that she considered important, had Bryan holding his breath and mentally gritting his teeth.

She stopped at metal door. It had an unusual yellow color. As she took the door's latch, she spoke softly, "Apprehension is showing on your face. Do not be concerned for your safety. I needed to show you this. It has worried me." Pain pulled on her eyes.

"I'm here with you."

"I was not worried about your emotional state," she said, "uh... but after you and I... after I conceived a child with you, my feelings struck me like nothing I could have predicted with all my knowledge. It struck my... what you call your emotional core... my heart."

"For God sake, what is this room?" Bryan asked. He couldn't keep the dread from his voice. In his mind, he expected a horror he hadn't seen, although nothing could be worse than his Louise in the Grey bastard's vat that he was going to destroy if it was the last thing he ever did. His poor dead Louise crawled across his mind. He told himself to think of something else.

Liana dropped her eyes. "It is not as bad as your Louise." She opened the door.

Bryan peered around her as she took one step inside the room. The room, perhaps thirty feet square, was well illuminated from the ceiling by two rows of fluorescent lights. Air from the room washed over Bryan with its staleness and a hint of something dank. A row of beds filled the space along the right side wall, with barely a gap for walking between them. In the center of the room, two long tables sat end-to-end, holding a small stack of paper-thin, flat, electronic display devices, approximately the size of a large book. Supplies for human-type writing, paper and markers of some sort, filled a small box positioned next to the displays. Chairs occupied both sides of the table. At the far end of the room, two toilet stalls stood out from the wall and a string of four sinks ran along the left wall. To their immediate left, in the corner, six metal chairs sat at a round table littered with crumbs of food.

Seven children and a female hybrid sat at the long table with the learning materials. A boy and a girl had one of the small electronic displays lying on the table in front of them.

The children casually looked up at Bryan and Liana for a moment with an uninterested expression and then went back to their activity, as if programmed. They ranged in age, by Bryan's guess, from five to ten or eleven. The group had five girls and two boys. The youngest girl looked five or six years old. The boys looked about seven and eleven. All the children wore the same jumpsuit type uniform of gray-blue. The girls had their hair tied behind their heads and the boys had short-cut hair. From his observation, all the children looked completely normal and not hybrid.

Bryan whispered, "This changes everything. We have to save these children... we have to."

"I am sorry for not telling you before, but…" Liana answered, leaning close to him. "My emotions are still developing. Our hope for destruction of this facility and our escape must be altered to include these innocent children. I did not know how you would react about leaving them behind."

"Now you know." As he glanced over the table, each child's face marked an impression in his brain. "I could no more ignore these innocents than our child that you carry. We will find a way. We will set them free so they can have lives of their own choosing."

He took her hand. She smiled at him and then checked the hall for a moment before turning back to the room.

Liana whispered, "I think my intelligence developed faster than the other facets of my human half. I have a theory that when the tiny life sparked within me, it sparked a new sense of communication, something on the molecular or quantum level, connecting the spirit of living beings, my spirit to our child. It could have triggered something in my brain."

"I'm glad. Liana, where did those children come from? Do you have any idea?"

"They were taken as you were taken, snatched from the earth with a transportation beam shooting down from one of their ships. I am sorry for what the Greys have done."

"Those poor children probably have no idea of what is happening to them. The Greys rip them away from their parents, their fathers and mothers, who will have their hearts broken the rest of their lives. What do the Greys do with them?"

Liana cleared her throat a little. "They teach them, evaluate their learning ability, and convert them into serving as liaison between Greys and humans, much like a hybrid. They use them to work with other children who are taken. They live all their lives in this facility."

"I know this facility is enormous… but still… why haven't I seen some children before this?"

Liana diverted her gaze to the floor. "Not all survive. I could not bring myself to tell you."

"Oh God." He sighed. "And of course, the ones who live on… never see the sky?"

"No."

"Have you ever seen the sky?"

"No," she said, her reply whispery and sad.

Something Bryan had read suddenly came to him, mankind's horror. "In our world's past a ghoulish government, during a war, exterminated innocent children because of their heritage. You would think intelligent travelers of the universe had advanced beyond such horror."

Liana touched the door latch; it clicked. Each child at the table looked at Bryan and Liana with placid uninterested faces and then in unison all of them dropped their gaze back to their activity. Bryan wondered from their manner whether the Greys controlled their minds, which was a fable he had heard one day floating across a table in a favorite student coffee shop near the university campus. How many hearsay stories grew from the seed of truth? Over coffee, those discussions of the far-out science, government oppression, and vast conspiracies, broke into the open like the sport du jour. Mind control seemed to fall into the favorite category covering UFOs. What wonders he could now recount to some of those smartass kids, sipping on their cappuccinos. Of course, they wouldn't believe him. No average person would swallow the incredible without proof.

Bryan said, "I… I haven't seen any older servant humans. I've only seen hybrids and they don't look older than thirty earth years." He had a suspicion about the answer and was sorry for throwing the darkness at Liana. He didn't mean to imply that she had any responsibility. The question arose simply from what he didn't see. If one assumed the military had constructed the concrete silos-of-hell into the bowels of the earth in their present form during the 1960s, then plenty of time would have elapsed for the existence of middle-aged or older human servants or for that matter, hybrids. Dauasi Ziebou could have been in his thirties. Liana was an exception. As he traced over the disturbing truth about those held within the walls, such as Liana, poor souls who had never seen a blue sky, he remembered something from Dante's Devine Comedy. *Abandon all hope, ye who enter here.*

Liana nodded. "You are right. But we will change it. We will bring hope."

Bryan looked at her, closed his eyes as he mashed his mouth apologetically. His gaze softened on her. "I'm extremely sorry."

"If a problem cannot be defined, it cannot be solved. This place is an abomination for any species. It is horrible." She glanced at him with a tear in her eye. "We must save them when the time comes." She paused. "My emotions are in turmoil. My feelings are still changing. My body is producing a different range are regulating chemicals. My logic is all I can trust for certainty."

"We are together now and always." He took her hand for a brief moment. "Shouldn't you get me back to my room?"

"Yes."

"Could you bring me something to eat?"

"Of course." She gazed at him with a somber face. "The testing you and I endured… was not entirely for you. They studied my responses to you. They are watching me more closely."

***

Bryan sat on his bed. Several minutes had passed since Liana pulled her eyes from him as she had backed out of his cell door. The vision of the captive children possessed him still. The ugly truth was that their minds served as nothing more than a playground for the Greys. Like baby birds raised in a covered cage, the Greys had stolen their potential to fly and find freedom. Those poor children, no doubt, had no awareness of their lives moving in a one-dimensional path, no awareness of their shortened destiny, and no awareness of any joy in their lives.

Their plight tortured him like his own enslavement. The people who had lost their children would have been insanely heartbroken. He couldn't imagine the pain of losing a child, one with his Louise or one with Liana. What a horrible heart-destroying time for a family, and it was no different than a situation where a human criminal grabbed a child from the sidewalk who was walking to school. He had received a strange blessing with the two years lying prone on the Grey's pest-removal table, awaiting his turn for the Greys to flush him away with their dissolving process. It had given his heart a little buffer for coping with losing his Louise, which he knew would linger in his brain forever.

How could he and Liana possibly escape with the children? His escape with her was near impossible. One plan after another seemed to fail his analysis because of one factor or another. He couldn't foresee how favorable events would transpire. He would have to take any bomb she could fabricate to the bottom level to create a diversion for her escape with his child and the other children. The number of variables exceeded reasonable logic and the Greys had too many controls. There was no way to predict the roaming spheres. He hoped Liana had a good idea.

A short time later, Liana cracked Bryan's door and handed him something to eat and drink. The curtness of her manner alerted him to search the hall, and just as he suspected, there it was, a spying sphere. Without a word she closed the cell door.

Chapter Twelve

Colonel Roth stood in front of his locker in the men's equipment room, pulling his shirt off in preparation to take a shower. The other men of his team were removing their clothes for a shower, storing their gear, or leaning against the lockers smoking. Winston leaned his back against a locker at the end of an aisle, pouring bottled water down his throat.

"Colonel Roth, Sir," Sergeant Mark Zane said. "Are we going back down? We didn't exactly complete the mission."

Roth grabbed a towel hanging from his locker door and turned around, strangling it in his hands. He faced five pairs of eyes down the aisle. The intensity of their gaze pushed on him, demanding answers. He knew they wanted what he wanted. He also knew what would happen if anyone got killed in the facility, especially down in the alien area. The secret staff meeting two or three years ago in a black facility on the subject had left no question about priorities. Of those in attendance, the older top brass, the representatives from the intelligence area, and the people associated with Defense Advanced Research Projects Agency, DARPA, only the old brass wanted the program stopped. They had said, almost to a man, that it was an abomination and worse than a deal with the devil. The technology that they had gained had come at too high a cost and much slower than the aliens had originally promised. Even the CIA analysts had protested that the military was being played for a sucker and that through numerous strategic gaming scenarios run on a super computer at the CIA, they had concluded with high probability that the Greys were working toward a planetary take-over. Based on what Roth had heard and seen, he figured the old-timers had called it correctly, but it seemed too late.

"Hell yes, we're going back down," Roth said. He nodded as if placing an exclamation mark behind his words.

"You know, Adrian, the big shit will hit the fan if the technology division loses this facility," Colonel Winston said. "I don't know. I've heard that some people at the top want it gone, but... I don't think they have the guts to speak in the open... afraid they'll be eliminated by a convenient heart attack. The foreign technology people pour millions every year into this sewer to keep it running. You and anyone else surviving after such a mission would get their asses court martialed and no one would know about it because it would be kept quieter than a graveyard. Hell, no one would learn of it through the Freedom of Information Act for five hundred years." He laughed sourly. "They would just get a black unit and terminate our asses."

"They can try," Zane said, his words rolling like a verbal gauntlet. "I'd give odds that I'd take a couple with me."

"Colonel Winston, it's not right that our people are swallowed never to be seen again, never to get a proper burial service, or their kin never to get closure over their death," Sergeant Blake said.

"Dammit, sir," said Mathews, "what cooks my ass is their damn arrogance that we can't look for our man. It's our facility. It's our damn planet."

"Gentlemen, there are many rotten things going on down there," Roth said. "As we were leaving today, I saw one of them wink at me."

"A Grey?" Captain Harvey said quickly. "I didn't see anything."

"At first I thought it was one them crossbreeds, but the man looked normal, like a human. I think he was sending me an SOS signal and that they were holding him against his will." He sighed. "Hell fire, that's what they do. They—"

"Don't go any further, Adrian, it's classified," Winston said. "You know that."

Roth shook his head. "I hate this! I should have gotten out a year ago. Twenty years' service is too damn long, especially when you serve it in Dante's hell."

Winston shook his head. "You're right."

"Screw it being classified. These men should know if they don't already." Roth's eyes narrowed. He mentally drifted off across the room. "They abduct people and perform experiments on them. They grab children too. Makes no difference to these bastards. There has been a rumor for years that they actually, somehow, eat humans. Our man is undoubtedly dead somewhere down there. But we should bring his body back home just the same. We don't leave anyone behind. We do have a code to follow."

Mathews said softly, "We don't leave anyone behind."

"Sir, how do you know all this?" Sergeant Zane asked.

Roth looked at Winston, who looked away. "Classified updates... reports," Roth replied. "However, the last one from a year ago was largely guesswork, extrapolation by some intelligence geek, because no one has ever gone down there and done a survey. There is a very old report in the database, made when the facility was commissioned, describing what those creatures were allowed to perform under the working agreement."

"How do they get supplies?" Zane asked.

Roth's eyes narrowed bitterly. "They have a hangar on level eleven where they come and go in their craft. As far as I know, Zane, that's the only access they have to supplies, other than the water, electric, air, heat, and maintenance materials like light bulbs that go down in the empty freight elevator. That's pretty rare. The last one I know about was two years ago. There may have been another in that time."

Karl Blake planted his foot on the bench that ran between the two rows of lockers, leaning an elbow on his knee. "Hell's bells, sir, why not cut off their electric or their air?"

Winston grinned at Roth.

Roth replied, "That wouldn't work. It would require us to shut down that part of the facility, and they have their own power circuit and backup generator. They could make their own air. We could get the plans I suppose and try tracking down the correct feeder line. Once their generator ran out of fuel, they'd probably raise hell and we'd have a bunch of three or four stars walking around up here kicking our asses. It's possible the Greys would flee their nest like a bunch of yellow jackets sprayed with bug spray, but I doubt it." He bounced his head, smiling, as if amused by a thought. "You boys wouldn't want your asses kicked out before your pension time rolls around."

Captain Mathews sighed. "If we go down there to bring back our man, we will face whatever firepower they have. I would bet a month's pay the device that one little sucker held in its hand was more than a cigarette lighter or a TV tuner." He sighed heavily. "And... I could live without the damn pension. There's always living off the grid in Alaska. I've thought about it a lot."

"That device was probably some sort of laser that could slice off your arm before you knew it," Blake said in an edgy voice, sounding full of nerves.

"In such a situation," Roth began, "we don't allow the weapon to be raised. We shoot first. I don't care if it looks like a Popsicle or a Bible."

"That's right!" Zane said. "We shoot first. This is our ball of dirt. When we going?"

Winston chewed on the inside of his mouth, bulging his cheek like he was chewing tobacco. "We should go soon... real soon."

Roth nodded. "I agree. Two or three days. Before any inspection. The fewer the brass, the better. They could foul up the whole deal... put us on lockdown."

***

The restaurant waiter carefully placed a hot plate of festooned salmon in front of Congressman Gutierrez and a small beef fillet in front of a spectacled elderly and partially balding man. The older man, wearing a dark-red necktie, crisp white shirt, and a gray suit, held his chin up arrogantly as he quickly glanced around.

"Senator Claybaugh, I appreciate you meeting with me for lunch," Gutierrez said. He noticed the senator's eyes and also chased his gaze around the restaurant, noting the rose-tinted Art Deco lights hanging from the ceiling, the puffy chairs, high-backed booths, and waiters moving in black waist coats like swarming bees. The eatery was broken into three large sections for dining and an area near the bar. Coming back to the senator, he said, "I've not been here before. It seems exceptionally nice."

"This is one of the best places to talk over lunch," Owen Claybaugh said, the soft light forming shadows on the age wrinkles of his face. "When my secretary said you wanted to meet here at the Capitol House, I knew you wanted to talk about something serious. You can feel free. There is little chance of anyone hearing us."

"I must say, your fillet looks extremely nice."

Claybaugh cut a slice and inserted it into his mouth. He nodded. "It's very good."

Gutierrez leaned forward, ran his eyes around the room again, this time without an obvious movement of his head. "Owen, I had a distressing visit from some constituents. One was a mayor from my district in Arizona.

Normally, I wouldn't chase this sort of thing but it raised my curiosity, my concern, and frankly, it scared me. These were all well-educated people. I expressed my concern, my doubts about my making any progress toward answers, but I said I would check. I owe that to my people. I try to keep my word."

"What the hell are you beating around the bush about? What's scaring you?" Owen frowned for a moment at Gutierrez, and then dropped his gaze to cut his fillet. He pushed his fork into it; his face seemed detached from the discussion as if the food was his primary concern. He held his fork over his plate with a hovering hand.

"I don't know if I look worried or not."

"Yes, I'd say you look disturbed." Owen raised his fork. His eyes watched Gutierrez and then he inserted the food in his mouth.

Gutierrez whispered, "Does the government have any agreements with a foreign organization, something sanctioning a joint research facility in our country?"

The question hung in the air for a moment, like an earsplitting milestone for him, adding weight to his heretofore inconsequential lunch meeting. As he studied Owen, it seemed to bring the specter of nervousness.

"Look old friend," Owen began, "whatever it is you're dancing around sounds like something you should ignore. Your manner tells me it's probably something that doesn't exist except on a nondescript budgetary listing within the darkest bowels of CIA, DARPA, or the military."

Gutierrez took a bite of his fish, glancing down at the table introspectively. This was new territory for him. "If you are a person who sees one pig fly, you might attribute the sighting to a hallucination. If you are a person who sees a pig fly one day and then sees it repeated sporadically over a period of years, then you might conclude a genuine phenomenon existed."

Owen stared at Gutierrez dumbfounded. "Can you say what it is?"

"Owen, people are being abducted by flying pigs," Gutierrez whispered.

"By cops?"

"By aliens in UFOs, dammit," Gutierrez whispered.

"Oh shit." His eyes slid left and right as if searching for someone watching. "Now I understand. I could get in trouble for merely discussing such a thing with you. Keeping our country and the world away from the edge of a precipice is a dirty business, a business sometimes calling for people to make agreements that makes any patriot puke. You need to drop your inquires on this topic… if you like living." He paused, dropping his brow, staring. "I mean it."

"What is the long term assessment of our survival in view of these visitors and their tampering?"

"I do not have clearance to know such things. I don't want to know either. I like living. Rumors exist about colonization."

"My God!" Gutierrez couldn't breathe for a moment. He thought he had heard a death knell for the earth. "What about our children and grandchildren? How can you live with yourself knowing this?"

Owen dropped his head somberly. "I have grandkids too. It sickens me. What's our choice? It may not be true. How could we… prevent it?"

"Backbone for God sakes… guts!" He glanced across the room and then back. "Owen, you're not on any intelligence committee as far as I know. There are things—"

"And I don't want any part of it either."

Gutierrez sat up, sipped his coffee, leaving the cup at his lips, pausing. "I would rather go to my maker with a fight than face the end impotently like a worm." In the back of his mind, he had a vision of a black political jungle, where the government animals chewed at each other's ankles, tearing away little pieces of the soul. The political compromises piled on top of one another in such a mess that no one agency or person had a complete and clear vision of the path of the country, and the world. Obviously, a paper trail leading to the decision maker wouldn't exist since the administrative orders would materialize mystically like subatomic particles coalescing on their own, forming the written word. The government was a sick person with multiple illnesses, taking so many pills, each pill interacting with another, and when a symptom disappeared no one could identify the curative. The term ghost government was, he thought, better replaced by ghost corruption.

Gutierrez pushed his chair back, reached for his wallet, and placed a hundred dollar bill on the table. "I'm sorry for bothering you, Owen. I had better leave you before you get in trouble."

Owen gawked at Gutierrez, stunned. "I... I didn't mean to..." Owen said.

Gutierrez walked to the entrance, the people, the tables, and the scurrying waiters a random blur. He felt like he did before his election, just another one of the victims who walked an American street. It made him wonder if there was a single person in charge. That begged a question: Did the president have knowledge of such radical deviations from traditional military preparedness?

The socio-political shadows that Gutierrez now walked through didn't resemble anything he had ever conceived while pursuing the office of a United States Congressman. It had never occurred to him that he'd fall into a dark cloud of secret government departments and ultimately fear for his life while serving his oath.

***

Gutierrez walked into a government office a short time after leaving lunch with Senator Claybaugh. Typical for

Washington, the office ceilings soared high overhead encircled by a crown of carved architecture that dated back to days of true artisans and cheap labor. A woman of fifty or so, in a modest gray suit with a rose colored silk-looking blouse, stood up behind her desk and smiled pleasantly with a reserved manner.

"Congressman Gutierrez," she said.

He extended his hand, taking hers. "Madeline, I appreciate the chance to talk with you on short notice." He looked around a little. This is a nice office. I thought the General Accounting Office would be more Spartan."

Madeline Harper shrugged and fought off a smile. "Even a director in the GAO can have a nice office. It's part history, too." Her mouth fell as her eyes grew serious. "What can I do for you? I must say your phone call sounded rather off the normal path."

"Is it correct that you oversee accounting functions connected to some people who provide a service for the government that the public doesn't know exist... uh, for various reasons... such as... which isn't my concern today."

Madeline's mouth dropped, then closed, and hardened. "Please remember I'm not at liberty to discuss some things just as you have your own oath."

"Yes, I understand and I wouldn't expect you to violate any covenants." He reflected, groping for the right collection of words, which could reach his question and pull back the curtain on an apparent black operation. "Have you seen any budgetary items that had a fuzzy explanation and possible connection to the operation of a secret facility... a facility unknown to congressional oversight?"

"What? I can't talk about such things. We see strange things all the time. Someone is always trying to get funding for their pet project or boondoggle. And believe it or not, the Inspectors General and our people try to do our best." She gazed at him with a questioning face.

Gutierrez met her eyes and wondered if she was waiting for more clarity behind his vagueness. "Have any of your contacts mentioned continuing programs from.. the time… from Truman or Eisenhower's time… perhaps connected to aliens?" he whispered.

"You must be joking." She rolled her eyes. "Why would some research be connected with illegal aliens from Mexico?"

"Not Mexico," he said softly. When their eyes met, he looked up toward the ceiling.

Her brow furrowed and then her mouth dropped. She sighed. "Oh," she whispered. She wagged a finger at him. "Trust me. You are digging into something that is darker than the Manhattan Project. I can't discuss budgets related to agencies doing national defense research work. You should know that sort of thing is extremely classified. Any program name, amount being spent, the rate, the administrator… all that's classified." Her eyes settled on the desktop. She breathed slowly then her eyes came at him more energetically. She leaned forward again and whispered, "Let's try this. There was a Freedom of Information Act, FOIA, request three or four years ago by one of those strange fringe science groups. It dealt with the budget for an arm of the Defense Advanced Research Projects Agency, DARPA. I saw two papers. There was an odd reference to something you might find interesting since you come from Arizona. That's as far as I'll go."

"What was the fringe science group making the request?"

"Something like… maybe BUFO, I believe." Her face turned stolid, cold. "Now you should leave."

Gutierrez reached across the desk and took her hand, finding it felt limp like a dead-fish handshake. She wanted him gone. He left her office without saying another word.

He drove his car to his government allocated parking space, parked, and sat behind the wheel listening to a symphony on a public broadcast radio station. He asked himself how much he wanted to risk in the pursuit of answers to satisfy his curiosity and satisfy his conscience on behalf of two people who didn't come from his electoral district, and who had likely died. Nevertheless, there was something infuriating about two people being plucked off the earth without a warning, without legal or moral authorization.

He reached to his inner suit pocket, pulled out his cell phone, and touched in a number for directory assistance. After he did, he abruptly wondered if a government agency would monitor his call to a fringe group. When a female voice came on the phone, he asked for the listing for an organization known by the letters, BUFO, anywhere in the country. He didn't know where. Moments later, the directory assistance gave him a phone number.

The forefinger on his right hand touched in the first digit of the number. He hesitated, thinking of rumors and wondering if they had any foundation in fact. He wrestled with his rationalization to go forward; it came from a simple idea. He wasn't seeking illegal information, only publicly released history. He continued dialing the number. An answering machine told him to leave a phone number without names. He repeated his number into the phone and hung up, thinking he had just wasted time playing a fringe group's illusionary games. Was someone monitoring their phone calls from an obscure technology center?

***

An hour later, sitting in his office the cell phone vibrated in Gutierrez's pocket. He thought of the committee he served on, wondering if they had called a meeting. Few people had his cell phone number. A shot of indignation rushed into his veins as he plunged his hand toward the phone.

"Hello," he said, his single word like a protest. "Who's calling?"

"Hey, man, you called us," a man said. It was a youthful voice.

Gutierrez was dumfounded. "What? Uh… is this BUFO?"

"What do you want?"

"I'm interested in a FOIA request related to DARPA and alien investigations."

"That stuff. Huh. Why?"

"Cause I'm trying to help find missing people. They were taken from my district."

"District? Who are you?"

"I'm a congressman from Arizona."

"Oh. Okay. Uh… even a congressman… uh, you need to know that you are treading on dangerous turf, stuff that can get you dead if you hit gold."

"I'm trying to help people find closure, to stop an illegal activity abusing our sovereignty, to send a signal that the earth belongs only to the human race."

"All very noble, but—"

"But what?"

"It's likely impossible and a death sentence for you and those around you… like family."

"I have no family."

"Are you certain you want to, as they say, go down the rabbit hole?"

"Yes. What can you tell me?"

"Not on the phone. We'll be in touch. Go to dinner downtown this evening."

Gutierrez heard the man break the connection. He swallowed hard, uncertain if he wanted to go forward, especially if it could mean terminal trouble. But hey, it was all probably smoke anyway.

***

The fading sun of early evening glimmered in orange streaks off the car windshields parked outside the restaurant window where the valet busied himself. Jagged shadows darted from the buildings, leaving angular planes of light and dark. Gutierrez sat by the eatery's front window probing his Greek salad with an exploratory fork. His cell phone vibrated in his pocket. Looking up sheepishly at the people around him, he placed the phone to his ear.

"Yes," he whispered.

"Congressman, do you still want to talk?"

"Yes. I'm in a restaurant right now."

"We know where you are. Pay for your dinner, leave a nice tip, and walk out. Be ready to climb into a green van in front of the valet parking station."

Gutierrez's mind flooded with questions and concern. "Okay…"

The person ended the call.

Gutierrez thought for an instant, asking himself if he wanted to plunge further into the cryptic security world. His hand went to his wallet and extracted two twenties and a ten. He walked to the entrance, his gaze covering faces as he passed, looking for eyes that fell on him and lingered a bit too long.

Outside he waved off the valet and rushed to a green van that squawked to a stop. The side door opened; he climbed in and quickly dropped onto a bench seat facing rearward.

"Sit here," a man in his mid-forties said, pointing at the seat facing forward. "We don't do names. So don't ask."

Gutierrez moved as directed. The man with long dark hair, big shoulders, possessing a somewhat bookish face with glasses, moved to the rearward facing seat, occupying the seat across from Gutierrez.

A second man, a little older with a short gray beard and bushy eyebrows, sat next to the long haired man. A third man, the youngest of the three, with shaggy sandy hair hanging out from under a blue baseball cap, drove the van at an easy speed, exercising patience with the traffic stops and starts.

"As I said before, you are dabbling in a dangerous area. In our FOIA request, we learned that the government is spending money on a facility that doesn't exist. That's all. There was a code number that I tried exploring further in the FOIA system and national archives. Someone had blacked-out all the other information. All I can tell you is that we think the facility is in your backyard, so to speak... and underground. Observations have documented infrequent trucks and choppers. And—once in a while, UFOs have been observed overhead, but we don't know if they are connected. We don't know if the UFOs are advanced military stuff. In other words, we don't know for certain if the government is working with aliens. This facility, we think, the government started building back in the mid-1950s or 1960s. It has been only in the last few years that stories have emerged from people, witnesses, because they were nearly on their deathbed and willing to take the risk of assassination. They described an underground complex. One man, a construction worker, declared before dying that it has its own nuclear power."

"All this sounds fascinating and clandestine, and good material for a science fiction movie, but I'm interested in missing people," Gutierrez said. His voice came sharp with an undertone of sarcasm.

"The aliens in that place take our people!"

"How do you know?"

"I talked to a sheriff from New Mexico who was called to investigate a decomposed female body lying out in the middle of a nowhere desert. Ordinarily, they wouldn't have been able to track the body, but she had a military type tattoo that they traced. The woman was from Reno. However, that wasn't the crescendo to the symphony. The kicker came when the medical examiner discovered what the body was missing. The body was sort of mummified, being that it was in a dry climate and no critters had chewed on it. All the conditions constituted a rare situation. Anyway, she didn't have all her lower internal female parts. They found a big scar that hadn't completely healed. So they checked nearby medical centers and hospitals, and found no connection. She hadn't escaped from a nearby hospital."

Gutierrez pulled on his jaw, staring at the floor of the van. "How does she connect with some phantom military facility?"

"UFOs my man. They are seen around that area. An observer belonging to one of the reputable UFO research groups reported two UFOs disappearing into the side of the mountain near where the military facility is allegedly located."

"So far I've heard two things alleged and not much in the way of a real connection."

"Excuse me, but are you trying to be obtuse?" asked the man with the gray beard.

The dark haired man said, "When the aliens completed their study of her they apparently disposed of her rather crudely… either on their outward journey or return. It all fits."

"Who in the government is supposed to be running this facility, DARPA, CIA, DIA or the Pentagon?" Gutierrez asked.

"It could even be NSA. It may go back to Eisenhower or Truman. We cannot help you any beyond this conversation." He hesitated. "I suppose we could drive you up to the gate, but they wouldn't let you in. We have no idea what type of classification you would need to get in."

"This is a waste of time," Gutierrez said. "I know someone else… someone… I can talk to."

"Be careful."

"Can you give me a map or directions to the entrance? How about giving me the phone of the UFO researchers out in that area who could take me to the gate of the facility?"

The long haired man, his mouth pinching with grudging acceptance, took out a pen and small pad of paper. He wrote something on the pad and offered it to Gutierrez with a flip of his wrist. "We know of one military person who might talk to you. He might seem oddly positioned but you can approach him safely. We interviewed him a long time ago and, although he didn't say anything overt, his tone came across somewhat sympathetic. You may know the man, General Mason Carpenter."

"Yes, I know him."

"It's your choice. I can give you the name of a man who lives out west, but he won't get you very close."

The man's shoulders slumped, Guterriez thought, seemingly from the recognition of his impotence. "Give me the contact information. If the general can't help, at least I'll have a backup."

The man removed a paper from a pocket. "Here are the GPS coordinates of the place, our guess anyway, and the phone number of Vince Harris. He lives out there. He can get you within a few miles if you can talk him into it. If I may ask, who are you looking for?"

"Two professors, Louise and Bryan Northfield. They held positions at Princeton."

"I'll mention their names to Harris."

Gutierrez took the paper and inserted it in his sock at his ankle. "Thanks for your help."

In a grave tone, the man said, "You must be careful with anyone you contact."

***

In the early evening in his apartment, Gutierrez picked up his cell phone, avoiding the landline, thinking the cell might be a safer communication device. He had never felt so hesitant to call anyone or so scared that he was plunging deeper into trouble.

"Whoever this is, better be someone I know," a gruff voice answered.

Gutierrez knew General Mason Carpenter from multiple appropriation discussions. He liked the general. "General, it's Congressman Gutierrez from Arizona." He wondered how he was going to broach the subject over a cell phone with a two-star general without the general immediately breaking their connection.

"Sorry for being gruff. Congressman, what can I do for you?"

"Mason, can you get me into a secret military base for a look-see?" Gutierrez held his breath not knowing whether he'd get fire or ice from Carpenter.

"You're joking."

"No."

"Excuse me, Congressman, what's going on?"

"It regards two missing people. You're probably going to hang up on me but at least hear me out." Gutierrez paused, listening for a click on the phone. "This base has the highest level in classification. It exists because of funding appropriations awarded by a committee, but it may not officially exist. I think you know I'm on the appropriations committee. So, I do have a tangential justification for a visit."

"Frankly, I'm getting a strange odor. Why is it so important for you to visit this nonexistent facility?"

"Like I said, because two people were abducted and quite possibly taken there... since the alleged activities at this nonexistent facility include illegal manipulation of the human genome to create who knows what... reasons for my oversight."

"Oh shit... you're talking... there!" The general fell silent for a moment. "You don't abduct people for that type of research."

"You do if you want a woman's female parts and a man's contribution." In his mind's eye, Gutierrez saw the general's doubting face.

"Congressman, what road are you trying to take?"

"I think the base is brutalizing our citizens illegally, abducting them and killing them. I think the base is operating in the dark with aliens from another planet. I think I could get killed trying to visit the place. The missing people I'm seeking aren't your average Mom and Pop, not that it makes any difference. I'm trying to help find two professors from Princeton who people saw transported up into a UFO."

"Holy crap, man. You don't want to go to that place. You should drop this foolish idea if you want to keep breathing. I can't deny or acknowledge any such activity by our government. I'm not ready to retire from the service yet or from life for that matter. I may not have family but I like living. You are not the first. Goodbye."

"Wait, wait, Mason. Please." A moment of silence passed. "Let's assume it is time for a military inspection, something that must take place to assess keeping personnel and funds being expended. Why couldn't I be part of an inspection? Why couldn't I get a clearance? There must have been an inspection over the years. Don't you owe me a favor?"

The general's voice came stern and cold, "There has been inspections. I've had that assignment. It has been a few years... not for... not since both political parties are at each other's throats. The intelligence people who protect this country cannot risk a 'bleeding-heart' politician going to the media. You know there are liberal brains that I don't understand, conservative brains, and socialist brains that think the world functions in a benevolent and understanding manner with goodwill for all."

"I know. I know we have to protect against the naive who need our protection."

"Many of our programs must remain at the extreme classification level for the sake of the country and for the sake of our planet, just like the Manhattan Project. Wait a minute. What favor?"

"Your future as one of the joint chiefs."

"That's a stretch."

"You know me. I'm a patriot. I've helped secure the funding you requested… for something you thought vital."

"So, this a shakedown."

"I don't operate in the gutter."

"Do you realize that there has never been anyone from any administration there since President Eisenhower was in office. I believe only two senators and maybe one congressman have ever been there. That's all… in all the years since it was built. That was in Eisenhower's time. I was tempted to resign after I was assigned to it and made my first visit. Even I don't know what happens on the bottom levels… and frankly, I don't want to."

"Things change."

"I'm sorry. This is a delicate area." The general sighed and made no sound for a moment.

"Don't you find the idea of a deal with… the—"

"…with the Devil… rather vile?" the general cut in.

"Yes. We are a sovereign country and regardless of a treaty or not…that was signed under, who knows what kind of coercion during Ike or Truman's time, the operation should be reviewed. Policy changes."

"We do need to visit that operation," Mason said, his voice dropping.

"Can't you do an unannounced inspection?"

"I was going to schedule a visit in few months. Frankly, I've been procrastinating on it. I could move it forward. I hate going there. I will have to include Brigadier Frank Warner, whom you may know."

"I've met Frank. Look, this is a lawful request I'm making, especially in light of the president's pressure to cut budgets for the military. You can tell Frank I'm trying to help save allocations. Hey... can... can you trust Warner?"

"Frank and I go back a long way. We've been to the War College together and served together in Iraq. He's probably the only guy I can trust. After I talk to Frank, I'll schedule one of our small personnel jets. This may happen today or tomorrow or the next day. Can you move quickly?"

"Damn right."

"One more thing. If he objects, it's over. Fair enough?"

"Yeah, but this has to happen soon. Less time for word to leak."

"I'll get back to you."

"Thanks."

Gutierrez turned off his phone and gazed off across the room. A voice in his head told him to drop the whole stupid idea and another thought told him that he was doing what was right. If he went that far on behalf of those poor people his conscience would feel satisfied. Perhaps he should leave word with an attorney so words of his sacrifice could be written on his tombstone if he didn't make it back alive.

Chapter Thirteen

Bryan couldn't sleep. From his cot, he gazed through the dark toward the ceiling. The clock displayed eleven fifty-seven. It felt like a late hour to his muscles. The past couple days had been remarkable even on the scale of walking among aliens. Any concept, a sequence of events, leading to an escape eluded his tired mind. He had grown weary and disappointed analyzing one scenario after another.

No sounds penetrated his chilly concrete cavern. Every time he was alone, facing his deep doubts, he couldn't avoid listening for signs of life. He had heard a door close once and there was the sound of dripping water in his sink when he didn't close the valve completely. He heard no motors or electrical transformers humming. He had heard the flow of air whooshing in the heating system twice.

He had his eyes closed for a considerable time, perhaps an hour, sometimes hearing his own breathing and sometimes finding it too shallow to hear. He started dropping onto sleep's feathery edge. Seemingly, at the precipice of restful peace, he sensed his own breath returning to him, flooding his face with moist warmth, no longer moving away freely. The change in the sound of his breathing tugged at his tired mind. He snapped open his eyes. Startled, he jerked his head toward the edge of the cot, his skin tingling.

A silver sphere hovered inches from his head. In a moment, it rose to the ceiling in an unhurried motion.

He looked toward the door for a Grey, but the door had not opened. He watched the sphere, his anger slowly overwhelming his initial fright. He sent a mocking face at the eerie visitor, guessing someone might have observation duty. The sphere shimmered and pulsated with a small change in its brightness. Several moments passed before he realized he couldn't remember what he had just thought, something connected to the Greys. His thoughts had frozen, caught in the middle of a thread of logic, in the middle of possible actions he could pursue, in the middle of a warning to himself to guard his thoughts. He checked the sphere again. He felt more aware. Concerns and thoughts of hopeful actions began connecting fluidly. He found his thinking pursuing their associations to their end, as if going backwards along a map, leaving the destination and returning to the origin. Then he remembered Liana's instructions and blocked his thoughts as they sprouted. He realized the sphere might have searched his mind. Liana's caution returning to his mind sparked his resolve. He stiffened, revisiting his computer artificial intelligence theories at Princeton, bringing them mentally forward as a diversion, as he felt the sphere probing for his feelings for Liana, probing for feelings toward Greys, and probing his desires for freedom. The only thing he could use for comparison with the sphere's intrusion was a feathery tickle inside his head. It searched for feelings regarding the presence of Greys on earth, feelings for cooperation, fear of dissolution and dissection, thoughts of hope, and feelings on self-sacrifice.

The enigmatic silver ball held its position over Bryan as if it had invisible eyes staring down at him, all while it tried absorbing his thoughts. Was a Grey sitting at a control somewhere looking back at him with its big black eyeballs? He had the distinct impression, a sixth sense, the operator of the sphere was sending him a message that he had to comply or die. He raised his head a little. He said, "Ham-Sah, Ham-Sah, Ham-Sah."

The sphere rose slightly and floated through his cell's metal door as if it was no longer solid material.

Bryan dropped his head to his cot. Perhaps he had won another battle. Perhaps not.

***

Early in the morning, Liana walked into a fourteenth level laboratory designated for cognitive study. She followed her usual routine in going there, obediently announcing herself to a male Grey, Nekzon Vagpok, as she entered. A female Grey accompanied Nekzon, a worker level Grey, Haagui Zielam, who was young in years. By her title, she had personnel responsibility.

Liana waited just inside the door for them to issue her directives for the day, maintaining her hybrid-servant deportment. She expected her encounter to transpire as usual, since she interacted frequently with these two Greys, either receiving orders for tasks or receiving orders to support another Grey. The Greys kept at their tasks.

As usual, Liana had implemented her mental barrier a short distance before entering the room. As always, she guarded her thoughts in the presence of these Greys. She had done it since her very early learning development. Now, with her changing body, she had to maintain a closer watch on her mannerisms.

In the past, she had welcomed her duty to monitor a new subject whom she would escort from the room where the Greys held humans suspended in time or held them ready for dissolution. Bryan had been a statistical outlier. Human's called it luck. The Greys frequently victimized new arrivals with organ removal surgery, gross dissection, or brain testing. Too frequently, the Grey's exploratory surgery resulted in her wheeling a failing subject to the room of tables where the Greys would reduce the once living tissue into molecular components. Occasionally, she worked with a subject on the teaching machine. Regardless of surgery, whether it was a clone, hybrid, or human, she rarely learned if the subject lived on or died. The time spent was an undeniable duty, and during her rapid maturation, she had carried it out with icy unemotional dispatch. On occasion, the Greys would perform mental testing like they did with Bryan.

Liana shifted her feet, still acting the obedient servant with her head slightly tilted downward. She maintained her eyes steady and directed away from the Greys who sat in chairs next to a table. Strangely, in her short life, she had only recently envisioned unleashing her resentment against the Greys for her enslavement and abuse of helpless creatures. She suspected such a feeling derived from a basal urge to gather human satisfaction from a physically rewarding outburst. Patience was a universal key and perhaps the prize of intelligence.

A light panel that was a holographic projection, serving as a control mechanism, extended two feet above the table. It was a vertical two-foot square, an illuminated sheet, like a book on its end. It formed part of a communications and computation device. Liana knew its function and operation, and had practiced at its control in unobserved unoccupied time. The female, Haagui Zielam, touched a spot on the projection, causing the whole display to collapse and transform into a palm-sized translucent, horizontal projection, with four touch-control points.

Haagui Zielam looked at Liana, her uncharacteristic broad chin moving almost nervously for a moment and then she spoke in a slow manner inside Liana's mind: "Your assigned subject, 9002, the male... his intelligence increased... after his experience on the learning machine. Since that exposure... he has shown improvement in mind communication. Markak has mentioned him. How is his cooperation? He is being considered for the next phase."

Liana sent a reply to the Grey's mind: *He has made much progress. He causes no problems except for his food requirements.*

Nekzon Vagpok spoke into Liana's head: "You talk physically with him frequently. Why do you do that, since his nonverbal capability improved?"

Liana replied thinking to him: *His communication has improved, although it requires more training time. I have him practice the skill, but I think he prefers the physicality of producing the sounds in his throat. He does not feel fluent yet.*

Haagui Zielam, blinked and asked in Liana's head: "Do you like communicating verbally with him?"

Liana maintained her impenetrable stoic visage, yielding nothing through body language or her thoughts. She thought a reply to them: *Verbalization takes time and requires effort and specificity to produce the correct rhythmic pattern of sound frequencies, what the humans call words. It seems more connected with emotional presentation than pure communication of ideas carried out by Reticulans.*

Haagui and Nekzon looked at each other, communicating.

Liana watched them, waiting dutifully, closing her mind to them, assessing what she had presented, giving them enough to prevent distrust. A sense of pleasure had taken her when she disclosed an activity to the Greys that they could not appreciate, that of physically speaking. Her feeling was primitive. Taking pleasure from their misfortune was beneath her intellect. However, the data on other high civilizations, records she had seen in the Grey's data system, indicated the higher species did not keep or need slaves. It angered her. Her anger was real. Her observation supported the premise that the Greys, the Reticulans, fell to the cosmic classification of intelligent thugs, and from what she had learned with the teaching machine, and the knowledge stored on the Grey's computer-type device, intelligent beings from other stars had warned the Greys about interfering on Earth.

Regardless, their warning hadn't stopped the Greys. Since she had learned of it, she had delved into her logic to predict the probability that one of the other intelligent universe travelers would come to rescue Earth from the Greys. Unfortunately, that low probability portended a dire future for Earth and humans. The humans would have to protect themselves. It also highlighted another question. Was a cosmic or planetary conflict, between the Greys and some other species, worse than the death and enslavement of the Earth at the hands of the Greys? She had, only fleetingly, pondered a need for a universal police to address the problem.

Both the Greys held their gaze on her for several moments. Nekzon Vagpok's protruding brow lowered slightly. Liana sensed that they had found the concept of vocalization and enjoyment difficult to assimilate.

Liana sent them both a thought: *I could configure a demonstration with subjects to facilitate your analysis of this behavior.*

The Greys looked at each other.

Liana remained motionless and clinical. She extended her sensitivity. She connected to their minds and their exchange as Haagui Zielam spoke mentally to Nekzon: "We could benefit from more data on the emotional response and on vocalization by this species. Perhaps we could use this emotional response in our control method."

With a steady authoritarian gaze Nekzon spoke in Liana's head: "Additional observations will aid our goal. It seems clear that as we move into their environment, the knowledge will facilitate our effort to develop sounds that can be used for mind control."

The female Grey spoke into Liana's mind: "Mettui Ouicil, you will arrange a demonstration this day with the subject. The subject will also be tested for suitability to serve Markak on an acquisition mission and suitability for a shared consciousness transfer study. The subject will support the location of higher level humans for the planned social control. If the subject fails to meet requirements for Markak, his scheduled shift to the biological modification phase will be advanced."

Liana lowered her head slightly, keeping her mouth rigid as her eyes maintained a detached coldness. She backed toward the door and walked down the hall, her mind rapidly analyzing the Grey's comments. Records she had collected in her head with her photographic memory allowed her to identify a flaw in the Grey's justification. Markak had never used one human to hunt other humans. The Greys had always studied a subject's potential by using vibrational energy and they had the capability of doing it from their craft while hovering above a target. They did not have a need for human or hybrid help and normally would have found that idea repugnant. Was Markak configuring a scheme? If so, was it caused by a suspected relationship between Bryan and her?

She didn't like them considering consciousness transfer for Bryan. It was problematic and extremely dangerous for the subject.

How many humans would the Greys observe in the laboratory before they answered all their questions and found satisfaction? Occasionally, she thought they acted like jealous voyeurs, extracting vicarious enjoyment from testing and inflicting pain on humans, rather than collecting scientific observations.

Markak emerged from a laboratory and walked toward Liana.

She stopped, feeling he wanted her attention. She respectfully averted her eyes to the floor.

Markak's words ran into her head: "Mettui Ouicil, the surveillance information shows the implant for your human subject, 9002, lost communication. Explain."

Liana mentally replied: *Subject 9002 may have carried out a physical activity that caused the deviation.* She pressed her hands to her sides and sent another thought: *When humans experience anger they can strike out and hurt themselves. He could have done that, striking his hand against an object. I will examine him and make certain he has an operating implant.*

Markak replied: "If his behavior has become troublesome, he may not be worth keeping for more tests, including the transfer evaluation." Markak paused. His brow moved down, covering his eyes slightly in a stern shadow. His words resumed in Liana's head, coming with a lighter cadence: "I had thought to utilize him on a mission, but now perhaps not if his mind is too unstable. He may only have worth through his genetics."

Liana felt his eyes searching her for emotional signals, body language. His comment struck her as out of character, testing and probative. She nodded slightly. Markak expected it; it was something she had observed early in her maturation as she studied other Greys near him. It was a reaction she found interesting given the elevation of his supposed intelligence. Even an advanced species like Markak had a weakness of the self, the inner cravings for recognition, and a desire for the esteem of others. He had an ego. This was strange for a member of a society where the individual belonged to the collective mind and had a duty supporting the good of the whole.

With his usual stern demeanor, he continued to the laboratory that she just had exited.

Liana resumed her trek down the hall, meditating on the objective of maintaining the current state of interaction between the Greys and Bryan. She considered looking at the Grey's schedule in their data system that they kept precise with their meticulous recordkeeping. It was risky. In those plans, she expected to find key dates for planned testing and possible missions outside the complex. One date would be for Bryan's termination. One would be her time for termination, which she assumed would occur sometime after she gave birth, if they learned of her pregnancy.

She stopped in the hall, paralyzed by her realization.

Her urination. She hadn't taken any precaution. How could she have been so careless with her thinking? She had overlooked it. *You are not as smart as you thought.* The Greys undoubtedly extracted information daily on her fetus from their data system. She needed to act quickly. The control system in the laboratory near where she had just met with Markak would work if she could return and gain access without observation by a sphere.

Perhaps she still had sufficient time for an escape with Bryan. Since the first encounter with him in the dissolution room, a confluence of events had occurred, the development of her baby, the termination dates, and the expectation of the military attempting the recovery of their colleague. She had detected the insatiable fury in the soldier standing eyeball-to-eyeball with Markak, fury that demanded satisfaction. Markak had probably detected it too. What of Markak's hint at ending Bryan? That was evolving into a critical question.

She needed to give Bryan more time, which could provide more opportunities to demonstrate his value for Markak. They both needed more time. She needed to keep feeding Bryan hope, until an opportunity emerged. From the data she had read while using the learning machine, hope and mental stimulation should help him avoid a rash incident or provocative behavior.

She marched to the stairs, conquering them energetically, realizing how much she enjoyed the physical exertion. It had to come from her human half. Her mind and body were still experiencing changes from the complex system of hormones inherited from Grey genetics and human DNA. She laughed to herself at the Grey's expectations for her, at what she knew of herself, and at what the Greys never would know. Perhaps she should place Bryan on the learning machine again.

Remembering Bryan's nourishment requirements, she picked up food and drink before continuing to his cell.

***

Liana opened Bryan's cell door. He was gone. She stepped into the room, her mind progressing through steps of analysis, evaluating alternatives connected with Markak's behavior pattern and his research programs. She dropped the food on the cot as a dark cautioning image crossed her mind. There was a low probability associated with Markak altering his plan and moving ahead with Bryan's termination. However, Markak did seem to have curiosity about the mental improvement Bryan achieved during the sessions on the teaching machine. Had that curiosity turned to concern? Another question arose. Was Markak controlling both her and Bryan, knowing how she had attached herself to him? Had he maneuvered laboratory tests and revised objectives, changing the endgame, a game where he was trying to keep her baby viable until the appropriate time he would have it taken. Of course, he could merely lock her in a room like Bryan. The weight of her feelings for Bryan registered in her heart unlike anything she had felt before, except her feelings for her child. She had to find him before they did something to him. She rushed out and down the hall, letting her intuition guide her.

***

A Grey standing in front of Bryan pointed to a laboratory chair. While similar to the chair used in conjunction with the learning machine, this one differed in its heavier construction. It reminded him more of a dentist chair from the nineteen-fifties, something used in an old horror movie.

He slowly sat in the wide seat and rested his palms on the naked metal chair arms.

The room with a high ceiling had bright white light pouring down from above, pushing the dreary unpainted concrete walls into the background. It felt warm, a fact that disturbed him. Why would they need a warm room? The room had no apparatus dropping from the ceiling, although it had two holographic control displays on waist-high cabinets. One was next to his chair.

The female hybrid that escorted Bryan from his cell to the laboratory stood at the side of the door poised to service the two aliens. The Greys and the female hybrid had the appearance of the laboratory team for another round of alien testing. Liana's absence made him wonder about the abusive limit of the test.

He began visualizing a flow diagram for a computer system to guard his mind.

Where was Liana?

The Greys moved around the controls, their steps gliding with an eerie poise, silently making their preparations, manipulating points of light.

Bryan caught sight of movement at the corner of his vision. Liana entered the room. She stopped just inside the door, her hands hanging easily at her sides, her eyes appearing slightly narrowed. Her mouth appeared tight and determined. He remembered her lesson and immediately held back displaying his pleasure at seeing her. He released a stress-bleeding breath and remembered his computer system mental exercise.

Liana raised a hand to draw attention.

Both the Greys stopped their tasks and focused on Liana. The taller Grey seemed to pull up his shoulders defensively, while the shorter one with a slight torso and detached manner, seemed to wait for the tall one to take some action.

Bryan heard her thought-communication to the Greys in his head. She started by acknowledging the tall male alien, Haazon Peutso-ui, who appeared indignant, and the shorter slight-of-build female Grey with a smallish face on a typically enormous Grey head. She was called, Haagui Tempok-uwe. Liana regarded the female hybrid, Dauasi Temgam, for a moment. From Liana's lesson, Bryan recalled the hybrid was a lower intelligence Grey-human clone. He found her ugly. Her sparse hair, similar to that of a ninety-year human, didn't help.

With fearless control, Liana told the Greys that Nekzon Vagpok required this subject for observations. As Bryan shared in the mental communication, he wondered how they would react, given their social structure. He felt a bit of satisfaction when the Greys stiffened and glanced at each other in a questioning manner.

Haazon Peutso-ui replied to Liana, saying that he had conversed with Nekzon Vagpok and Markak only a few moments ago. Markak had revised the testing schedule, authorizing the evaluation of the subject for intelligence, mental stability, and documentation prior to staging for biological reduction and molecular simplification.

Liana nodded, showing obedience and stepped to the side of the door. She glanced at Bryan, her face like a stone statue, lacking any emotion.

Seeing her cold manner, he sat forward, raising his arms to draw the Grey's attention. "I was already tested," he said verbally in a strong voice.

The tall Haazon Peutso-ui turned to Dauasi Temgam for a second and then quickly toward Bryan. The Grey's thoughts shot into his mind: "You will comply with more testing now or we will take you to molecular simplification."

Bryan nodded and sat back in the chair.

The female hybrid restrained his legs to the chair. He looked at her, connecting his eyes to hers for an instant.

He felt sorry for her creation, which in her case, had experienced deviation in the Grey's methodology. She hadn't received the better benefits of human DNA. Her head was too bulbous and looked grotesque over a virtually nonexistent chin. Long hair would have helped her. If she wasn't doomed to the Grey's termination cycle, she was the spinster type doomed to care for a cat, a parakeet, and to live with an umbilical to a television displaying forty-year-old game shows. He sighed. Here she was, temporarily gainfully employed torturing humans.

He looked down and wondered why they needed bindings?

The two Greys approached Bryan, one holding a helmet-shaped apparatus obviously devised to cover a head; it was similar to that of the teaching machine. The object, composed of tiny glowing spots of light lying on the surface of a translucent film, didn't have any wires for connection to a master control and the individual lights didn't appear to have a connection to each other. The Greys lowered the headgear on him, instead of assigning the manual task to the hybrid. The hybrid stood unobtrusively out of the way awaiting the Grey's orders.

Bryan lifted an eyebrow at Liana, showing that he had noticed the Greys doing some of the physical operations. She remained still, regarding the operation with only her eyes, ignoring his attention.

The headgear, now in place, wasn't unpleasant, at least for the moment. It extended down just past the edge of his ears. Haazon Peutso-ui motioned to the hybrid and as she moved to a holographic projected display, Bryan felt a nervous tremor in his hands.

A rectangular display glowed with life in front of him. He could see through it as if he were looking through a slice of vapor.

Everything Liana had told him washed over him like an ocean wave. With an instant of appreciation for her, he controlled his thoughts, preparing to block any of their probing for memories or previous activities, especially actions counter to the Grey's control and existence.

Haazon Peutso-ui manipulated a control on the projection console a few feet away and then turned, observing Bryan.

Like a whisper, vaporous at first, and then more intense a word repeated in his head. The word was soldier. Bryan thought he detected another groups of words floating just below the surface of conscious recognition, but dismissed them. The display screen in front of him showed three pictures. A command ran into his head for him to stare at the picture for the word they had given him. He washed his eyes over a picture of a woman with a child, a soldier in dress uniform, and a soldier in combat dress lying on the ground with a large bleeding wound in his head. Bryan held his eyes on the bleeding soldier. He realized he was doing something counter to his nature but he felt compelled. A sense of sadness struck him.

The word, friend, slid into his thoughts, seemingly part of the communication with one of the Greys, similar to prior encounters, and then a secondary thread of words sifted through his thoughts telling him food came from the Reticulans and imprisonment came from humans. They showed him three pictures: a Grey, a military officer, and a hybrid. They instructed him to select the one for friend. While connecting the mental-ribbons of words and meanings associated with the pictures, another burst of words cut into his head. The energetic word-string repeated. It told him to use his barrier. Immediately, he knew it was Liana's message. He knew he shouldn't look at her. He selected the picture of the military man.

Again the stream of instructions poured into his thinking, telling him to stare at the word that he had heard. The display showed a picture of an apple, a picture of a house, and a picture of a mathematical equation. He looked at the equation. Warmth ran over him, a sense of careless freedom.

He recognized a new word in his head. Life.

My computer work, remember it!

The Greys presented a picture of a dead human, a burnt landscape, and a picture of a alien standing with a smiling human. They told him to select the picture closest to his feeling for life. He selected the burnt landscape.

He dug deeply into his mind. *Hold onto the barrier. A neural computer structure. What type of expandability could be achieved for commercial work?*

A thought question came into Bryan's head: "Who do you trust?" The aliens displayed three images, a snarling wolf, a soldier pointing a rifle at him, and a happy human woman holding a Grey-looking baby. He indicated the snarling wolf as his choice. He wanted to grin from his amusement but continued his game.

Bryan fought to slow his mind. *Hold the barrier.*

The test pushed deep, giving him a dull ache in his head. He had to keep controlling himself. He couldn't let them win. *Remember threshold logic and network functions.*

Another word, comrade, and a group of three images came at him. The first image was a dead human woman, the second was a dead human man, and the third was a dead Grey. Bryan selected an image of a Grey lying dead. A sense of anger and then despair ran through him, bringing tears. He realized he had failed at keeping control. He gathered himself from the smothering emotional storm.

Clear it away!

They had tinkered with the emotional part of his brain, hormones, and the pituitary gland, making him cry. Bryan envisioned a wall in his mind, fighting to block the false feelings. He wiped his hand across his cheek, removing a tear.

The word, obedience, and images of a human kneeling before a Grey, a Grey bowing to a human, and the image of a human lying dead, flashed into Bryan's head. A command directed him to choose the meaning of obedience. He selected a human lying dead.

Another instruction-word-string slid into his thinking. The fragment he got was the word, world. His mental barrier stopped the rest of the string just as he began drifting. He looked straight ahead, drawing up his strength, tensing himself, his face determined.

The two Greys looked at each other, their bulky brows moving and wrinkling their foreheads. They seemed engaged in an energetic discussion. After a moment, they turned to Liana.

She faced them without any facial reaction.

Bryan heard the mental exchange that Liana apparently shared with him. A Grey spoke. Bryan wasn't certain which one. It wanted to know how he had blocked their efforts and maintained cognitive control.

Liana sent a question to the minds of the Greys as well as Bryan, asking the Greys what test procedure they had employed with this human subject.

Haazon Peutso-ui stared at Liana, telling her something.

After a moment, Bryan heard Liana's mental-echo of the Grey's comment. The Grey had said their study was about evaluating unconscious control, compliance, and potential for complete programming. The order had come from Markak for them to evaluate his mental malleability for one of their control programs and check his inconsistent mental behavior. Markak had predicted that the subject was unsuitable for programming, unsuitable as a mentor to new subjects, and barely usable as a Kuikui, which wasn't needed with the current research plans." Bryan worried about Liana's encounter with the aliens.

Liana covered her face with a curtain of calm.

He understood her effort to display calm and tried to do the same, although his concentration was waning. He didn't know how long he could continue with his diverging mental barriers. He refocused on holding his mind on his computer laboratory, on the graduate assistants with their projects, trying to avoid involuntary leakage of plans or his fears.

Words came into Bryan's head, Liana's words. She spoke to the Greys mentally, telling them that this human subject had multiple sessions on the learning machine and had his intelligence improved, and his ability to control mental communications. She advised them that by using him in their mind control testing, they could damage the opportunity to place him on the learning machine again, which could contribute to Markak's research with a rare and valuable subject. With this subject, Markak could gain insight into the potential threat of the species. She added that testing him again could adversely influence the work performed by Nekzon Vagpok and Haazon Temtso. Continuing, she added stolidly that her purpose was only to identify ramifications related to obtaining quality and reproducible observations in their research. She said she would await their instructions.

The two Greys conferred. Haazon Peutso-ui tilted his head slightly, drew himself up with purpose, as they continued exchanging thoughts. Haagui Tempok-uwe appeared merely to listen, moving her head twice as if agreeing.

Bryan, unable to detect the Grey's thoughts, glanced at Liana. From her plain appearance, he couldn't conclude whether she had overheard any of their conversation. Had her comment exposed an organizational chink in the alien's flawless genius to the light of logic? Perhaps Markak was playing games.

The female Grey waved her spindly hand over the console, closing it down, removed the head apparatus from

Bryan, unstrapped him, and exited with Haazon Peutso-ui following her.

Bryan got up from the chair, relieved that the ordeal had ended, his gaze tracking the Greys walking down the hall.

"Liana, what was that all about?" he asked verbally. "What was the Kuikui?"

"A mind control study, trying to see if they could give you suggestions and commands with reliability, and stop your thinking. The Kuikui is a human bio-bot, a type of human drone... human with a brain implant. It is a human totally controlled and once implanted the subject cannot go back." She glanced down the hall and back at him. "Are you feeling satisfactory?"

"Yes, I'm fine. It's strange, but I did get a sense that they tried to brainwash me."

"Brainwash?" she asked.

"Mind control... program my brain."

"I may have just created more aggravation for Markak and another incident that could elevate his suspicion of my behavior. You need to follow me to the learning machine. There is something I need to do with you."

"What happens if he discovers the purpose of our actions?"

"Our escape probability would plunge."

Chapter Fourteen

Liana marched with urgency down the hall. Her face radiated intensity. She took Bryan on the same floor to the teaching machine. Instead of facing a chair with arms waiting to wrap him in horror, they now offered an embrace with a hopeful promise.

She moved to the machine's console, saying nothing about him sitting in the chair for another exposure to the signals that sent bursts of information swarming inside his brain, ultimately and miraculously increasing his intelligence.

"You don't want me connected to the learning machine?" Bryan asked. His tone carried his confusion.

"Not this time. I have tasks." She spoke in an even voice, but detached.

"I would like another session on the machine."

"Yes… in a moment."

Even though she said little in that moment, it revealed more of her person and he was glad for it. Liana's tone and her focus took him back to his wife; it was the way she partially tuned distractions out during an important task. The mannerism, the exposure of that personal trait she had just shared with him, he took as an indication of their growing bond.

Standing off her left shoulder, he watched as she manipulated the touch-beams on the holographic display. She placed the head unit over her head. Her hands touched areas of the display. When she stopped and removed the helmet with its pin-point lights, she turned to him.

"I've checked the schedule of their planned activities, all their various programs that the Greys have formulated and recorded in their system. I mentioned it before. Through thousands of years, they have developed an unwavering behavior of recording complete details for everything. They are fanatically fastidious about it."

Bryan laughed with a stifled breath and smiled. "Your amazing vocabulary... where did you get it?"

"I memorized one of earth's dictionaries the Greys had in their data system."

"Are you a savant?"

"No. Far from it."

"Never mind my wonder and please continue."

"The dire potential... I looked at their future actions targeted toward us." She gazed at him, her eyes dropping at the corners a little, and then they grew hard with purpose.

"What's the bad news?" he asked. He frowned. "I see it in your eyes."

Her voice came low and measured. "They know I am carrying our child. I suspected it. They plan to keep me until they take the child. After that, they will have a child and my DNA, and won't need me for a slave. They intended to scan your brain." She looked at him with sympathy, appearing reluctant to continue.

"What do you mean I was to have my brain scanned?"

"The data system shows that a drone scanned you last night in your cell."

"I had a strange night. I woke with a silver sphere hovering over my head. I had a faint throb in my head and a recurring question about seemingly disconnected things."

"That is when it was done."

"Is there any way to detect what they learned? I think I tried to block its penetration."

Her eyes darted away from him. "We need to use the teaching machine. Sit in the chair and place the headgear on while I reset the controls."

Bryan dropped between the arms of the chair, slid the head unit on, and watched Liana manipulate the controls.

"Okay, close your eyes and relax."

Trying to bleed the tension from his shoulders, he blew a breath through his puckered mouth. He felt a sense of light and energy running around in his head, and exploding thoughts.

After a few moments, Liana whispered, "All done. Open your eyes. Hand me the head covering. There's another task I need to get out of the way before we can go."

After easing the unit off his head, he looked at her, waiting for an update on his future, anything, a frown or a smile.

"What?" Liana asked.

"Oh, wait," Bryan said. "Yes. I have memory of the probe, the sphere's searching. I remember the feeling, like it was hovering at the threshold of my thinking. It was searching thoughts related to control, organizations, country infrastructure, and my fears. The connections are faint and fleeting, and more from the past." He hesitated, his head feeling jittery. "That damn sphere."

Liana concentrated on the controls. "Spheres are useful if you know how to penetrate their control procedure," she said preoccupied, as her fingers moved rapidly over the illuminated touch-control locations.

"I'm glad you understand them."

"The schedule originally had an optional procedure listed for you, injecting a nanobot into your body, which they designed for humans. It is the implant. It is for total control, monitoring, and tracking. It travels to your brain where it takes over. You would become the bio-bot that I mentioned to you. But that information entry was changed. The second entry stipulates the presence of a behavior problem that necessitates termination. A note indicates the nanobot had a high failure projection." She paused, seemingly checking something on the control panel. "Two should work fine. There, that completes our work for now."

"These creatures are persistent little bastards."

"What? Oh yes, they have had eons to practice." She paused and then her face became chillingly cold. "You can no longer think that our escape is only for us or our child. Their schedule includes a slow progression toward population infiltration using a wave of hybrids, altered children, and bio-bots, which the Greys will follow. We escape to save this world from them."

"I can understand them wanting to dissolve me into protein juice, but why would they want to terminate you?"

"I am not as compliant as the others. I am not a robot. My mental and communication skills are not the same as the usual hybrid. They have had time to study me and subsequently may fear that because they cannot penetrate my thoughts, they cannot control me. I think they realize that I am a big problem. Markak may suspect that I am something they never anticipated in all their genetic tinkering."

"What does that mean, Liana?"

She dropped her eyes. "I'll tell you in time." She rose from the teaching machine controls.

Her revelation, while not pleasant and hopeful, gave reassurance from the perspective that she'd be fighting at his side and they'd either escape or die together. Even though she operated only in her concrete world, he found her an enigma and amazing after seeing what she could do and what she knew. She inspired him just like Louise. Her remarkable intellect encouraged him.

"How much time do you think we have?"

"My estimate is weeks for me and days for you. The next step for you after mental testing is DNA manipulation and chemical treatment... and then the table." She stood and ran a hand across her stomach.

Bryan inched closer to her, his eyes moving down to her stomach and back up again. "May I touch your body where the baby is?"

Liana's eyes grew large for an instant, and then as she understood, her face softened. She took his hand and moved it to her stomach, allowing him to feel her. He smiled, gazing at her longingly. She wiggled her lips a little, leaning toward him. He kissed her, wrapping his arms slowly around her. Her lips relaxed, giving to him, then pushed on his. In a minute they parted, gazing at each other, smiling.

"Liana, you know, even though we've only been together a few days, I truly love you. This is very strange for me since it took months with Louise."

"I have learned love from you and I love you, too. We must take care." Abruptly, she checked the door. "As I have said, the Greys have formidable intelligence."

He nodded.

"Have you had anything to eat?" she asked.

"No and I am hungry. If it's safe perhaps we could talk for a time… perhaps… in case I don't make it."

Liana frowned at him. "Positive thoughts cannot hurt our situation."

***

Liana left the door open as she walked over to the table in the nourishment supply room. She placed two food bars and a glass of liquid on the table in front of Bryan, and continued retrieving her own food.

As he raised his head to sip his drink he caught sight of movement in the hall. A silver sphere floated along, stopping, hovering, and observing them from three feet outside the door. "We have a friend."

He waited for her reaction as she turned.

She sat down at the table. "It is of no consequence."

Bryan continued, holding his drink in one hand as he bit into a food bar, finding its composition to have a granular texture and tasting like chicken or turkey. The liquid was a citrus-influenced concoction that brought a welcome freshness to his mouth, regardless of the faint metallic aftertaste. Liana nibbled on a different food bar that had a granola-appearing surface that reminded him of something he had purchased in a grocery store back in New Jersey.

He checked the sphere using only his eyes, took another bite of food, and enjoyed watching Liana for a few moments. "I was just thinking. What I find incredible is the rate at which you matured after the Greys removed you from the surrogate." His voice was a barely audible whisper.

She acknowledged the sphere with a long gaze, sending a message that she knew the Greys were watching her. She rose and closed the door with a casual sweeping arm. Sitting back down, she replied, "Yes. It is quite interesting. However, my appreciation for life and its wide diversity has rapidly matured. I have thought much about the one who carried me and feel great appreciation. I do not know who she was. I was never allowed to meet her as I grew. As I said before, hybrids are nothing more than throwaway replaceable servants. Some of the hybrids do meet their mothers. Horribly, according to what I have found in the Grey's database, she died. That is all I know. They may have disposed of her. It is a hideous waste and not consistent with highly intelligent beings. Thanks to a random positive event of chemistry and biology, I became a gift from your wife and able to carry part of her spirit into the future. Remember me telling you that I came from your Louise's DNA?"

"Of course I remember. But... when did you finally come to realize your place in the Grey's social organism?"

"Perhaps thirty of this planet's sun risings and settings before the Grey's assigned me to monitor your awakening."

"You mean, days?"

"Yes, although a day has no meaning down here."

He looked at the door and smiled at her. "Is it okay for you to shut out the sphere?"

"Bryan," she said, "it can pass through the door like it is vapor, if the Greys so desire."

"I didn't know if... wait... I saw one do that after it sponged my brain while I was sleeping." He stopped, gazing off. "I just happen to think... if it can go anywhere... then what about us and..."

"Yes. Do not worry now." She took a bite of her food and then her gaze fell softly on him. She didn't speak.

"What?" he asked. "Do you want to ask me something? I feel it."

"Are you comfortable with me... and the fact that I am part... ?"

Bryan hadn't heard her express anything with such emotional insecurity. She sounded as if she needed reassurance about her humanness. "It may not seem like much of a consequence but humans like knowing our DNA chain. In a way, it comforts us, helps us feel connected. Now, Louise's family chain is your family chain. I'm very glad to be with you—for who you are, regardless of your DNA chain."

"That sounds nice. My Grey component most probably came from donors living here or possibly from the repository the Greys brought with them from their home planet. The Greys do not care about any spiritual connection between a child and its birthing parent or its hereditary line, except for the components composing the DNA and what manipulations they can achieve, moving closer to their goals."

"What are their goals?"

"As near as I can conclude, they want improved physical ability, faster mental increases, longer age, and perhaps most importantly, reduction of DNA replication errors... a clean DNA resource."

He stared at a spot on the floor in absentminded reflection, sliding back in years to times more pleasant and simple. His voice emerged with a longing tone. "We appreciate who came before us, appreciate the origin of our line of DNA, if you will. It may be primitive but I suppose it helps us feel we aren't alone and that every one of us belongs to something beyond us. We don't actually refer to DNA much. We celebrate age and long lives. It's probably because we don't live that many earth years."

"The Greys live several hundred earth years. They have worked to increase their longevity and their methods of producing young Greys, using their problematic cloning. You know, the Greys are not matured in a living Grey female as they were thousands of years ago. And that may have contributed to their soulless existence and their disregard for the life of other creatures. They are grown in a type of incubator... actually there is one on level thirteen. That is where I was birthed... down there." She stopped. Her brow rose. She said, "I hate what they do with living beings... animals or intelligent species."

Bryan, seeing her expression of deep feelings and concealed sensitivity, tapped his hand on the table to break away from the depressive tone. He raised his head energetically. "So what is their planet like?"

"All I can tell you is what I learned from their data system. Remember, I have not even seen this planet's sun or sky." She blinked several times, as if in thought. "Their civilization is around forty or fifty thousand years beyond where humans developed electricity. Their planet has a red sun like yours. They fear their sun's hydrogen consumption rate, which forms helium in a fusion reaction. They fear the hydrogen is decreasing. They have been seeking other planets to inhabit. Their planet is larger than this one, but it is at a similar distance from their sun, so they have liquid water, and an oxygen and nitrogen atmosphere. Their gravity is a little higher."

"The gravity explains their smaller bodies."

"Yes. Their planet experiences higher temperatures in their warm season and colder temperatures in their cold season, all due to the shape of their orbit, which is more elongated than Earth's. They have two moons, several active volcanoes, and two salt water oceans. Their population went through several cycles of change, arriving at the controlled numbers they have now. Their control of population with their birthing and DNA manipulations hasn't changed for the last ten thousand years. Their manufacturing is regulated and is limited to creating artificial food from constituent molecules, and robots for labor such as ship construction and cleaning debris created by the weather. They control the weather reasonably well, maintaining a balance in the planet's energy cycle. They don't need to manufacture anything like cars or other goods since what they use has a long lifetime."

"No wonder they control the population... equilibrium with resources."

"That's part of it. The individual in their society has responsibilities to the collective, which they perform from their own housing compartment. They spend their non-collective time attached to the learning systems. They have no activities out in their environment. Their energy comes from conversion devices that extract energy from the universe. They have a more complicated name for it, but Earth science calls it dark energy. They have a large effort in their space exploration, building many ships, which is where the most intelligent of their species employ themselves. They have colonization efforts on several planets, so their species will survive if their sun starts to expand. The drive to colonize other species and worlds is in their collective mind with unbridled control from cold logic. They are driven to spread their system. They believe their way is best."

Bryan envisioned a robot colony, as if his dreams of artificial intelligence had existed for eons and had formed its own society, all its members moving according to a single computer program. "If they thrive with a collective mind, do they have a central governing body?"

"They have a central committee that establishes controls; it changes through a consensus of the members. Members are picked based on intelligence every two sun cycles." She sighed, sounding tired. "They have no religion and do not believe in a supreme creator of the universe."

"Do you believe in a universal creator?" His uncertainty about her feelings came out in his voice.

"I do." She looked at him thoughtfully. She ran the back of a finger down his cheek. "There are so many civilizations in the universe, recorded by the Greys, many of which have existed tens of thousands of years longer than the Greys. And from what I have learned, most have such a belief, derived from the way the universe came into existence, that it was not always here, and the obvious cause and effect logic."

He nodded. "Thanks for sharing that."

The corners of her eyes dropped. "The Greys are a spiritually dead civilization. They have no activity in art, recreation, sport, or enjoyment."

She sat back, folded her arms on her chest, and studied him as if waiting for his reaction.

As he gazed at her and at her very human worried face, he wanted to make everything all right for her, and while doing that he'd like to escape to daylight himself. Talking with her was all he could think of for the moment. A reflection slashed across his mind. It was the last time he talked with Louise in a reminiscent manner. He told himself that Louise would have liked Liana. What was wrong with him? Liana was Louise, in a way, and much more.

Bryan pulled on his face, absentmindedly brushed a finger across his nose, and sighed. "I haven't talked about family for a long time," he said. "I guess I should since I may not be around much longer."

Her eyes closed easily. "You know better than talk like that."

Her reminder surprised him, brought back a feeling of courage, adding to his admiration for her. "Sorry, you're correct." He scratched his neck, resetting his mind. "Continuing with my life's resume... my father worked in a factory... in manufacturing, and my mother worked in a county government office reviewing and filing records. We lived in a small town in the state of Pennsylvania, which is near the east coast of the country. I always liked science and computers, and in college I decided to study computer science and artificial intelligence."

Liana leaned forward. "That is interesting about the computer study. The Greys moved through the development of artificial intelligence technology and eventually stopped. In their data of the learning machine, I found they concluded that the risks greatly exceeded the benefits. I found a report indicating they had a scare about ten thousand of their solar cycles in the past. It seems they created an artificially intelligent device that eventually began altering its own programming code and its behavior rules, began replicating brain components, altering its power generation to make it more autonomous, and it eventually killed several Greys."

"Some of our scientists have proposed the same sort of thing for computers here."

"After quite some time, the Greys discovered they could create and control biological forms just as easily, and terminated all their efforts in artificial computer intelligence. They still use computers and large knowledge databases. When they moved to using biological robots, they disregarded the fact that the biologicals were alive and had a spirit."

"Interesting."

A moment went by without them speaking.

Bryan whispered, "The things I remember about my family are the holidays and birthdays. Our holidays, days we use for celebration, brought family together with food, gifts, and remembrances. Humans bring their lineage together to celebrate their connection, their common origin. With your DNA from Louise, maybe one day you can meet some of her family. That would be your connection in the human chain of evolution."

"How long were you with your Louise?"

"Three years."

"That was not very long. I am sorry for you."

"You and I will live for her. I have room in my soul to love you like I did her."

Liana closed her eyes for a moment like she was visualizing something. "In the future, I will consider meeting some of the humans connected to my genetics. My feelings are far from that point." She pressed her lips together and blinked. "You should know everything."

"What?"

"I just happened to think… I never told you about an abominable form of genetic work the Greys have carried out down on level thirteen."

"More ghoulish horror?"

"There are creatures down there that are part human and part earth-animal." She covered her mouth with her hand. "They have released some of them into areas of the earth."

Bryan wondered if she would cry. "Don't worry, we will end it. It's not your fault."

She looked at him with tears forming in her eyes. Her voice crashed to a whisper. "I could have had animal DNA. They could have made me with…"

"Honey, you don't have anything but Louise's beautiful DNA and part of a Grey's form of DNA. I know a female when I see one." He paused and then his eyes danced. "Didn't you look in the data system at the report on their procedure used to bring you to life?"

Her eyes brightened. "Yes. I did look."

"You are fine. Correct?"

"Yes. But…"

"Forget that horror. You're fine. I love you. And you have me beat by a mile."

"A what?"

"Just a figure of speech." He shed a long breath and gazed warmly at her. "You're fantastic."

Chapter Fifteen

The door to the nourishment room opened. A female hybrid stood in the doorway with the silver sphere still hovering in the hall a few feet behind the hybrid.

Liana had only seen the female a few times, including occasions in their sleeping quarters. The female, a large-boned Grey creation with brown hair cut to four or five inches, had a large masculine head with bony brow typical of a Grey and large almond-shaped dark eyes. Her small mouth formed a grayish thin line.

"I am Daulak Gufbou," the female hybrid said with an uneven voice that sounded dry. "We are to talk."

From the hybrid's name, Liana positioned the five-foot visitor's probable function in the servant staff. By her name, she was of the lowest intelligence level, a Grey-human clone, and the Greys probably only used her for errands and simple labor. Daulak was not one of the better genetic accomplishments. Liana's face became stern as she stood and faced Daulak. She felt disgust and a touch of amusement at Markak's trivial game.

"Daulak, your voice is dry," Liana said. "You must not use it much." Liana expected a sudden announcement of orders or a repeat of the previous words. "Come and sit at the table. Drink something for your throat."

The hybrid stepped over to the table with small erratic jerks in her movement, her balance appearing impaired. She pulled back a chair and sat, looking at Liana. "That is true, but I do enjoy using my vocal capability," Daulak said.

"Are you here to get something to drink or replace some of the food compartments?" Liana suspected that neither of those reasons fit into the chance encounter and its curious timing.

"I would like something to eat," Daulak said in a hesitating manner.

"A food bar?"

"Yes, a sweet one. I like those."

Liana retrieved a bar from a compartment and placed on the table in front of Daulak. Liana sat down on the opposite side of the table. She glanced at Bryan and then Daulak who took a bite of her sweet bar and began chewing. "Did you have any other reason for coming here?" Liana asked.

"I was ordered to find you," Daulak said, sounding as if Liana was a distraction. Daulak smiled at Liana with eyes that seemed detached and unaware.

"What is the reason for you seeking me?"

"I do not know." Daulak looked down at her food.

Liana felt a twinge of insult and instantly realized her thought was unusual and strange, nearly an embarrassment, as if she had surrendered to animal mentality; it insulted her intelligence. "What were you supposed to do when you found me?"

Daulak blinked, tilted her head, and looked off. Her voice emerged with a lilting tone. "I was ordered to talk to you." She paused. Her eyes settled easily on Liana. "I almost forgot. Markak ordered you to go to his level and support work with new arrivals. So, I am here. I am telling you his message."

"Thank you," Liana said.

Liana sent a thought to Bryan: *Bryan, the presence of this low intelligence hybrid, whose normal assignment is common labor, indicates Markak is scripting some sort of entanglement scenario. He sent the hybrid to distract me and prevent me from attending to my assigned subject. It means the Greys plan to do something with you and do not want me protecting you. I believe they know my feelings have grown for you. They are ready to end us.*

He nodded.

Liana studied Daulak for a moment with a hint of amusement in her eyes, and then with an absence of emotion, she rested her hands on her lap. "I believe we are approaching a turning point," Liana said aloud.

The hybrid, Dauasi Ziebou, stepped into the doorway, his shoulders drawn back, his chin raised, and a spot gleaming on his forehead. He glared at Liana. "You are to attend Markak on level fourteen to help with new arrivals," Dauasi said, enunciating the words strongly.

"Markak has acquired new human subjects," Liana said. "Is that correct?"

"Yes. You are to proceed to down to him at once." The hybrid's voice was jarringly harsh.

"We were just discussing that with Daulak," Liana said plainly.

"Markak sent me to help her."

She eased her chair back and stood. Her face showed only calm. She looked coldly at Dauasi Ziebou for several moments, thinking.

Bryan's eyes moved from Dauasi to Liana. Daulak sat passively at the table as if awaiting instruction.

Liana sent a stream of words into Bryan's mind: *It is time to set a chain of events into motion. I have to play Markak's game but I will protect you no matter what happens.* She turned to Dauasi. "Dauasi, will you escort this subject to his cell?"

"Yes."

"What if... while you're gone?" he asked. "I don't like the looks of this."

"I'll find you." Liana turned abruptly like she had flipped a switch and marched briskly into the hall.

***

After she disappeared from sight, Bryan sat in his chair, leaning back with his arms folded on his chest. He guarded his mind, burying his growing anxiety. He furtively observed Dauasi, waiting for a command to leave for his cell. Daulak rose from the table and walked to the door.

Bryan sat forward. "I would like to finish my food before going to my cell."

"Finish quickly," Dauasi said.

A silver sphere entered the room and took position just above the door, just before a male hybrid and the male Grey, Haazon Temtso entered.

The two hybrids and the Grey communicated. Dauasi Ziebou and Daulak Gufbou abruptly walked out of the food room, seemingly with sudden purpose, disappearing down the corridor.

Bryan sipped part of his drink. He felt compelled not to move easily, giving Liana time to check out Markak and then execute her plan, whatever it was.

The hybrid and Haazon Temtso stood along a wall away from the door inside the room. Bryan thought they were negotiating through indecision on something.

The hybrid faced him. "I am Daukul Juibou, and you are to come with us for more instructional time on the learning machine," Daukul said.

Those words sent a chill over Bryan. "More time on the teaching machine. You are going to make me very smart?" He fiddled with his glass. He started to get up, his thoughts searching for a way to delay the situation. "I still have some of my drink remaining. May I finish it?"

Daukul Juibou turned to Haazon, his eyes darting, seemingly processing the communication from the Grey. "Do it quickly," Daukul said, frowning.

Afraid to push his luck, Bryan used two attempts at the last portion of his fluid before he slid his chair back and stood.

Down the hall they moved in a single line, Bryan following Haazon, and the hybrid walking behind him. The silver sphere followed the hybrid like a rear guard. When they approached the elevator, Bryan realized their destination wasn't the teaching machine, which was on level twelve where they were.

Inside the elevator, when the Grey touched the button for thirteen, Bryan thought of dissolution tables. Was he about to disappear by the Grey's disposal system for humans? The changing weight on his feet as the elevator dropped told him that he'd soon face a liquidating shower. He protected his mind with jumping thoughts of university work. He flashed on actions he could take to escape their turning him into protein soup. A fragment of an action, a low risk option, flitted through his brain. He tilted his body to the right while inclining his head from the right to the left. He bent at the knees, stood straight for a moment, and then dropped limply to the elevator floor. He sprawled, lying on his side with his face against the cold metal floor.

Haazon looked down at Bryan, his alien eyes searching, blinking, and suspicious.

The hybrid moved his head acknowledging communication from the Grey and stood menacingly over Bryan. "Get up," Daukul said aloud, harshly.

Bryan stiffened his mind, protecting it against the Grey and the silver sphere, pushing his thoughts to visualize the last paper he wrote in his university work. After a moment, he felt the eerie cool touch at three locations on his forehead, the Grey's creepy fingers. He fought an urge as it pushed into his brain, trying to activate his muscles to locomotion.

***

Liana stepped from the elevator at the bottom floor, anticipating deviations from the usual routine, immediately evaluating the area, and looking for hovering spheres. She felt an urge to race after answers that would further her understanding of Markak's plan. The urge came, she was certain, from her human emotions.

She saw nothing, no hybrids, no Greys, only an empty corridor. The circumstances fell within a range of events she hypothesized and felt she should succumb to buy more time. The deviations confirmed Markak had made a decision, first get rid of her subject, keep her isolated until time to take the child, and then terminate her. Markak's subtlety with which he moved to terminate Bryan and her was amusing. He could have simply taken Bryan and her to a laboratory and operated on them.

Did she have time for further checking? She walked briskly, checking three laboratories. She didn't find Markak or any other staff, which further confirmed her analysis. She ran back to the elevator hoping she hadn't taken more time for the confirmation step than she should have. Clearly, Markak intended for his operatives to take Bryan to the dissolution tables where they would remove a troubling influence within Markak's domain of horror. A horrible vision formed in her mind. She hammered the button in the elevator to go up to level thirteen.

A possible answer to one of her questions, the reason for not taking the simple path to terminating Bryan and her, fell into her analysis. Markak's gambit possibly included a psychological twist; perhaps the alien leader valued the observation of her developing human behavior in relation to her child's growth.

Liana burst from the elevator at the thirteenth floor and ran down the hall toward the room with the dissolution tables. Markak's minions had locked the door. She focused her mind, trying to detect thought-communication beyond the door. At least one hybrid and one Grey occupied the room on the other side of the door. Uncertain about the presence of a sphere, she whistled a sequence of recognition tones she had programmed into three spheres. A thought-level signal came to her from a sphere on the other side of the door. She commanded it to disable the door lock.

The door clicked.

Liana snatched the door open and stepped into the room. She immediately saw Bryan lying on a table. He didn't move. She looked for threats that could stop her or harm him. The only staff that would confront her were near the dissolution table. The hybrid, Daukul Juibou, and the male Grey, Haazon Temtso, snapped around from the table's operation, tensing at the sight of her. Neither the hybrid nor the Grey had a weapon. Liana's eyes returned to the table. The operation lights on the table told her it was set to dissolve the occupant and not induce hibernation. The table's covering began its slow descent from the ceiling. The tissue rendering fluid would start when the covering had completed its travel. She pushed a mind-command into the sphere, sending it down the hall.

The Haazon waved a signaling hand at Daukul. Daukul, a rare five-foot-eight hybrid lunged toward Liana, his hands spread like claws, reaching for her throat.

She slipped gracefully to the side of his lunge. Simultaneously, she sent a thought into the Daukul's mind. The hybrid paused and stood erect, dropping his arms impotently at his sides. His eyes fluttered.

Liana brought her focus to the Grey. Haazon's black eyes held onto her as he recoiled, hunching its shoulders defensively. Liana felt the Grey trying to probe her mind. She pushed with all her concentration into Haazon's mind, delivering another mental maze. She didn't know if it would work on the Grey. The Grey stopped moving and closed its eyes.

She rushed past the immobile Grey and hybrid to Bryan. She grabbed his arm and pulled him off the table. He landed with a thud on the floor just as the covering found its closure position. The dissolution fluid poured from above the table, washing across its vacant surface. Her heart shuddered for a moment and then she detected Bryan's thoughts. *He is alive!*

He moaned and rubbed his head.

Liana stooped down to him and caressed his cheek with the back of her hand. His eyelids moved and opened. He smiled at her.

"I'm glad you came when you did," he said, his voice raspy. "I didn't know how long I could fight them before I found myself on a table being dissolved."

"I'm glad you used your training," she said beaming at him.

"Yes."

She lowered her head a little as her mouth drew tight. "You... you were on the table when I arrived."

Shock exploded in his eyes. "Oh damn, I could have been..."

"Is that the physical structure or a curse word?"

"The curse word, damn. We'll work on that later."

"Okay, we must go quickly. Now, we must hide and stay away from Markak's trap until I can take us to the next step."

"What's the next step?"

"Waiting for the military and their search for their man." She studied him.

"You're thinking of using a military invasion as cover for our escape?" He frowned.

Her face stiffened. "It's a critical part, but precipitating it is problematic. I don't have complete control of all the events that we face."

"What?"

"All we can do is try."

"How can we avoid spheres that pass through doors?"

"By virtue of a sequence of beneficial cosmic events on the local scale. If they happen our probability will improve... like luck."

He laughed. "Since when do you use the concept of luck?"

"What can I say? It is my human part coming out." She fought a smile. "I have to acquire my devices."

"For the reactor room?"

"Some additional ones as well." She wiggled her nose like she was amused and eager. "We must go now. We must stay together. I don't know how long my mind puzzle will work on these two."

"I have no intention of leaving your side, ever."

They rushed from the room, jogging down the hall.

Bryan slowed. "Wait a minute," he said, breathing heavily. "I know how to influence the timing on the military."

Chapter Sixteen

Bryan ran with Liana down the hall on level twelve, fascinated by her incredible focus. Their movement made him question whether they could evade detection. There was no telling if or when the military might provide an opportunity for escape.

She stopped and opened the door to a long narrow room. Inside, feeble light spawned heavy shadows, making Bryan stare into the void for a moment before he could see no one occupied the room.

"Wait by the door," she said, closing the door.

Platforms designed for sleeping formed a line along one side of the room. A three or four inch thick pad covered the supporting surface.

"This is my sleeping quarters." Liana reached under her bed platform and removed two devices. "Give me your right hand," she whispered.

She took his hand, held one of the devices near his thumb, pushed a slide, and then she touched a button on the instrument. "Disabling the tracking implant again."

"Thank you. Now, where do we hide and for how long?"

"You said you had an idea. Whatever it is we must also consider gaining access to the freight elevator on this level so we can load the children at the opportune time."

"Will the children go without causing a fuss?"

"They are children and sometimes they question, but the Greys trained them to obey." Her eyes darted for a moment. "We must leave this room and hide. You must tell me your idea on the way. Ready?"

"Yes."

She cracked the door and peered out looking for Greys. "It is clear."

They scrambled down one hall and then another, stopping at an unidentified insignificant looking gray metal door. Liana stepped into the room that was only illuminated by the light from the hall. Bryan followed, halting abruptly as the door closed behind him, creating total darkness. The door latch clicked. A dull click at the wall brought a single light to life overhead.

"We're hiding in here?" Bryan whispered. "We are hiding in a maintenance closet with mops, brooms, and buckets.

"It is never used. I have never seen any of these materials used. We need time. There is not any better place to wait."

"We can't stay here for long. They'll find us with the spheres. Won't they?"

"Possibly." Liana dropped her head, staring at the floor in thought. "We will need to create a diversion in order to save the children—and ourselves. Based on their thoughts, I expected the military to invade by this time but—their action may not happen in time for us. I cannot understand how I miscalculated."

"You're only human." Bryan moved to the wall, moved a bucket out on the floor, and sat on top of it. "If you can safely make your way to the room with the tanks, I know how to stir the hornet's nest."

"What?"

"Bring the military down for a confrontation."

She stared at him.

"When I was in the tank room, I saw the severed arm from a military person. It was in the second vat. It had an identification patch on the remaining uniform sleeve. Could it be the man the military is trying to recover?"

"It could. I never saw a military man in the halls or laboratories. I did see an entry in the data system about a man who was not tested. The entry indicated his mind failed testing. The Greys assigned him to chemical processing. They recorded his origin as, elevator, which I have never seen. The Greys identify where they acquire new arrivals with planetary coordinates."

"If we could send that whole arm up in an elevator with the uniform attached, I would bet the military would come down here ready for battle to recover their man. The patch on his uniform read, Dreamland."

Liana nodded. "That identifying word matches the word I saw in a meeting on the military's level. If we do this, many military humans will die. Not just those who come down to take back their fallen comrade. Do you feel you could handle the moral question of destroying those lives?"

Bryan caressed her hand. "This facility is a cancer eating at the heart of my country and this world. Look at the horrors the military and Greys knowingly condone and carry out. I've heard that some people say these technical efforts, biological atrocities, and genetic violations are necessary to protect the country against other countries on the planet, but the Grey's motives are as perverse and black as the criminal humans authorizing this place with their backs turned. Cancers need cauterized and excised. It looks as if it's up to me and you to set the world back a little closer to balance." He paused. "Yes, I can handle the removal of a cancer. One of the elements in that removal is the destruction of the reactor. That will make this place uninhabitable, but I'm concerned about the Greys escaping."

Liana pulled her hand back, clutched her mouth for a moment. "I have other events to entertain them—if we get an opportunity. I am concerned about how long we will be able to hide before they find us and if the military will come. The military is vital!"

Bryan didn't like the word she used. It was the first time he'd seen her so uncertain, so worried. "It looks as if we sleep here tonight," he said. "The bundle of towels behind you on the shelf would help to fight the cold concrete floor."

***

It was ten-thirty in the morning when the Gulfstream G650 jet taxied from the runway over to the parking apron near the terminal building. Gutierrez descended the steps of the jet, following General Carpenter and General Warner, both dressed in crisp military uniforms, representing their responsibility with dignity. Looking toward the terminal gate Gutierrez saw a man holding a sign with the name, General Carpenter, on it. Next to the man was a Cadillac sedan, a roomy model from at least five years past, one made before downsizing took over. At the top of the small terminal was a sign for the Jicarilla Apache Nation Airport. He felt a pang of indecision, wondering if he had made a mistake in coming.

Carpenter looked up. "My kind of sky... not a cloud."

"Too bad we couldn't find a trout stream somewhere," Warner said. "Gutierrez, do you fish?"

"Yes, but never for trout. It looks too difficult."

"Nah," Warner said. "I could help you catch one in an hour."

Outside a door to the small terminal, Gutierrez noticed man who wasn't doing anything except smoking, standing with one hand casually draped from a trouser pocket. The man was definitely watching. Gutierrez couldn't decide whether he should feel worried or not about the guy. He glanced at the rental car and back at the man, nearly connecting eyes with the unflinching character. He remembered Harris and wondered if the UFO investigation group was watching for him.

"Okay, gentlemen, now is your chance to change your mind," Carpenter said as they approached the rental car.

"I have to go," Gutierrez said.

"I didn't flatten my ass in the plane to turn away from responsibility," Warner said.

"Sir, are you Carpenter?" a man said, standing beside the car in jeans, white shirt, and tie, holding the cardboard sign with Carpenter's name on it.

"Yes. Is this my car?"

The man gestured toward the car. "The keys are in the ignition. It's all yours. Your staff aide took care of all the paperwork. It's not a new car but she's in excellent condition."

"Very good. Thank you." Carpenter walked to the driver's side.

"Shall I open the trunk for your luggage?" the rental car man said. "Although, I don't see any luggage."

"That won't be necessary," Carpenter replied. "This is a short visit."

"Okay then, thanks for your patronage." The man nodded and walked toward the terminal door.

Carpenter looked over the top of the car at Gutierrez and Warner. "Gentlemen, climb aboard. We only have seven or eight miles." He pointed to the north. "See that rounded peak. That's where we're going."

Chapter Seventeen

Bryan felt Liana move against him. It seemed like morning but he wasn't certain. Her body lying against him reminded him of his Louise and brought back a memory of his previous life. They had lain with their backs touching after Liana wasn't comfortable with Bryan facing her and draping his arm over her. She had apologized about her nascent emotional state and then professed her love.

In Louise's pragmatic mind, she would have wanted him to continue on with his life by finding a new companion just as he would have wanted the same for her. He and Louise had their youth, their family-formation years ahead of them. Liana was the most incredible female he had met since Louise and they would keep Louise's memory alive in a child—if they could survive.

"I didn't want to wake you," Liana whispered, sitting up.

"I just woke. Are we escaping today?"

"The random variable is the military. I must go to the tank room and dispatch the horrible invitation on the elevator, provided the body-part is still retrievable."

"Do you want me to go with you?"

She shook her head. "If I run into someone, the questions would cause hostility. By going alone, I can fabricate some ruse." She gazed at him sadly. "I know it will be hard for you to wait, not knowing how the plan is taking place, but that will have to be your burden and task."

"You're right. Go ahead." He pulled a food bar from his pocket and held it up. "You want a bite before you go?"

"I will have more control without those molecules being processed in my stomach."

"Please knock three times and then two when you return so I know it's you." He thought for a moment. "May I give you a kiss before you go?"

Liana leaned over to him. He kissed her.

"I like that custom," she said with a smile.

"Please be careful. I love you."

She turned back to him. "I love you, too."

***

Down on the fourteenth floor, Liana pushed open the door to the stairs, searching in both directions along the passageway. No one. She emerged as if nothing unusual was taking place, adapting the demeanor of an obedient-hybrid, posture properly erect, walking with an unrushed pace toward her objective. She calculated that she would encounter one or more Greys on this level before she had completed her task, especially since Greys frequented this level more heavily, moving to and from the laboratories.

As she moved down the hall, she quickly considered the possibility of failing because of her human emotions. She immediately purged that doubt with her confidence and determination that the logic functioned supremely. At an early point when she questioned her own development, she researched the Grey's data on the maturation patterns of clones and hybrids. What she found had amazed her and precipitated a question about the thoroughness of the Grey's science. Nevertheless, here she was. Her metamorphosis these past few months, her explosive body changes, had caused her to make an occasional self-evaluation. Her development speed was more akin to a Grey, but her biology was more like a human's. The development of the child she carried and its gestation time was unknown, and unpredictable, even to her vast intellect. She guessed it might be close to that of humans.

Her new reason for escape and the planned destruction was more imperative than ever, but with innocent lives at risk it necessitated new safeguards. The equation had too many unknowns. Once the body-part was delivered, the military criminals overhead had to invade the Greys. If only she could prevent the Greys from combining their observations, forming a thorough analysis, and seeing her pattern of treachery. That was the Reticulan's strength and it was also their weakness, their need to cluster and pool their knowledge, their obsessive interdependence.

Liana turned down the hall leading to the vat-room. After she'd walked a few paces, the Grey, Nekzon Vagpok, and the male hybrid, Dauasi Suibou, emerged from a laboratory and stood at the side of the hall. Dauasi Suibou, about five-foot with an ill-nourished gaunt face, stood behind Nekzon. A weapon hung at Nekzon's waist, one of the cylinders, and it told her that Markak had issued an alert about her. Nekzon's shoulders pulled in as he stared at her. His mouth was hard, angry.

Events had taken place as she had strategized, although too quickly. She kept walking, ignoring Nekzon as if the day was normal and she was completing her usual duties.

Words began entering her mind, words from Nekzon, telling her that Markak wanted to discuss her human subject with her. Liana sent a reply thought: *I have a task to complete first. I will proceed to Markak quickly.*

Nekzon replied into her head that she was to stop the present task and immediately meet with Markak. For a fleeting instant, she read into Nekzon's Reticulan mind and picked up a deep hostile thought that Nekzon had failed to block. It was added indication that Markak had planned her immediate termination in addition to Bryan's. If they took her fetus now, it might not survive, even with the Grey's technology.

Liana looked down at Nekzon, blanking out a basal human emotion of disgust, blocking any mind probing he attempted, maintaining cold detachment. With explosive concentration, she pushed a logic-maze into his mind, including with it a hint for solution, and a mental picture of the supply closet where they had hidden during the night. In the next instant, she gazed at the hybrid, whose face suddenly contorted with confusion. She jammed a logic-puzzle into the hybrid's mind, not providing a hint for solution or termination.

Nekzon stood motionless. He appeared paralyzed, arms hanging impotently at his sides. His eyes slid closed. She saw his eyes moving under his eyelids like he was fighting disorientation and searching for something. She suspected he was engaged in a search for the key to unlock the maze.

Liana studied him for a moment, assessing her influence on him, considering whether she had set in motion what she had anticipated. Bryan may not have felt comfortable with her strategy but eventually he would play his part, if only the military would help in a timely manner. She removed the weapon from the Grey and hid it in her clothing.

She rushed into the room with the tanks, the Grey's biochemical holding of surplus tissue. Just inside, she found the tank that Bryan had identified. On the floor near the tank, she found a three-foot grappling device. Leaning it against her leg, she lifted the lid on the tank. A sickening stench, rising from the liquid, hung heavy in the air. She coughed, cleared her throat, and wincing against the smell, she continued. The liquid surface heaved and fell in miniature swells as it circulated. It presented no objects that she could see. She probed down into the liquid with the retraction arm, feeling objects bump against it. Part of a man's torso bobbed into sight and sank. She stirred the bottom repeatedly until an intact severed arm, including hand and fingers, circulated across the surface long enough she could nudge it to the side of the tank. Battling a sensation deep in her throat, something she hadn't experienced, she grabbed the body part with her hand, detesting the touch and smell. At the upper region of the arm she confirmed the identification word, Dreamland, and then she noticed a ring on one finger of the cadaver part. Perhaps those two elements of identification could entice the military to visit. She closed the lid, went to the corner of the room, and gazed down at a pile of discarded victim garments. She wrapped the arm, still dripping the disgusting tank liquid, in a lightweight human's jacket.

She ran down the hall toward the elevators. As she passed Nekzon still locked in her mind puzzle, she felt an emotion that she knew was human. It was satisfaction. It enfolded her as she considered the Grey learning how it felt existing under another creature's control. A second thought struck her; his inability to extract himself from the tangle in his mind. She needed him to recover so he could carry out his part in her theatrical tragedy, but she had no time to double-check him. It was funny how she was counting on a Grey to help with their own demise.

At the freight elevator, she signaled for a car to descend. A rare feeling of anxiety folded over her as she waited for it to arrive. She checked the hall for approaching Greys or an unfriendly sphere. Her concern was normal, although it was more human than she appreciated. The freight elevator seemed slow. It would be vital later. The elevator rattled. At last, it opened. Sadness rose inside her as she looked at the fragment of a human man in her hands. She could see in her mind the Grey's horrid act, the destruction of a soldier, by her analysis, in retaliation for a trespass. She reverently placed the soldier's arm in the middle of the elevator car's floor with the military's Dreamland patch facing the open door. She pushed the elevator button, sending the enticement up to the military's level. It was a taunt that a dutiful soldier couldn't refuse and she hoped they would plunge into the Grey's hell for their fallen comrade.

What if the Greys had completely scared the soldiers the first time, scared the courage from them? She had to get a message to them, a bit of insurance to ignite their fury.

At the left of the freight elevator door, she opened a dust-covered metal box hanging on the wall, and removed a dirt-laden emergency service telephone handset. It was possible that it didn't function and hadn't been used since the time of construction. She touched in the number written on a faded instructional sticker inside the box. The phone rang and rang and after she had counted twenty rings, she obtained a reply.

"Are you having trouble with the elevator?" asked a man, his voice showing his surprise. "Who is this? Who is down there?"

"Listen carefully," Liana said. "I have a message for Colonel Roth. The missing soldier he is seeking can be found on level fourteen in a room full of tanks holding human body parts. If he comes, he should not attempt recovery without sufficient weapons. Is that clear? If he wants his comrade, he should come today before the Greys dissolve the body. And please allow the freight elevator to descend as quickly as possible after the package has been removed. It is vitally needed."

"Who is this?"

"Tell him a friend called," Liana said. She hung up and closed the service telephone box, waiting for the elevator to return.

She hated enticing men into a conflict where many would no doubt die. She had no love for the Greys and these humans perpetuated evil. Humans served as test specimen under manipulation of a superior intelligence, a species dangling technology like a piece of meat before a starved animal. Something popped into her mind, a passage she had read during the months of her raging hunger for knowledge. The philosophical literature spoke of doing little harm to prevent great harm and misery for millions. The ill-smelling plan of hers was perhaps just that, but great risk awaited the children, not to mention a whole country.

A noise came from the elevator as it arrived. Liana went inside and looked up at the ceiling. Panels a foot-square formed the top of the elevator car. Three round can-lights provided light and a ventilation fan occupied the center of the ceiling. She reached up to the metal grille of the fan, pulled on it, testing its attachment. As she figured, the grille tipped downward with a spring-clip holding the opposite side. She removed one of her detonators, a hand-weapon, and a piece of cloth from inside her clothes at her waist. She wrapped the items to prevent them from vibrating and a party discovering them. She placed the package on the upper surface of the grille and replaced it. She looked up at the fan, checking if the bundle was visible, picturing in her mind possible future events. She thumped the grille with the back of her hand, checking for any attention-attracting rattling sound. Nothing.

Liana ran to the stairs, making her way back to the closet and Bryan.

***

Colonel Roth stood over the dismembered arm of a brother-soldier lying on the floor outside the elevator. He beat a clenched fist into his thigh as he seethed with blinding anger. Mathews, standing next to Roth with his arms folded on his chest, his mouth fixed with bitter determination, shook his head. Sergeant Blake looked on with a grimace from the side of the elevator.

"Colonel, sir, I couldn't leave it in the elevator... and... sir, someone called from down there... called on the elevator service phone," Sergeant Blake said. His eyes darted from Roth to Mathews and back.

"Who?" Roth said, frowning at Blake. "What?"

"It sounded like a woman... and—"

"Woman?" Roth said, his voice like a blast of air. "What did she say?"

"It was so fast... something like, 'The missing soldier is on level fourteen in a tank of body parts.' She said we should come with plenty of weapons and we should come today before the body is dissolved."

"Dissolved!"

"Yes, sir."

"My God," Mathews said.

Roth squinted as he clenched his teeth. "Those bastards." He stopped. "Blake, did we identify the ring on the hand?"

"Yes, sir, it's Sergeant Bauer's."

Sergeant Zane walked up to Roth, his eyes sweeping the floor until he stopped two feet from the arm. "Colonel, sir, I hope we're going to go get the rest of him."

Roth pushed a cigarette in his mouth, his brow pulled up as he glared transfixed at Bauer's arm. He pulled a gleaming silver lighter from his pocket, flicked it once, and raised the yellow flame to light his smoke. "We have to," Roth said sternly. "We don't leave men behind."

His cell phone rang in his pocket. He frowned. "What the hell?" He snatched the phone to his mouth. "Colonel Roth."

"Adrian, this is Vince."

"You shouldn't have called this phone."

"Hey, since you saved my ass with my wife the night I got blasted on tequila, I figured I'd let you know that two generals and some plain-suit dude just picked up a car at the airport thirty or forty minutes ago. I just happened to be delivering cleaning supplies."

"Any names?"

"One was Carpenter."

"Okay, thanks." Roth pushed his phone in a pocket as an alarm blared in his brain. He looked at Mathews and Blake. "We're going to have an unannounced inspection within hours... maybe one, maybe more."

Zane shook his head. "My butt-pucker factor just shot up three notches. Maybe we should wait a few days until the inspection has been finished and everything is back to normal. If we have an arm, there's no hurry to gather the rest of his body—unless they really would dissolve it."

Roth pulled the cigarette from his mouth and flicked off the ash. "Maybe it's time the brass learns what happens to our people." He sucked on his cigarette with one eye closed, avoiding the smoke.

"What are you thinking?" Mathews asked. His eyes narrowed as if suspicious and expectant.

"No. We go as soon as possible. Besides, they have never inspected anything below level ten. They can't go there without violating the damned agreement with those Grey bastards." His gaze drifted down the hall as his voice emerged thin as an afterthought. "By the time the inspection arrives our team will either be toes up or the Greys will be just a bad memory. If they court martial any of us, I'll go public. I'll mail a disclosure to so many media outlets that they'll think it's snowing."

"They'd shoot us first," Mathews said, his voice heavy, dry.

Roth turned to Zane. "Go quietly and tell our team to prep immediately for a recovery mission, descending from this floor in fifteen minutes. Anyone who wants to stay upstairs is free to do so. Make certain everyone wears the vests with the plates in case we run into one of their funky ray guns."

Zane laughed under his breath as a diabolical grin seemed to sign his mental-last-will-and-testament. "The quickest trigger wins. We can kill those Grey suckers if we can hit 'em." Stopping, as if struck by a sudden revelation he said, "I don't know what would be worse, a court martial or getting sliced by a blue beam from a ray gun." He paused, glancing at the floor. "Maybe we should wait, sir."

"Get after it, Sergeant."

***

Liana knocked three times and then two on the closet door, eager to feel Bryan's reassuring and supporting eyes. She opened the door. The light was off. She wondered what had happened. Then she saw him lying on the floor on top towels spread like a blanket. The light from the hall shown on his eyes. He popped up as if startled. She felt a little relief.

"You fell asleep?" she asked, slightly amused.

He blinked a few times and cleared his throat. "I thought the light might attract attention from under the door so I turned it off. A few minutes after I laid down, I think the stress got to me. I dozed off."

"No harm done and the light was a good idea."

"Did you send the package to the military?"

"And I called to give them a warning."

"I wonder how much time we have."

"I ran into a Grey and gave him a head full of cobwebs to keep him busy for a while. I believe it is around late morning, so it is going to be a long day and night... and if the military does not come... we could..."

"The message has to stir up the soldiers. It has to."

"I hated to do it, disrespecting a corpse and initiating violence."

"Please come over here and sit next to me. I'd like to hold you in case something goes off the rails."

"What?"

"In case of a malfunction in the plan," he said with a subtle smile. He held out his left hand.

Liana eased herself down to the floor beside him, feeling the warmth of his hand on her waist. She turned to him and found his eyes.

"It's fantastic feeling you next to me," he whispered. "You might find it silly, but humans like to hold each other, like to touch, like to kiss. Maybe it's electrical." He grinned and moved his lips toward her.

She couldn't wait and pressed her mouth on his. *If only the moment could last forever* she thought. She pressed herself into him, sending her arms around him, squeezing him to her body, feeding a hunger that had grown quickly in the short time she had come to know him. She knew it was her human half and she loved it.

After a moment, Bryan drew his lips away.

"I understand why you like to touch," she whispered.

"Liana, is it too early to dream about us?"

"You do not really think like that do you?" she said. "We cannot fail." She thought to share some of her thinking and statistics she had worked out in her head, but she needed his head clear for the coming confrontation that she had anticipated. She rested in his arms.

***

A short while later, Bryan winced in pain and moved his leg from its position on the concrete floor. He looked down at Liana's head resting on his stomach and at her peaceful and unwrinkled face. He brushed his hand across her hair.

Something thumped against the door.

Her head popped up. She hesitated for a moment, thinking, and shot to her feet. Bryan jumped up. Liana watched the door.

The door opened, pouring in light. Out in the hall two male hybrids, Dauasi Ziebou and Dauasi Suibou, blocked the door. Two Greys stood a few feet behind the hybrids, Nekzon Vagpok and Haazon Temtso.

Inside Liana's head shot commanding words that they must follow Nekzon Vagpok and Haazon Temtso.

She slashed her gaze across their hands and bodies, noticing that Nekzon carried a weapon. It was clear Markak had ordered them to use it if she didn't comply. Nekzon would slice her in half without the slightest hesitation and smile as he was doing it. She knew this encounter preceded Markak terminating Bryan and her.

She steeled herself, drawing up one of her unemotional faces and thinking of preserving Bryan's positive attitude, she turned to him. "We must go with them. Please do not make any overt motions. They are prepared to terminate both of us at any moment."

He nodded. "I thought I heard the command too," he whispered.

Liana looked at him strangely, as if impressed. She wanted to say something to him but couldn't with the two Greys nearby. And she couldn't tell Bryan of her gambit. She would shield her thoughts, open some of them that she wanted accessed, and offer hints in other fragmented thoughts. She had human hope.

Over a short time, she had observed that her mental capabilities confounded the Greys, and she had detected increasingly cautious communications from them. She would not underestimate them, having seen too much of their chillingly evil control. Markak stood out as the primary threat to their lives and she had concluded that he stood atop their intelligence level. Bryan and her meeting with him required supreme delicacy despite the likelihood their deaths quickly approached. She began moving into the hall.

Liana turned to Bryan, realizing he was sending her a thought stream. "Stop, Bryan. Others may understand. Use verbal."

Bryan's brow rose. He nodded. "I hope our package achieves the desired provocation in time," he whispered.

Several feet into the hall, a stream of words rolled into Liana's mind from Nekzon, telling her that Markak would deal with her severely. Markak would interrogate her.

Nekzon pointed a finger toward the elevator.

Outside the door, Liana noticed Bryan's face. "I see doubt on your face," she said softly. "I share some of the same fear, but there are many possibilities to unfolding events."

He touched her hand.

When the elevator door opened, the two hybrids watched suspiciously, drawn into tense sentinels, as Bryan and Liana walked into the compartment. Liana got the sensation that they wanted an escape attempt and found their behavior surprising malevolent. They all descended in the elevator.

On the way down, Liana, looking for indicators of coming events, observed that Nekzon had a faint muscle movement in his jaw. She sensed that he was struggling with something and it appeared he could barely control his anger, possibly because of the mind puzzle she had given him. She had humiliated him. She smiled to herself. He had done well with her mind-puzzle. Nekzon's throwback to past evolutionary emotions like hatred and retribution was instructive and curious.

Releasing a sigh, she thought of the programmed timer for the explosives that caressed the waterlines. She visualized in her thoughts how the waterlines would, when blown, flood the bottom floor with water. A thought of explosives in the spacecraft hangar on level eleven rolled through her mind. Then she thought of Markak.

Nekzon raised his head sharply as if alerted, stiffening in preparation to take action, his eyes froze in concentration on Liana.

Bryan clenched his jaw.

Verbally Liana said, "Do not despair, Bryan, they dance to my waltz. I just waved my baton."

He frowned at her, trying to make sense of her comment.

Chapter Eighteen

The elevator door opened at the Grey's bottom floor.

Markak approached the elevator followed by two Greys, a tall male with an abundance of facial lines, Haazon Peutso-ui, a female Grey, Haagui Zielam, the male hybrid with the bumpy head, Daukul Juibou, the small female hybrid who needed a wig, Dauasi Temgam, and a female hybrid obscured by the taller Daukul Juibou.

Dauasi Ziebou, standing at the rear of the elevator, nudged Bryan in the back with his fist and then pushed Liana to exit. They stepped from the car, shuffling forward, stopping a few feet out from the elevator, facing Markak and his entourage.

"This looks like the end for us," Bryan said aloud in a whisper.

Liana glanced at him and back to the gathering. "There is still hope. Remain calm."

"Maybe." He sighed loudly and suddenly lunged across the few feet toward Markak. Surprised by the irrational act, Markak jerked backwards a step, but too late. Bryan wrapped one arm around the tiny alien waist and took Markak's slender neck in his other hand. Markak's mental commands attacked Bryan's concentration. He screamed at Markak. Markak's eyes exploded with shock. Markak's support group backed away from him as if taking a tactical formation. Nekzon reached his hand to the cylindrical weapon at his waist.

"Bryan, you can't win by doing this," Liana said in a calm voice. "Think about it."

"I am," Bryan yelled.

Markak raised his free arm and pointed toward a hybrid at the back of the group. Dauasi Ziebou moved past Liana and stood a few feet from Markak's party.

"Daulak Gufgam, Markak requests you to step forward for recognition," Dauasi Ziebou said aloud.

A female hybrid with red-blonde short hair moved forward. Her head, while larger than a human and more like a Grey, had the human female gentle jaw and chin. The hybrid stepped through the group and stood a few feet from Liana.

"Louise!" Bryan said on a burst of breath.

"Please Bryan, it is not her," Liana said. "It is a clone. Don't be manipulated."

Markak held an open hand toward the hybrid.

The female hybrid looked at Bryan. "I... I am your companion," Daulak Gufgam said with a voice that was faintly feminine and a tone of something else unidentifiable. "You can live with me."

"What in the hell have you done to my Louise?" Bryan screamed. He tightened his grip on Markak's neck. "You bastards!"

Markak pointed to Dauasi. Immediately Dauasi Ziebou said, "You can release Markak or we can kill Daulak Gufgam."

"Bryan, she's a Grey-human clone," Liana said softly. "It is a horrible copy of your Louise. The clone does not know you or remember your past. I never knew who she was. I never saw your Louise and we have no mirrors. Please remember our future. Please trust me. Do it for our child."

He looked at Liana and released his grip on Markak. He lowered his head and stepped over to Liana, taking her hand.

"I'm sorry," he said.

Nekzon walked immediately to Markak, the two of them communicating mentally. Nekzon moved a hand in a small gesture like he was making a presentation. They gazed at each other for another moment. Markak nodded.

Liana suspected Nekzon had just shared her thought-information with Markak and Markak was performing logic analysis on it. Just then, she felt Markak creeping into her mind, searching instead of communicating. She thought of an explosive with an activated timer, she visualized the time set for the detonation, which approached within the current earth-time hour. She thought of a failsafe and the confidence that there wasn't any way to stop the explosion. In her mind's eye, knowing Markak was monitoring her thoughts, she saw all the bulkhead doors exploding, allowing a flood of water, a torrent plummeting to the bottom level and all levels occupied by the Greys. She envisioned the nuclear reactor melting without cooling water. With Markak still on the mental telephone line, she sent a thought to Bryan, reminding him not to think about helping with placing the explosives, which she knew he would for a fleeting moment, long enough for Markak to acquire the thought. In her mind came an image of a sphere going to the hangar to activate explosives.

Markak became still as his brow rose.

His eyes grew larger than Liana had ever observed. She sensed he was engaged in evaluating his alternatives to stop the flood and prevent the reactor meltdown. She detected Markak's fleeting thought of a weapon slicing Bryan across the midsection. Markak's mental sharing told her that he was through dealing with problems caused by her and Bryan.

The rattle of a mechanism in the freight elevator's operation drew her attention. Its floor indicator changed from fourteen. It moved upward, raising her hope with it.

Markak turned sternly to the female Grey, Haagui Zielam.

Liana picked up part of Markak's message to Haagui Zielam. He told her to rush to the room containing the emergency controls, where she had to activate the emergency water cutoff, the control at the facility's surface that regulated water for subfloors. Nothing was to slow her or stop her. Haagui scurried grotesquely down the hall, moving faster than Liana had ever seen a Grey move.

Markak and Nekzon looked at each other for a moment and then both regarded Liana. Liana thought she saw a hint of amusement on Nekzon's usually inscrutable face.

Nekzon glared at Liana and pointed toward the opposite wall of the corridor. With the other hand he reached to his waist and removed his cylindrical weapon. Liana backed toward the far wall with Bryan at her side.

"I am sorry for my miscalculation," she said in a soft regretful voice. "I do not feel bad for reaching the end with you, but our child... will never see the sky."

He pressed his mouth into a resolute line. "You did your best."

***

When the freight elevator arrived, Colonel Roth pushed the control to hold the car. He stood at the door, watching his men move into the car, anxious to collect his missing man.

His cell phone rang. He hesitated with an angry frown and then grabbed it. "Colonel Roth."

"Sir, this is Corporal Blackwood, at the reception area."

"The main gate?"

"No sir, here in the building... up front. Two generals and a congressman are here for an inspection. It's to take place as soon as possible."

"The generals are already in the building?" Roth said. He looked at the questioning faces of his men, who all began shaking their heads.

"Yes, sir."

"Take them to my office. No. Wait. Order the congressman to leave. Only military are allowed. I don't care if the president is here. Have the civilian wait outside the building. If that doesn't stall them for a while, then take all of them to my office. General Warner is the only one who can authorize a civilian."

"Sir, I think one of them is Warner."

"Remind the general that I have local safety discretion. We have an unsafe situation that I'm currently troubleshooting. I'll be there in thirty minutes. I repeat... the civilian goes." Roth closed his phone. He stepped into the elevator car and hit the button for the Grey's bottom level. "To hell with the generals," Roth said. "We're going. Safeties off."

Zane and Blake slapped their hands together above their heads.

* * *

The elevator rattled.

Markak turned toward the door.

Liana fixed her eyes on it for a moment and then glanced at Bryan, her face sharing her hopeful fear.

Markak's bulky brow lowered as he warily watched for an explanation. He turned to the hybrids. They quickly lined up side-by-side on his right. He looked at Nekzon, their eyes holding a connection as their minds seemed in communication for a moment. Markak, like a ghostly specter, pointed at the wall behind them, opposite the elevator. He glared at Liana with morbid attentiveness.

Liana heard Markak speak in her head: "You served a part in an experiment and you confirmed our premise for hybrids functioning as a colonization force. Hybrids can cohabit and breed with humans. Our trial is over. You will now discard your attachment for the human."

Showing no emotion, she thought to Markak: *No. I cannot break a spiritual trust.*

In her head, she heard Nekzon: "Stand next to the subject. Markak will observe the termination of your life and your subject."

Liana replied to Markak and Nekzon: *You will destroy a child conceived during your experiment.*

Swiftly Markak sent her a thought: "The experiment will be easily repeated. You no longer have value. Do as ordered. You have failed compliance."

She pressed her back against the cool concrete wall, clasping Bryan's hand. It was clear by the way Markak reacted, giving his personal attention, ordering Nekzon to bisect their bodies with the ray weapon, that the experiment was only a part of the situation. She had embarrassed Markak, the Reticulan leader. A lowly hybrid and her subject had tarnished Markak's reputation and opened doubt to his intelligence and management. She found the scenario amusing, the way Markak wanted a dramatic execution, reducing himself to violence characteristic of a lower intelligence species. It seemed he needed to save face.

"Bryan, I didn't know that they had cloned Louise," Liana whispered. "I had seen her infrequently but not knowing what I looked like, I couldn't compare myself to her. No mirrors. The reference about the clone in the data system made no connection for me. I'm so sorry."

"Liana, I love you. Forget it."

Nekzon raised his weapon. He pointed it at Liana.

The elevator rattled loudly.

Nekzon snapped around, looking at the elevator.

Liana squeezed Bryan's hand. "Perhaps the dance is underway."

Bryan frowned at her with a quizzical expression.

The freight elevator door opened.

Twelve soldiers poured from the elevator like molten steel, moving fluidly into combat formation opposite the Greys. Each soldier carried a tactical machine gun, grenades, night vision glasses rotated up from view, and communication devices at their throats with connections to ear pieces. In their defensive posture, they sighted their rifles at the Greys and hybrids.

The Greys and hybrids formed a tense line, backing up three paces as the last soldier stepped into position.

Nekzon moved over to Markak's side, disregarding Liana and Bryan.

Liana nudged Bryan to move a few feet down the hall, away from the line of military weapons.

Colonel Roth stood in the center of his soldiers with his gun raised like a lance and his eye sighting at Markak's head.

"We want our soldier's body!" Roth said. "We know you have him. We know you took him and butchered him."

Markak turned quickly to the hybrid, Dauasi Ziebou.

Dauasi Ziebou instantly stepped next to Markak, looking at Roth. Dauasi Ziebou spoke, his voice mechanical and calm. "We do not have a body. We do not have a soldier."

Roth's eyes narrowed and his jaw muscles hardened. "That's a damn lie. You can't hide behind any treaty. We're not leaving until we get our comrade's body."

A whooping siren screamed, echoing throughout the concrete cavern.

Roth shot his eyes at Captain Mathews.

"That's from the nuclear reactor, sir," Mathews said, his gaze moving back to the Greys. "That's big trouble!"

Liana pulled Bryan two more steps down the hall toward the stairs. "The Greys shut off the water," she said.

Bryan's face looked as if he'd had an epiphany. "To prevent your flood." He grinned.

"We'll go soon." She moved three more steps, watching the confrontation at the elevator now from thirty feet away.

Dauasi Ziebou faced Roth again. "One of your people has disabled and shut off the water going to the reactor cooling system," Dauasi said.

Dauasi turned toward Liana.

"That mutation is trying to blame us," Liana said. She knew she was acting irrationally but she felt invigorated. She nudged Bryan. "Shout and tell Roth that Markak is lying about the soldier."

Bryan yelled, "Roth, Markak lies. He has your soldier and he shut off the water to save his own ass from being flooded. He knew the reactor would melt down like Chernobyl. But he doesn't care. He couldn't survive a flood but he could the radiation. He can fly away."

"You bastard," Roth shouted at Markak, instantly aiming his gun Markak's head. The soldier standing next to the elevator, holding its door open, stepped up to the firing line.

Liana tugged on Bryan's hand. "Now."

They scrambled to the stairs that were now only a few feet away. They climbed as fast as they could. From behind them, at the confrontation, machinegun fire erupted in a cacophony of random bursts and continuous streams of bullet-concussions mixed with cries, squeals, and an eerie humming-whoosh.

Liana paused on a step. She slid a cigarette-size object out from her garment at her waist, pushed a spot on its surface, and replaced it. After a moment, an explosion rumbled in a distant area of the concrete structure.

"What was that?" Bryan asked, puffing for breath.

"Your explosives on the waterlines."

Arriving at the twelfth floor, Bryan and Liana ran to the children's housing and training room. She opened the door while he kept watch in the hall. When she stepped into the room, a female hybrid, Daulak Gufbou, and a female Grey, Haagui Tempok-uwe, rose from their chairs. They remained motionless as if confused by the sudden visit and change of routine.

Liana sent a thought: *How are the children today?*

Haagui replied to Liana in thought: "They are fine. Why do you visit?"

Almost before Haagui had finished, Liana pushed a thought-puzzle into both the hybrid and Grey's mind.

The hybrid started raising her arm and stopped. Her hand slowly dropped to waist level, appearing as if she wanted to shake hands. Her eyes glazed and she stared off in the distance. The Grey stared ahead, motionless, as she fought for the solution of the Liana's mental maze.

A constant shrill alarm replaced the whooping siren. In the distance, Liana could still hear gunshots, although their frequency had dropped.

She waved her hand for Bryan.

"This is a bunch to handle," he said as he moved close to the door.

Liana sent a command into the minds of the children to follow the man to the elevator. In unison, the children stood and walked, accepting her as an authority figure. Bryan escorted them quickly to the freight elevator as Liana followed.

The precious time that the Grey's stole from the children was another horror. She pushed it away and rushed ahead, calling the freight elevator to their level. An ominous feeling struck her. A soldier could have reopened the elevator after it had closed. She hadn't accounted for possible damage to the elevator during the firefight.

"What's wrong?" Bryan asked. His eyes hanging expectantly on her reply.

"I overlooked something."

"The elevator's not coming up?" he asked.

Liana heard the building fear in his voice. "I need you calm and clear thinking," she said.

He mashed his mouth in disappointment. "Sorry. I'm at your side."

"I feel a vibration in the elevator shaft," she said. She looked around the hall. "The alarm we hear must indicate the reactor is approaching complete failure. The core could superheat the water and blow. That was a consideration I made but there was not any definitive answer. We still have a little time to get out."

He grinned nervously. "We will just do our best."

The elevator made a rattling noise. Bryan looked at Liana with wide eyes and back at the door as it opened. Inside the car burn marks spotted the walls and the edge of the door, giving testament to a fierce and deadly firefight below.

Liana shot a mental command into the children's minds to move into the elevator. "Quickly, Bryan, push them in the elevator," she said aloud.

Bryan spread out his arms, herding the innocents, walking and nudging them into the elevator.

In the center of the elevator car, she reached up to the ceiling and lowered the fan grille. From its top she brought down a package and opened the bound detonator and hand-weapon.

"Take the weapon," she said, holding it out to Bryan.

He looked down at the cylindrical-shaped device. "How do I use it?"

Liana said, "Point the narrow end at your target. The front button on the side turns it on and off, and the back button activates it like a trigger." Liana stooped down, comforting a crying little girl.

Bryan checked the children. "We're all in. Let's go."

Suddenly, a hybrid, Bryan's clone, and a Grey, Haagui Zietso, the male with the strange wide eyes, rushed up to Bryan and Liana. Bryan's eyes instantly located the Grey's weapon. It was identical to what he held.

Liana stood motionless for a moment, gazing at the Grey in uncharacteristic helpless horror.

"Bryan," she whispered.

He held out his weapon. With his eyes on the weapon, he fumbled for the front button. At the same instant, the Grey took his weapon from his waist and raised it toward Liana. Bryan hit trigger button.

A silent blue-white beam extended from his weapon. The eerie beam burned a perfectly round hole in the center of the alien's chest. Bryan's jangling nerves moved his hand in an uncontrolled path from the Grey's chest, out its right side, continuing on into the left side of Bryan's clone hybrid. The Grey and the hybrid collapsed to the floor, their flesh laid open and bloodless. Bryan fumbled to find the off switch, ending the beam.

Liana hit the door control. "I am closing the doors!"

The door closed and the elevator began its upward travel from level twelve.

She pushed the detonator control in her hand, and looked at the door, listening. A faint low frequency hum became audible. Its intensity increased and then it throbbed like a big whirling machine out of balance.

"What is that?" Bryan said.

In a moment a deep rumbling accompanied the throbbing, which Liana anticipated would in a few moments, encompass the whole wing of the building. The elevator shook as they rose past the last floor controlled by the Greys, the eleventh level, the Grey's spacecraft hangar."

"What did you do?" Bryan asked.

"That little tremor was my sphere creating harmonic oscillations within the structure, weakening the concrete and steel composing the ceiling and support columns of level eleven. The other rumbling... well... you'll see. You better hope I allowed enough time for us to make it to the surface before it blows."

"Before what blows?" he asked.

Liana looked blankly at him and then she turned to the elevator lights, watching them indicate level two. "One more floor," she said. "Children, as soon as the doors open you must follow us outside the facility. Do not stop to look around. We are going out into the open sky, which you may not have seen for a long time. It may make you squint, but it won't hurt you."

The elevator stopped. The doors opened. In the hall, military personnel scurried like ants whose nest had been trampled, running random directions.

"Out the door, children," Bryan said. "Quickly, quickly, follow Liana."

Liana walked fast across the open concrete cavern, heading toward a bright light, daylight in the window of a door, twenty yards away. The line of children with Bryan at the rear fell back a little.

"Hurry, children," Bryan said, nudging a boy.

Liana slowed and looked back. "Hurry, children!"

At the exit to the outside, Liana led the children through a personnel door. Bryan picked up the last child, now a little girl, running with her in his arms.

Liana ran out and down the approach road, leading her entourage, passing a parked car.

A man sitting in the car, climbed out, watching them dumfounded.

"What's going on?" he yelled.

Liana continued toward the edge of the road. Bryan turned back and yelled over his shoulder, "Get away from the building!"

Liana, at the edge of the road, pointed to its sloping berm. "Children lie down on the slope. Hurry, Bryan, get off the road! Everyone keep your head down." They dropped to the side of the hill, beside their children.

The man from the car ran across the road, rapidly dropping to the ground next to Bryan.

"What's happening!" he said.

"Not now," Bryan said.

Distant thunder rumbled and shook the ground. Liana looked at Bryan, her face reflecting an aura of satisfaction.

Inside the building, a geyser of boiling flames blasted out of the elevators and stairs, sending a torrent through the personnel exit door in the building's dying breath. The complex shuddered, racked by Liana's justice. Exterior concrete walls cracked, shedding chunks of concrete, the beginning of its collapse. A pyroclastic storm of yellow-orange flames blew out the two fourteen-foot high, semi-truck access doors, sending them cartwheeling down the road. The doors then slid across the pavement like skipping rocks thrown across the surface of a pond, one landing partially on the road and the other off the road in a barren gravel area. The explosive wave blew debris into the sky, which was followed by billowing smoke rising from the roof of the facility. Debris rained over Bryan, Liana, and the children, like a tickertape parade.

After the blast had dissipated Bryan checked the building. "Let's get out of here while the place is still collapsing," he said.

"Yes."

He got to his feet, gazing over the collection of young faces, extending a hand to Liana. She took his hand and stood, waving for the children to get up.

"What happened in there?" the man asked, getting to his feet.

Bryan looked at the man suspiciously. "We are leaving. You can stay if you like."

Liana pointed to Bryan. "Children, this is Bryan. Follow Bryan."

He took a small boy's hand and began walking. "Okay, we're all going to walk quickly down the road. Follow me. Liana, you want to make certain we have everyone moving?"

"I'll take the rear." She raised her hands toward the sky. "Children, look up at the sky. You are safe with us." Liana listened for the children to speak but none of them said a word as they began looking around. She knew they needed time. They would talk very soon, especially with the way they looked around at what they had forgotten or had never seen.

Bryan marched hurriedly down the access road, leading the train of children.

Liana checked behind them at the man following. She didn't feel comfortable about him. He showed no sign of classification and looked like a non-military person.

As they marched along, the sky pulled her gaze upward, joining the children whose insatiable eyes pierced the barrier free sky, running across the desert, marveling at the plants.

After a few minutes, the sounds faded in the distance.

A soldier in a white sport utility vehicle raced past headed toward the complex, the writing on its door identifying it as base security. Bryan watched it pass. The man behind Liana waved at it.

"Don't do that," Bryan yelled.

"What? Why?"

He continued walking, looking over his shoulder. "They will lock you up for being here."

The man didn't reply and merely glanced back longingly.

"Liana, what was that second explosion that blew out the doors?" Bryan asked. "I only expected the reactor coolant lines to blow... and that strange vibration... as we went up in the elevator."

Another security vehicle shot past headed to the facility. Bryan watched if the man following would wave. He didn't.

"That was a ruse I used for Markak, a sacrificial bishop so I could place him in check. I left him two moves. Drown or fly away. He shut off the water so he would not drown. He caused the reactor melt down, knowing he'd have time to escape in his craft on level eleven. It was an obvious choice. The second blast was my checkmate. I exploded the fuel storage tank on the first level of the east-wing of the facility and with it, the east-wing access doors to the Grey sublevels. It behaved as I expected, pouring down the east-wing freight elevator, spilling onto each floor, vaporizing, exploding when it reached the bottom. Then it collapsed floors on top of the Grey monsters. I conservatively estimated the whole structure would collapse once the concrete reached close to twelve hundred degrees on one of your temperature scales. Concrete's compressive strength drops and can no longer support the floors above. Gasoline burns around twelve hundred fifty degrees taking into consideration intermittent fluctuations."

"How did you... how did you get there?"

"I altered the control directives for a sphere, employed it locating the fuel tank, and used it to travel up and plant the explosive."

"The spheres functioned like a type of drone for your chores?"

"They had limited physical manipulation abilities, but functioned quite well."

He beamed at her. "You amaze me. Okay, I'm ready to get out of here. By the way, where did you learn chess?"

"The teaching machine."

"Of course."

A mile farther down the road, they came to a gate across the road and an empty gatehouse. A pickup truck with huge tires sat on the other side of the gate with three men standing beside it, watching the smoke rising in the distance with binoculars.

"How do we get out?" Bryan said, looking over the fence.

"I guess we climb," Liana replied. She glanced up at the sky. "It is wonderful." At last she could see part of freedom.

"What?"

"The sky."

"Yes, it is," Bryan said. "What about the fence?"

The man behind the group stepped up. "I can help lift the children," he said.

One of the three men from the truck approached the fence, a stocky man, nearly six feet tall with round face under a red baseball cap. "If it wasn't for the security that's stationed and patrolling all over this area I'd hook my winch on the gate and pull it down with the truck."

Liana studied the man, feeling uneasy about him. She sent a thought to Bryan: *We must be careful with new human encounters.*

He looked at her. "They are safe."

She nodded.

"Yeah, the security people... I think they'll be busy for a long time," Bryan said. "They had a massive explosion. We escaped."

"Okay, then," said the man. "I'm Jack Taylor by the way."

"Hi, Jack, I'm Bryan Northfield. Can we do this quickly?"

"You're Bryan Northfield?" said the man behind Bryan.

Bryan turned. "Yes." Liana looked on suspiciously.

"I came here looking for you. I'm Congressman Gutierrez from Arizona." Gutierrez extended his hand.

Bryan took his hand. "I'd say you're a little late, right, Liana."

Liana looked the man over, her eyes stern, showing her caution. "Government man?"

"Yes," Gutierrez said.

"Bryan," Liana said, thinking their journey wasn't over.

He shook his head, preoccupied with the fence. "Thanks, but not now, congressman."

"Perhaps we can talk later sometime," Gutierrez said.

"I'll think about it. We've had all we want of the government."

"Fair enough. I understand. I came here at great risk myself. Perhaps I can help with your anonymity."

Bryan froze as if struck by a sudden thought. "Oh God, that's right." He stared coldly at Gutierrez. "What about witness protection and a sizeable whistleblower award... since my pension and other assets are likely out of reach?"

"Bryan, you know any governmental connection weakens the obscurity needed for protection," Liana said.

He nodded. "I'm sure you're correct in your assessment."

"It would be a privilege," Gutierrez said. "I make no guarantees."

"Give it some thought." Bryan turned to the man on the other side of the fence. "Okay, Jack."

Jack turned to the second man, a tall gray-bearded man with a western hat. "Cal, let's tear this gate down for these folks." He walked over to the winch line at the front bumper and unrolled the line as he walked it to the fence.

Bryan glanced at the burning complex and then watched Jack hook the line onto the fence. "Gentlemen, I'd like to get out of here as fast as we can. Two years was long enough."

Liana patted his shoulder. "Do not worry," she whispered. "We are free. My checkmate finished the installation."

"Hello, you two," said a third man from the truck, who had short graying hair, a bushy gray mustache, and expressive steel-gray eyes, standing at the side of a front fender. "I overheard that your name is Bryan Northfield?"

Bryan frowned for a moment. "Yes."

"I'm Vince Harris. Bryan, you're the reason I'm here." Vince waved at the congressman standing behind Bryan. "Hi, Congressman. I'm with the UFO study organization. I followed you out here."

"Mr. Harris, yes, nice to meet you," Gutierrez said.

"Okay, get back," Jack said. "You never know where the metal will fly." He waved to Cal who was behind the steering wheel of the truck.

"Okay people, you better move," Cal shouted out the truck window.

Jack motioned with his hand. "Take it back slow, Cal."

Liana and Bryan moved the children several feet back from the fence. Gutierrez stood next to one of the children.

Cal rolled the truck away from the fence, slowly tightening the cable going to the gate. The truck shuddered as its four wheels fought for grip against the gravel. The gate gave inches at its top as the support posts bent. With the sound of straining metal, the truck creeping, the bolts in the metal straps that wrapped around the posts sheared off and the gate's hinges ripped away from their steel posts. The truck pulled the gate across the gravel road, leaving Liana, Bryan, the children, and the congressman an open path to freedom.

"Children, hurry through the opening," Liana said, her voice rising with the sound of urgency.

They all crossed the breach in their prison fence, stopping a few yards away.

Jack disconnected the cable from the fence and began rewinding the winch.

"I feel better now," Bryan said.

Harris stepped over to Bryan and Gutierrez. "The congressman came here with two generals thirty or forty minutes ago," Harris said. "I came to see if they would let him in, and to see him ruffle feathers by digging into this black facility."

"They wouldn't let me in," Gutierrez said.

"It's a good thing," Bryan said, acknowledging Liana pridefully with a grin. "You may not have survived."

"The congressman informed our group that American citizens, free people, were held prisoners in there," Harris said. "He came looking for you and your wife." Harris looked at Liana and back at Bryan. "So, there was a big explosion?"

Bryan turned to Gutierrez. "Thanks for coming, congressman, even if you were a little tardy."

"You are welcome. I might be able to help with a new life."

Harris extended his hand to Gutierrez. "Congressman, nice to meet you."

As they shook hands Harris frowned. "How did all of you... you escape the facility... it was a black government research... wasn't it?"

"I didn't, but they did," Gutierrez said.

"How did you get out?" Harris asked.

"I'd say the facility was pretty much destroyed, right Liana?" Bryan said.

Liana nodded demurely. She was now concerned for their health. "I would agree with that assessment. Additional detrimental conditions exist with the exposed plutonium from the reactor meltdown and subsequent atmospheric debris. We should travel."

"Meltdown?" Gutierrez said, surprise in his voice.

"You mentioned helping," Bryan said. "Congressman, I would greatly appreciate your protective and financial help but you should be very careful if you have any interest in living to old age."

"I'll give it considerable thought."

"His help is problematic," Liana said softly.

"They're right," Harris said, glancing from Liana to Gutierrez and back. "Excuse me... are you... you are Louise, Bryan's wife?" Harris asked.

Liana looked at Bryan, thinking she needed to exercise caution in her new world. She watched his eyes narrow and then she heard the thought he sent her: "You can say you are Louise if you want, until we are away from here." She sent a thought back to him: *Thank you. If it is necessary.*

Bryan threw his arm around her. She smiled at him, posing for Harris.

She spoke into his mind: *I will need an identity for human society and I would feel privileged to be known as Louise.* She quickly heard his reply in her head: "To me you will always be Liana and my wife." Liana leaned over to Bryan and kissed him on the cheek.

"This is my wife," he said.

She spoke sternly, "These children came from the bowels of that prison of horror. Grey aliens abducted these children and their abuse was condoned by the government. Their lives could be ruined. The Greys brutalized, dissected, and manipulated horrors in genetic breeding programs. Unless you saw it you would never imagine the hell that existed." Liana glanced skyward and then turned toward the underground prison of ghoulish horror. Black smoke boiled up from the carcass of the unholy partnership, polluting the brilliant blue sky.

"If only I had some... a little documentation... proof," Harris said.

Gutierrez rolled his eyes. "It would get you dead."

"It's destroyed," Bryan said. His voice was edgy, at the precipice of emotional shock, as his eyes filled with tears. He cleared his throat.

Liana patted him on the shoulder with a sympathetic gaze. "You are fine."

"Mr. Harris, can you get all of us into your truck and take us to where I can rent a van?" Bryan asked. "I hate to beg but can I borrow some money from one of you? The aliens took my money."

Harris laughed. "I'm told they do that." He looked at the children. "Shouldn't be a problem. Seven children, you two, and the congressman... you'll all fit in the back of the truck."

"Thanks," Bryan said.

"Bryan," Liana said sternly, "we must obtain distance from the radioactive material that is carried by the smoke."

"Oh wow, I forgot her comment," Harris said.

Bryan glanced at the smoke and turned to Harris, Jack and Cal. "Gentlemen, can we go now?"

"Yes, damn fast, as far as I'm concerned," Cal said.

"Where will you go?" Harris asked. "My organization would like to interview you, document your story."

Bryan laughed sourly. "Not on your life. In fact, that's probably what it would cost."

Harris appeared dismayed. "You need to help your country."

"I already did and so has my wife. The bastards cut out one of my kidneys." He took Liana's hand. "I think we're going to find a new home somewhere. Right, honey?"

Liana smiled guardedly, as if hiding a secret. "I think someplace north," she said. "Do you not think?"

Harris frowned, seemingly at her speech.

Bryan grinned at her. He laughed. "I think you read my mind, honey."

Liana gazed off across the arid scrub landscape, up at the sky, and at the truck.

"I can't change your mind about your story?" Harris said.

Bryan clenched his teeth. "Not on—your life."

Chapter Nineteen

A week later, Bryan and Liana sat on the porch of their rented home in Montana. The twilight of the August evening had draped over the trees.

He sipped his coffee, hanging one leg over the other in his Adirondack chair. "I think you like my coffee."

She didn't turn from the pine forest, watching the tops of the trees lose their orange-tainted green as the sun retired, leaving behind a crisp scent on the spawning evening coolness. The peace from such a simple experience had never crossed her imagination and could never have existed had it not been for Bryan. She was indebted to him for giving a different birth to her life. Probabilistically, her chances of escaping the Grey's and the fortress of horror before meeting him had barely condensed into a concept. Her intelligence could have provided the tool to an infallible plan, but he had brought her spirit, the spark of a child, and surprisingly, his wonderful love. The child inside her and the love he had given her had forged the plan and made its execution imperative. It didn't bother her that his mind occasionally compared things she did to memories of his first wife. Strangely, in a way he was comparing twins, given her genetic origin.

She found his contentment restful to her own feelings. He was teaching her how to appreciate simple things. She enjoyed their growing relationship and had to keep telling herself not to over analyze everything between them. His love was real. A perverse wrinkle took her face and she tilted her head. "Yes. I am learning to like your coffee drink. You are certain it will not hurt the baby?"

"Yes, yes. There's never been any research indicating problems."

"I believe you." She sent her attention to him. "I have been thinking."

"What?"

"After this baby... if it is fine... I would like another... one conceived out here in this peace."

Bryan nodded, letting his eyes close for a moment. "I would love that too."

She pulled in a long breath and sighed contentedly. "I like this remote area of Montana."

"It was a good choice. Maybe we can make an offer to buy this place."

"How does that connect us to your public records?"

"Our public records. You are home, honey, so it's our records."

She bobbed her head. "Yes."

"I worry about having new identities through the FBI witness protection. Since we're dealing with only cash routed from our whistleblower money in a Swiss account, we should be fine... although we must remain watchful and stay away from computerized systems that can be hacked and tracked."

"I agree."

"I think you like the fact that there are not any government people or a town for a long distance."

She flashed her eyebrows. "True."

"For me, I like having several minutes warning when someone is coming. I like being self-sufficient... except for food. I like no wires, no phone, and no one watching."

"No one has come, Bryan. And without implants, the others will not find us either."

"We must never let our guard down. They can come any time, snooping, trying to suck information from my brain, from your brain, from anywhere they want. If that congressman, investigation man or the other two men start talking about seeing people walking out along that facility access road, who knows how many visitors we would see. I'm worried I didn't cover our tracks enough setting up the cash disbursement from the Swiss account. I'm worried about the government snoops. And I'm worried the congressman will make a mistake."

"We can add a few more scanners down the road and throughout the approaching forest. We still have the weapon."

"Yes we do. How long until its power fades away?"

"Not for many years." She sipped her coffee and looked at him. "I could make something more powerful."

He frowned and after a moment he grinned.

She craned her head back. "Living in that dark place, I never imagined the freedom of such a sky with the night views of all the distant suns and galaxies."

It was quiet for several moments. A tree toad in the distance collaborated with an owl, providing an evening diversion. A bird cooed in a nearby tree, joining the night's symphony.

"What's that sound?" Liana asked, tilting her head.

"A Mourning Dove, I think."

"But it is evening."

"Mourning as in sadness."

"I like it. It is soothing."

"Liana, what do you think about the children recovering?"

"We will keep them on the program I formulated and keep them on the home schooling. When they are ready to go on their own, we will pray they have learned their lessons." She knew he'd pick up on her last reference.

"You're sounding at home with that spiritual reference." He looked up at the darkening blue of the sky, now just dark enough the stars shown.

Liana heard his thought about looking at stars with Louise. "Bryan, if you cannot keep the horror of that night from your mind when we sit out here, we should stop sitting out on the porch like this."

He smiled at her. "You know some couples say they can read each other's minds after they've been married for several years. Here we are and you have always been able to get my thoughts."

"I love us just the way we are," she whispered.

"That brings me to a question that I've wondered about ever since you placed me on that teaching machine."

She dropped her eyes to the wood plank floor. "How smart am I?" she said. Her eyebrows arched. She had pondered if he would ever ask, and if so, how soon. From what she had read in his mind it did not make much difference and was more curiosity than anything.

"Yes. That's the question. Since you put me on that machine, I know I could make some real contributions to artificial computer intelligence if I worked on it. With my new intelligence, I also know that it would be a mistake for our world." He sighed. "So where do you think your intelligence falls?"

She looked into her cup of coffee, serenity gracing her brow. "I am what you would regard as a serendipitous occurrence... a freak accident... even by the malevolent Reticulan's calculations. They did not know me thoroughly. I would not let them. I always blocked my thoughts from them unless it suited me otherwise. My intelligence level is four times that of the Greys... at least four times higher than Markak... anyway."

Bryan lurched forward, nearly coming out of his chair, spilling coffee on his right leg. "That makes your... is that right... that your intelligence level is around twelve hundred?" His brow nearly buried his eyes as he considered the impossibility.

Liana's eyes widened. She twisted her mouth with amusement. "Yep." She frowned. "And do not think of me building a spacecraft using their technology. I saw it flash through your brain."

"Nah, I love living here with you too much to attract strange visitors."

She smiled devilishly. "However, I may create something to make some extra money if we need new window coverings or a refrigerator or a new truck."

The End

About Craig L. Andrews

Craig L. Andrews is the author of the novel, *The Ninth Martini*, released in 2013 and the novel, *Until The Day*, published in 2015, both by Solstice Publishing. Alternative Books Press published his novel, *Chronicle of Stolen Souls, The Legacy of Fathers*, in 2014. Moonshine Cove Publishing released his novel, Sky Fishing, in September 2015. He has also self-published, *Broken Toy, A Man's Dream, A Company's Mystery*, a biography of a man whose small company patented a toy mouse (true story) Micky two years before Walt Disney's Mickey Mouse (available on Amazon). Prior work includes two novels from the horror genre, published by Commonwealth Publications, *The Godmanchester Stone* and *The Bed and Breakfast*. He holds a B. S. and an M.S. degree in physics, and has authored physics and automotive engineering papers.

Social Media Links:

Twitter: https://twitter.com/CraigLAndrews
@CraigLAndrews

Facebook:
https://www.facebook.com/Craig.L.Andrews.Publishing

Goodreads: https://www.goodreads.com/CraigLAndrews

If you enjoyed this story, check out these other Solstice Publishing books by Craig L. Andrews:

Until the Day

When Christine Lockwood, the daughter of a wealthy doctor falls in love with Michael, a butcher's son, she learns a horrible truth about her money-hungry father and that he'll do anything to stop her from reaching for her dream. Obstacles fall like rain, washing away her dream and Michael's efforts to prove himself, taking us to the surprising ending of Until the Day.

http://bookgoodies.com/a/B00XI18O38

The Ninth Martini

A former SEAL, Zack Hawkshaw, on assignment to the CIA is pushed into a mission that might require him using a skill he swore he'd never use again. The thrill ride takes him over the world, ending on the homeland where Zack faces his nemesis in a final confrontation with the clock ticking down. Once you start you'll have to read to the end.

http://bookgoodies.com/a/B00DYB8JKK

www.ingramcontent.com/pod-product-compliance
Lightning Source LLC
Chambersburg PA
CBHW051521260626

47170CB00003B/725